Steve Smith lives in the Scottish Borders. He is married with children and grandchildren. He enjoys writing, reading, walking, gardening, astronomy, amateur-dramatics and charity work. He has written poetry and stories for many years. This is his second novel.

I0452752

CREATION FARM

Steve Smith

Southdean Books

CREATION FARM

First published in 2014

ISBN: 978-0-9576185-0-3

*The community and characters described in this book are
entirely the products of my imagination and bear no resemblance
to any person living or dead or to any community in the United
Kingdom.*

To Caroline,

Briony and Andrew.

.

Cover design by Andrew Smith:

Andysmith-creative.co.uk.

Behance profile:

Behance.net/andyartdirector.

Acknowledgements

I would like to acknowledge the help of the following for making this book possible:

My wife, Caroline, for her patience, proofreading and support.

My son, Andrew, for his innovative cover design for 'Creation Farm.'

Peter Flannery for his invaluable help and advice.

Inga McVicar from 'Full Paper Jacket,' for her honest appraisal.

'The Economist.'

'Celtic Christianity and Nature' – Mary Low.

'A Song Book for Boys in Camp and Club,' for the extract from 'The Quartermaster's Store.'

CREATION FARM

"Science is a first rate piece of furniture for Man's upper chamber if he has common sense on the ground floor."

(Oliver Wendell Holmes Snr. – 'The Poet at the Breakfast table,' 1872.)

Prologue

Blip..!

It is well into the night and the scientist feels as if his head is about to explode. He pinches the bridge of his nose, trying to ignore the stiffness in his neck as he stares at the array of screens. The work is relentless. Forcing his eyes back into focus he scans the scrolling digits and symbols, watching for the telltale red coding that will alert him to any problems.

In principle there should be two staff members monitoring the process – either two specialists or a scientist and a technician. The management protocols require this. Standards have fallen recently - a fatal procedural slippage.

Blip..!

A single line of code flashes in green brackets. The scientist hits return and the stream of numbers continues. He performs the action with the enthusiasm of someone on automatic pilot. He has been sitting for hours each day in front of the screens, occasionally checking the data, updating his electronic records and backing up the saved information. The process of creation is precise and achingly slow.

To either side, the other monitors display graphic representations of the developments that are even now taking place in the nutrient baths and super-cooled isolation tanks in other parts of the complex.

Blip..!

The scientist scans the line of code, this time bracketed in orange.

Enter - for the zillionth time - enter!

He hits the key as a hard-faced security guard walks into the room. The scientist gives a nod and a weak smile - unreciprocated. He has worked for the Falcon Research Centre for five years and still the guards make him nervous.

His shoulders sag with relief as the man gives the room a last searching look and turns to leave. The sound of the sealed door closing is a barely audible *shlunk*.

He stares at the screens, at the endless string of letters and numbers generated by the computers. To the layperson it would seem like gibberish, some indecipherable code.

To the scientist it is the language of creation – this block here gives the structure of certain proteins, here the rate of metabolism and the complex molecules being produced - variations on a billion themes. It has been the same for months. The work is agonisingly complex. Even for him, a committed team member, the novelty has worn off.

Blip..!

Green brackets - the scientist hits the key.

Blip..!

Orange, God I need some sleep.

He leans back in his chair, closes his eyes and clasps his head with both hands. One of his debilitating headaches – the exploding kind, could be just around the corner.

Blip..!

He hits the key without even looking then swings back into an upright position.

That's it – I'm calling it a night.

The scientist hits 'return' and enters the password to temporarily shut down the process, saving the data.

He completes his report, which effectively states there is nothing to report. He leans back in his chair, eyes closed, then stands up to leave the room, letting the system close down automatically. He knows it always does. For that reason he misses the moment when the brackets round the fatal 'Blip!' flash an angry shade of red.

One

James Humble always remembered the day when he found himself inexorably propelled towards danger, yet could not resist the challenge before him. It was a day when his life changed forever.

At six a.m. on a warm Saturday in early September, walking in the deep woods, he sensed profound change. The growth was abundant and lush. The ancient conifers had been overtaken by ash, beech, birch and oak. The odd mature Scots pine stood out amongst them, its pinkish bark gnarled and flaking.

The sky was huge – an azure dome with a few trailing clouds. Around him was *Caithland Forest* – one of the largest stretches of woodland in the country. If you lacked local knowledge, map and compass skills, you could be lost for days. James Humble loved it.

The natural world was a source of fascination for him. He stopped to examine a red fungus growing close to the earth, lying down on his stomach to take a photograph. The image would be logged in his notebook and added to his extensive records. To Humble, the forest was an ecosystem complete in itself – a composite personality. He was not surprised to sense its moods after all his explorations there.

Humble ran fingers through his thick, black hair, scanning the surroundings. His face and hands were weathered and he carried his lean frame like a man accustomed to the outdoors. Reaching the crest of a slope from where he could trace his route, he stopped for a moment to look down on the community of Candywood.

The small township straggled along the narrow valley of the River Candy in the brooding hills of the Scottish Border Country. It derived its unusual name from the native woodland, which had once covered the valley sides – an ancient royal hunting ground, *The Candy Wood.*

Humble had been part of this community during his childhood and teenage years. The inheritance of the family business anchored him.

The place is in my bones, he thought.

The township was technically in Scotland but was so close to the border that some of its properties straddled the boundary. Its population was distinguished by variety, with descendants of the original inhabitants and a proportionate number of people from all over the U.K and beyond.

Candywood had its own dialect, an argot formed from a mixture of Border Scots, Northumbrian, Cumbrian and locally coined *slanguage.* It was known as "Candy" or "Candy-Tongue." In this area, families had swapped the same genes for generations. Humble's own family however, were vague about their origins.

Rebellious during his twenties, he had taken off after his University years, working at various jobs in England, Germany and the Netherlands. His father's early death from cancer had brought him back at the age of twenty-eight. Younger brother was in Edinburgh with a safe Government job. His sister, aged twenty-four, about to produce her second child; lived in Carlisle.

Catherine Humble had taken her husband's passing badly and had become a depressive recluse.

Her death followed two years later. James was left with the business to run. To his surprise he found he had a flair for it – genetic or learned.

Known locally as "The Anything Shop," it was hugely overstocked, a hobby as well as a business. If an item wasn't available, Humble was famous for writing it down and ensuring it was there in future. From marmalade to mousetraps, Humble's had it. Attention to detail was the key.

The region was known as *The Three Valleys,* a reference to the three rivers converging on the borderline marked partly by the River Ling. The other rivers, the Candy and the Whitegrain, flowed into the main stream. The default climate was once moist, with frequent mists known as 'Wet Blankets.'

Not any more, he realised. *It's changing.*

An unusually hot summer had dried out the bald, brown hills, refreshed by a few spasmodic bouts of rainfall. The rivers clattered along the squeezed valleys and dark Caithland Forest wrapped itself around village, farm and cottage like the closing fist of a giant.

Gazing down at the place, Humble felt old memories gathering. It was a weakness...too much introspection. The shop provided grounding now but there was still a maverick streak in him.

Dropping down from the rise, he looked about with clear, blue eyes. His practised gaze caught sight of a tall, thick-stemmed plant with arrays of yellow flowers clustered tightly along its stem...

A mullein? – Unusual around here.

Like the other forest flora, the mullein was vigorous and robust. He moved towards it, taking out his notebook.

16

This specimen was one of the largest he had seen. He would photograph it and compare its measurements with previous records.

Plunging through the vegetation, Humble was suddenly aware of something else, a movement. He turned and caught sight of the largest rat he had ever encountered.

It was grey-brown in colour and the size of a badger. Rats are normally wary of humans but this creature looked at him and bared its teeth before moving on. He followed it carefully, watching the thick tail move like rope through the grass. Not quite believing what he was seeing he slowly brought out his phone to take a picture.

Unreal, he thought. *Super-cats yes, but super-rats?*

The giant rodent moved deeper into the forest, along a rough trail. Humble stepped quietly. The rat continued through the undergrowth and he became aware that a boundary fence was ahead.

It was the double security fence of the *Falcon Agricultural Research Station*. The outer barrier was similar to a deer fence with locked gates set into it at intervals.

The inner fence was three metres tall made of tough steel mesh with a curved section added to the top, holding coils of razor wire. Electric conductors were clearly visible. Notices were placed just on the inside. They read,

AGRICULTURAL RESEARCH STATION. NO ADMITTANCE TO THE GENERAL PUBLIC. ELECTRIFIED FENCE. DO NOT APPROACH.

The legend, 'Falcon Research Ltd.' and a telephone number were shown. There were warning signs showing lightning bolts and the ubiquitous health and safety notices, black writing on yellow…

DANGER OF DEATH.

Humble knew almost every part of the forest except the interior of the research centre. This section was called *Falcon Woods* and had been separate before the mass of Caithland had overwhelmed it like Birnam Wood coming to Dunsinane. He knew the fences ran through the forest to its edge then continued, curving round to form barriers through and around the densest areas. Weatherproof cameras had been fitted to the taller, inner fence.

The rat was still moving and with astonishment he saw that others were joining it. They were variously coloured brown, black or grey and all were enormous – rodents from Hell. They squatted by the outer fence and Humble took picture after picture, disbelieving yet excited despite his customary caution. Then his attention quickly veered away.

On the inside of the inner fence was a man on his knees, slumped near the base of the barrier. He guessed the man may have sustained an electric shock from the inner fence, throwing him backwards. He moved forward to help the casualty, looking for a way over. He could scale the outer fence he realised – it was not electrified and he was fit. There was a gap between the two. Not knowing how he would deal with the electric fence, Humble decided to have a closer look, then paused. He could hear people approaching. Warned by some deep instinct he retreated into cover quickly.

Two security guards appeared, armed with truncheons and machine-pistols. They sported military-style uniforms with a Falcon logo.

Humble drew further into the thick undergrowth, crouching down. The two guards roughly lifted the man, who wore work overalls with the same logo and began to drag him back into the depths of Falcon territory. He had time to register that the man looked Asian or Middle-Eastern, before he disappeared with his captors.

Uncharacteristically he felt angry and ashamed. He had hidden, letting the man be taken away,

But what could be done against armed men? Quickly he backed off further along the track to a safer area, reaching the edge of the forest and the path back to Candywood. Walking quickly, he took the minor road to the village and slowed down,

Almost seven, he thought. *Have to get back to open up.*

He gathered himself together, needing a few minutes to think. Inside the shop he paused for breath. Raw emotions shot through his mind. He was sweating.

Fear was not normally his companion but an inexplicable dread had gripped him during the encounter, a fear as dark as the forest. His mind was a whirl of chaotic thoughts and emotions. Yet he had a dogged stubbornness, which sometimes served instead of courage. There was some steel in him. He was not about to let this one go.

Ting - a - ling!

The shop doorbell sounded. A customer entered. It was the local police officer, Marcus Burn. To Humble he was about as welcome as a Jehovah's Witness.

All I need, he thought, but maintaining his professionalism said,

"Hello, Marcus, good to see you."

Burn brought with him a small eddy of dust and a whiff of freshly-laundered uniform. He smelled slightly of after-shave. Burn spent only part of each week in the area, the bulk of his duties being elsewhere. It was therefore necessary for him to tap any local knowledge. The shop was one of the best places to do this - a gossip and information exchange.

He had the build of a rugby player, thick neck almost disappearing into his broad shoulders. It had earned him the nickname, 'No Neck.' His face was broad too, topped with thick red hair and a squashed rugby nose.

He was in his early thirties, a similar age to Humble but they had differing backgrounds. Burn was a townie – brought up in Cruiksdale, just less than an hour to the east, by road.

Humble didn't like Burn, didn't trust him. If Burn asked him any questions he would give him as little information as possible but he was still confused, out of breath and sweating. Burn could see it. Knowing Humble's habits he sensed where he might have been. He began by asking for an item he knew Humble stocked,

"A book of first class stamps, Jim, please."

"No problem, Marcus, anything else whilst you're here?"

The shop-owner braced himself for the real reason Burn was in the shop. The police officer had arrived early, knowing the store would be quiet. He noted Humble's agitation, saw his clothes were wet and muddy in places and that there were sprigs of bracken stuck to his outdoor trousers…a policeman is trained to observe.

"No thanks. Have you visited the forest recently?" Burn asked.

Humble placed the stamps on the counter, took a deep breath,

"I'm planning to go soon. The exercise is beneficial and I need material for my regular article. Why do you ask?"

Humble wrote a wildlife column for the local newspaper, *The Lingdale Gazette*. It was entitled *Country Cousin* and reported on the seasonal changes in the wild areas around Candywood. He wondered why no one else seemed to have noticed the abundance of growth or spotted any super-sized animals. Perhaps they were keeping their powder dry, afraid of ridicule.

"Just thought I should caution you not to go near the research centre," said Burn, fishing for a reaction. He passed over a ten-pound note. Humble kept his face impassive.

"Why in particular?"

"They're not keen on people approaching the place – worried about their security, you understand."

"I know there are bloody great fences running around it."

"You know the Falcon Centre then?"

"Know of it. They keep themselves well out of the public eye. I've no idea what lies beyond that perimeter. Is there something top secret about it?"

"I'm much too lowly to be told about that," Burn said, "I've just been asked to check if anything out of the ordinary has turned up. The company is concerned about sightings of people who shouldn't be there. Division has asked me to investigate any security risks."

"Oh. I get it. Classified stuff."

"I didn't say that and I'm not privy to that kind of information. Besides we have a Data Protection Act in this country."

"So I've heard. Other acts too. There's always an act to hide behind but we live in a remote region. All sorts of things could happen here. Who would know?"

"There's nothing sinister, just normal security," said Burn, "It's a research station not a government listening-post."

Humble did not respond, keeping to practical matters,

"Here's your stamps and your change, Marcus."

"Thanks. Not much left from a tenner these days."

The policeman took the items from the counter and turned to go,

"I know you often walk in the forest but take my advice, Jim and steer clear of Falcon."

"Well, I might want to chase up an idea or investigate the plants and animals, the strange absence of the usual biting insects; anything like that. It's what I do for fun," Humble said.

"Take my words seriously. They don't want to be troubled. Leave the place well alone. See you again."
Humble raised a hand as the officer left,

What was that about?
His reticence with Burn was deliberate. He had learned the hard way to keep his mouth shut.

Sightings of large felines were occasionally made in the area, probably crosses between feral domestic cats and Scottish wildcats from the north. It was known there was a shortage of female wildcats and the males had been migrating south for years.

In April when he had reported a particularly big beast he had been taken seriously at first. Eventually he had been dismissed as an eccentric - *The Cat Man*. For some time afterwards he had been referred to as, "Pussy" by some elements in the district.

Now standing in his shop watching Burn drive off, he thought again about those encounters. He kept his photographs of plants and other evidence in his flat above the shop, with a collection of found items built up from his wanderings. He was a squirrel when it came to interesting discoveries. His vast collection, his notebooks and databases, were regularly updated.

At the time of the cat sightings he had found the temptation too much and emailed an article to the local paper about unusual animal and plant growth, emphasising the super-cats. It was not well received. The Editor of the Lingdale Gazette, Dick Shepherd, telephoned him from Gillerston after Humble had sent in his copy,

"Look, Jim, I'll get straight to the point. Your usual stuff about the countryside is great but I'm looking to cut out the bits about over-sized animals and plants. People are going to think it's weird. Our readership is just not into that stuff."

"But, Dick," he countered dismayed, "It's an interesting development. It really needs to be an article in its own right. I can expand on it and include photos …"

Shepherd cut across the flow,

"Jim, we're a small country paper. People want to hear about farm-stock prices, local activities, anniversaries and sport. Things like this scare them. They literally won't buy it. You could send it to a bigger paper or a specialist magazine but not *The Gazette*. Sorry."

He ended the call.

An unkind thought had formed in Humble's mind,

Dick...well named.

Shepherd had a point, however. His job was to sell papers, not speculate on strange theories but Humble remained convinced that the forest held secrets. Either the authorities knew and were covering up or they were genuinely unconcerned.

Taking the opportunity whilst the shop was still empty, he raced up to his flat and put his notebook into the bulging box-files of records.

He sat down heavily. Someone had tried to escape from the Falcon place. That someone had ended up unconscious at the foot of an electrified fence, dragged away by security guards with guns! Guns! - In the U.K! Something was going on...the oversized plants and animals were just part of it. Something was going on and Humble was determined to find out more.

His experience of the outside world, his observance of the succession of 'suits' who had run the country for decades, together with knowledge of the local culture; had led him to trust few people, to remain enigmatic, to ride the zeitgeist. His intense curiosity, however, was driving him on. He would not be intimidated...he would return to the forest and next time he would not run away.

Two

As his assistant, Humble employed Mrs Gill, a conscientious middle-aged woman he knew as, Stella. On weekends and some occasional days, he needed another worker. Her name was Louisa Moscadini. She would be in at nine.

Saturday was the busiest day so extra help was needed. The bonus was that his dark-eyed assistant was startlingly lovely, with an olive complexion and a near-perfect figure. She had a butterfly tattoo on her right shoulder and a tiny blue bird above her left ankle. Humble's fantasy was to find out if she had any others.

He was smitten but his reticence kept him from making a move. Louisa was a student at Northumbria University, Carlisle, in her final year of a Business and Marketing degree. She was twenty-six and a native of Gillerston, west of Candywood, where her Italian-descent family had a café and a fleet of ice-cream vans.

She breezed in exuberantly as usual, removing her headphones, shaking out luxuriant, black hair.

"Hiya, Jim. Ready to rock n' roll?"

He closed his eyes briefly,

"Er, yes. I've just had a visitor as it happens."

"Oh?"

"And I saw something when I was taking an early morning walk – something I didn't like."

Humble told her about the police officer's visit as she listened, with her gazelle eyes fixed on him. He needed to share his concerns with someone and, abandoning caution, went on to tell her what he'd seen, what he hadn't told Burn.

"Is this for real? I mean this is Candywood."

"The outside world has penetrated even here," he said.

"It's like something on T.V."

"Possibly, but the guy at the fence had something to do with the research facility. He was wearing corporate clothing. There was a Falcon logo on his overall."

She moved close to him putting a hand on his left arm. Humble tried to hide his reaction.

"I'd love to have been there," she said. Her voice was a little deep for a girl but it was music to him.

"Nothing exciting ever happens around here. Thanks for sharing it with me. I can understand why you're wary about Marcus Burn. Even though he's a cop he's a creep. Maybe I can help."

Humble was besotted with Louisa and couldn't help recklessly confiding in her. She scrambled his brain. Her liking for the crime genre in books, films and T.V, led her to see herself as something of an amateur detective, once considering joining the police. Family pressure however, meant that her ultimate destination would be marriage and the business.

The Moscadinis were practising Catholics, another barrier between Humble and his part-time assistant. James had no certainty about religion, just a vague idea that he should attend Church occasionally and try to be respectable – difficult with Louisa around.

"Thanks. I'll keep you in the picture. I may yet have to tell the truth about this if the police keep asking questions."

"Of course. But maybe we could do a little digging ourselves seeing as we know so much about Candy."

She winked.

Gossip was a cottage industry in Candywood and much of it passed through the shops, the watering holes and the houses, zipped along the main street and became more distorted as it went like Chinese whispers. The place was a goldfish bowl.

Candywood was at the heart of the Border country. Historically, families had fought each other as well as the other side. Their loyalty had been to kith and kin, or more accurately, tribe. They had lived short, violent lives in an unforgiving countryside and their culture had not entirely died out.

Marcus Burn knew this as well as anyone. The concept of obeying the law was at best a tenuous one. People were kept in line through fear of character assassination. On occasions a small group of men might take someone to a quiet place and deliver a hard but lasting lesson.

The Reverend Morton Parke knew this too. A red-haired Ulster Presbyterian, he was the local Church of Scotland Minister. His face looked as if it had been flattened after several blows from a spade, without any effect, except possibly to the spade. The forty-eight year-old clergyman worked the community in a highly professional way, aided by his very able wife, Margaret, who handled the Guides, the Village Hall and other organisations.

His church had a monopoly on locally organised religion apart from a small neo-pagan cult, *An Bile Buada*, which kept a very low profile. He was never sure which local people were members. It tended to favour Celtic mysticism and had an obsessive interest in trees.

Parke's lank figure was striding up Lingdale Street when a police patrol car cruised by. He knew it wasn't Burn...he had a Land-Rover. Other strollers were craning to see what was going on. When the vehicle stopped outside Humble's, some of the strollers suddenly altered the direction in which they were walking.

The Minister headed towards the shop. Humble might need his help. Passing the *Lingdale Arms*, he noticed the side door was ajar. It was a signal that the place was open for business for certain customers. If you knew the signal, you could get an early drink in there before official opening hours. Voices drifted from the building, amongst them one he recognised from its volume – Vincent "Rocky" Craggs, the landlord, who had obviously spotted the patrol car.

"What's the Law doing here at this time of the morning?" Craggs' voice asked.

"Dunno, Rocky," replied someone whose voice the clergyman couldn't yet identify.

"You been up to somethin', y' wee chancer?" continued Craggs in a bantering tone. Now Parke's acute memory placed the other speaker - "Sticky" Hagg (real name, Peter or Pete), known for his inability to leave a bar, hence sticking to it. His voice was like sandpaper, from years of smoking,

"Naw, no' me, Rocky, ah wis here a' night."

"So you were, Sticky, so you were. How could ah doubt it y' old piss-head?"

There was the sound of someone being slapped on the back and an accompanying gasp. Rocky was a big man.

Parke was immune to swearing. His previous church had been on an estate in Belfast controlled by paramilitaries. He tried to avoid cursing himself but was not prissy about it in others. It wouldn't have got him far in Candywood. He wandered a little way along the street, pretending to examine the village notice board.

Humble was thinking of the old song…

"There were rats, rats, as big as alley cats,
In the store, in the store,
There were rats, rats, as big as alley cats,
In the quartermaster's store;
My eyes are dim I cannot see….'

Dismayed at the unexpected arrival of a police car, Humble left Louisa to mind the shop and ushered the officers into the back. There were two of them – a sandy-haired W.P.C with a lightly freckled, unsmiling face, who looked about fifteen and a taller, older-looking male who eyeballed Louisa as she headed into the shop to deal with the first customers. Business would be brisk until the gossip had run its course.

"Mr. Humble," the male officer began, "I'm Sergeant Dalveen and this is W.P.C March. We wondered if you could tell us if you've seen anything unusual in the forest recently."

Burn must have sent for reinforcements, Humble thought. *What exactly is going on?*

As with Burn, Humble played dumb, giving nothing.
He hoped they had him down as a hick with little grip on reality. Many people outside Candywood regarded the

place as being full of eccentrics, escapees from the real world, criminals and inbred half-wits.

"Our colleague, P.C Burn, is concerned about the Falcon Research Station," continued Dalveen. "We've had his report. It's possible that security there has been compromised."

"I don't know about that," said Humble. "It's hard to get near the place anyway so I would think the security is pretty watertight."

"We're told you walk in the woods regularly, Mr. Humble," W.P.C March said suddenly, shifting on her feet. "If anyone has spotted anything suspicious it would be you."

Her mouth was a thin line,

"For example have you seen anyone watching the place, moving near the fence, possibly taking photographs?"

"No, nothing," Humble said, refusing to be drawn out. He wasn't going to have some callow, female cop intimidating him.

Dalveen's phone signalled. It was Marcus Burn. Humble felt acutely aware of the straining ears in the front shop. He was glad the door was closed. The officer returned.

"P.C Burn has spoken to the management at Falcon," he said. "They explained that one of their staff had been slightly hurt during the course of his duties. Slipped and fell whilst clearing a ditch. It happened early this morning near the perimeter fences."

"They were concerned someone may have witnessed the incident."

"You're in the habit of taking walks out there. Are you sure you didn't see or hear anything? P.C Burn

30

told us you appeared agitated when he spoke to you just after your shop opened."

Bastard, thought Humble.

"I'm sure," he lied surprisingly easily.

"The security guards at Falcon are authorised to carry weapons under certain circumstances," continued the sergeant, "Terrorism and so on."

He made it sound as if there was nothing unusual about armed guards at a non-governmental research station in the U.K.

Agricultural research for God's sake! What's so secret about that?

"We'll ask P.C Burn to keep an eye on things. You should stay away - let the professionals do the work. There are cameras placed on the perimeter fences around the station. Anyone who approaches will be caught on film and hopefully identified."

He looked directly at Humble, who tried not to react but was inwardly worried. He hadn't thought of the cameras. A cold serpent writhed in his belly.

The officers readied themselves to leave. Dalveen spoke again,

"I repeat it would be better not to stray close to the facility in future. I'm told they're doing important work and they like to be left alone. This area is lucky to have a place like that to provide jobs. Not much else going on is there? If it expands there'll be more work. Good news for everyone so it's best to leave well alone. Goodbye and take care."

He gave a brief, curt nod before both officers moved to the door and passed, carrying an air of solid authority, to their car. It moved away down the street to the west of the village, presumably to rendezvous with Marcus Burn.

Humble closed the door between the front and back shop and leaned against it, thinking. He felt annoyed, knowing he had been warned off again. It had the opposite intended effect. It aroused his innate stubbornness.

Three

Humble and Louisa planned to look up *Falcon Research* on the Internet as soon as there was a break in business. Curious locals had left after failing to extract any information. Parke had offered to help, his acute senses telling him there was something out of order. Humble had given him a brief explanation of the incident. He trusted the Ulsterman. Parke had a mind like a razor and he was straight and loyal to his friends.

"I can guess what you're thinking, Jim."

"What?"

"You won't be able to resist doin' some investigatin' for yourself. I know what you're like. I've often thought that Falcon is overly secretive but the police don't give these warnings out for nothin'. You could land yourselves in a pile of trouble if you're not careful."

His face held a serious expression. Humble's eyes shifted sideways,

"I know, I know. But I can't help wondering why we aren't being told more about it."

"It's doing agricultural research. It's providin' jobs and puttin' money into the local economy. Do we need to know anything else?"

"Yes," Humble said, "We do. There must be more to it than that. The police said there were armed personnel there – for "security reasons" – why would you need armed people at an agricultural facility? Do they think someone's going to steal some of their oats?"

Louisa giggled. They looked at her without smiling. She shut up.

"Just tell me you won't do anything stupid. If you must look around out there be careful. At the slightest sign of danger you have to back off. We don't need any heroes here. It's important to be sensible."

"I'm not talking about taking on Falcon single-handed. I just need to know what else they're doing there. If it's harmless they have nothing to hide do they?"

"There was the report in the *Gazette* when Falcon opened," said Parke. "You remember, 'Local research facility supports our community. The future's bright for jobs in Candywood'. The Director – what's his name, Dallas; gave talks to the Community Council and other organisations."

"That was in the early days, so why all the secrecy now? Why has their approach changed? Have they gone into dodgy, experimental areas? I have to know. I don't trust the police on this one."

"I don't know what they're up to. Just be careful that's all and keep me informed...and if you drag this young lady into it you'll be responsible for her safety."

"I can take care of myself you know, Mr. Parke," said Louisa. "I'm tougher than I look."
The minister changed tack,

"Remember some of those other crack-brained stunts you've been involved in, Jim? *I* certainly do. There was that time you slept out in old Blackhope Castle to see if it was haunted. Then you tried to track down criminals from Carlisle who you were convinced were hiding out in the forest."

"They were, Morton. Don't you remember? They broke into the school in the days before the security alarms were fitted. They helped themselves to food from the kitchen and washed in the school toilets."

34

"They were only caught because I saw them moving off during one of my morning walks in the woods."

"Granted, you were right on that occasion but the supernatural stuff was a bit over the top – tryin' to take photos of the ghost of Hob Hill for example, or pokin' about that abandoned churchyard in the middle of the night to investigate some old legend. Then you were convinced *An Bile Buada* was a coven, which got you into all sorts of strange situations. There was that protestin' up at the Clyde over the nuclear subs, goin' to London to demonstrate against the Iraq War; not to mention the big cat sightings."

"I did see the cats, Morton. And now I've seen giant rats. I have the pictures to prove it. And thousands of people thought that war was unjust – even you."

He was becoming defensive.

"I know, but take my advice, "said Parke, I'd hate to be sayin' prayers for you if this thing gets too serious. Stay in touch."

With a long look at both of them, he left. They waited for the door to close on Parke's retreating back then Humble located his iPad, half-listening for the shop bell.

He kept the machine in the back shop together with his now ageing laptop but Humble was still reluctant to part with his desktop computer in the apartment above the shop.

"I hadn't realised you'd been so active, Jim," Louisa said. "You're a more interesting person than I thought. Mr. Parke means well but I hope you're not going to let him put you off, are you?"

Louisa moved close to him as he tapped the tablet. She had one hand on his left shoulder. He sensed her warmth and struggled to remain composed. It was hard. Briskly he scrolled along the touch screen,

"No, I'm itching to find out more and I won't be deterred, but there's nothing here about Falcon Research. Plenty of other references though...birds-of-prey, courier services, even a car; nothing much else."

"What about the O.S map?"

"I've looked - nothing. Here let me show you."

He reached over to his desk and pulled out the Ordnance Survey map for the area. His finger pointed to Caithland Forest.

"There are no buildings marked and no name - just a space," he said.

"I think military buildings are shown in the same way. They're there but without names. Could Falcon be linked to the armed forces do you think?"

"It's possible. Who knows?"

"Well I'd like to find out. Why don't we both do some investigating?"

Humble thought he would love to do some investigating but of a different kind. The shop bell rang. They postponed their conversation.

∗

Morton Parke felt concern for Humble, especially when the shop-owner gave in to his insatiable curiosity. Back at his house adjacent to the church he confided his thoughts to Margaret,

"He's off on one of his wild goose chases again. Louisa Moscadini is eggin' him on I'm sure of it – she's a bit too free and easy if you ask me."

"Morton, you're being too judgemental. He's a feller in his prime looking for fun. This can be a boring place for the adventurous and Louisa's a lovely, intelligent girl."

She smiled faintly at him.

Parke looked at her,

"Margaret, she's got tattoos."

"A lot of them have. Doesn't mean they're not respectable."

He frowned,

"Take those girls from that wild family down on Pine Street – the Guffocks. The three of them mothers before they were out of their teens and not a husband between them. One even went to Carlisle to work and came back with another child. No sign of the father."

"Your prejudices are showing, dear. You're not supposed to have any in your line of work. We've had this conversation before. These things have always happened. Their families look after them in their own way. At least they're not on the streets, taking drugs, drinking or selling themselves. Louisa is from a good Catholic family."

"Since when did that count for anything? " Parke said.

"Let's not go there."

He was startled. After all their time together Margaret could still surprise him.

"Where do you learn these expressions?" he asked, "Facebook? Twitter?"

37

"No. It's just the way young people speak these days. You have to talk a bit like that if you're going to understand them. The world's changing quickly and we have to change with it if we're going to reach out to people. Besides I don't use social media much - only just started really. It can be fun. Our computers are not just for Church business. I'm actually thinking of getting an iPad."

Parke shuddered. He was inclined to think electronic communication-gadgets were a waste of time if not dangerous.

"Anyway," she continued, "With regard to Louisa's religion. This is not Glasgow or Belfast. Sectarianism has no hold in Candywood, thank God. That's one of the reasons we came here, remember?"

"Aye, you're right. We still need to think how we can help the lad and make sure he keeps out of danger. I don't like that Falcon place or that Marcus Burn for all he's a copper. I'll have to keep an eye on young Jim for the good of his health."

Margaret made no comment.

*

The father of one of the children Parke had mentioned was at that moment preparing for a busy evening in the Lingdale Arms. He was Rocky Craggs and the girl in question was Shannon Guffock, aged thirty-one. She and Rocky had got together when his marriage was failing. She had two other children to different fathers. An amicable arrangement existed between Craggs and Shannon's family involving generous cash payments, free drinks and favours when required. In return no claims were made directly on him and Shannon was able to live her life as she pleased.

As often in Candywood, the facts were generally known but rarely discussed except behind closed doors. Rocky was forty-two and had been married to a woman named Kendra. She had run off three years ago and the last he heard she was working in a club in Carlisle. The owner was her partner.

There were two children from the marriage. Ann-Marie and Michael were now teenagers. When Kendra jumped ship they had opted to stay with Craggs. Some locals had briefly referred to Kendra as a *slapper* but this soon stopped. No one risked annoying Rocky.

Sticky had already arrived and was on his usual bar stool. The other regulars would wander in later. Cooking smells from the restaurant kitchen drifted in - burgers, chicken curry and chips.

A man who could almost be described as a giant, Craggs looked as if you could run a tank over him and he would get up. He was known for his banter and quick tongue. He ran a tight ship.

"Got that bloody room finished yet, Bridget?" he called to the cleaner. "We'll need the lounge in good order for the meals tonight."

"Aye...nearly there. Do ah get extra if ah stay longer to polish the cutlery an' the glasses?"

Bridget was of indeterminate age and seemed to have been there forever - in with the bricks. A tiny stick-like woman and a conscientious worker, she was nobody's fool. Craggs answered,

"Don't try yer luck, woman. Just get on with it will ye?"

She pretended to be upset…

"Ye're a hard boss so ye are, Rocky."

He laughed. It was a joke they shared. Bridget was a diamond.

"It's true, Rock. You *are* a hard boss."

He turned. It was Samantha Leoch, the owner of Brookbank Riding School. She was thirty-two, generously-proportioned and attractive in a healthy, country way with rich, auburn hair. She and Craggs were rumoured to be an item. No one knew for sure. They liked to keep the locals guessing.

She smiled and looked coquettishly at Rocky,

"Are you going to be free later, tough guy, when the pub's quiet?"

"Maybe," he said. "Depends how the night goes." Leaning over the bar, she spoke in a low voice,

"I'll be back then – big feller. Don't work too hard. Save some time for me."

He watched her supple, confident movements as she left.

*

In the middle of the afternoon the shop was suddenly empty,

"I'm game to have a closer look at Falcon," Louisa said. "I know you're going to and I can't resist the chance to investigate it. Can I come with you - please?"

She had her right hand on his left arm, the other placed on his chest. He was having difficulty feigning indifference. Louisa realised the effect she was having on him and pressed home her advantage,

"We'll make a good team. It would be an adventure. It's so boring round here sometimes, I could scream."

"Could be dangerous…you heard what Morton said."

"Please, Jim, pretty please with a cherry on top. We'll be careful. You could get someone else to go along if you're worried."

He thought of being alone with Louisa in the forest,

Another person would get in the way. On the other hand she's clearly a risk taker, even a little reckless.

He felt the responsibility…

"Kirk Andrews might be interested. He's very sound and keeps a cool head. Would you be okay with that?"

Humble was thinking furiously,

Kirk is older and married and he's supposed to be a pillar of the community.

"Yeah, great. When do we start?"

"What about tomorrow," he suggested, "Do you have to go to church?"

"No, I can say I'm doing some studying with one of my flatmates, Kath. It'll be okay. I'm not a great one for church anyway. Thank you."

She kissed his left cheek then, overcome by an excess of excitement, stood up on her toes and kissed him on the lips. The shop bell rang and they separated hastily, looking in the direction of the door. It was Samantha Leoch. She smirked,

"Not interrupting anything, am I?"

Four

In a laboratory building inside the Falcon complex, work was finishing for the day. Some of the scientists lived on site within the extensive grounds. Those who were not involved with classified, experimental work were bussed out to Gillerston or villages in the district.

Workers from Candywood had routine jobs and returned home at five. They had no knowledge of the other purposes for which the complex had been established several years ago, on the site of a former chicken farm. More land had been acquired from the local Highwater Estate and the area had been extended far into the forest.

It was a very secure, double-fenced zone of considerable acreage. Security personnel worked shifts together with certain specialised staff. Falcon operated around the clock.

A Falcon scientist, Doctor Aashish Prahalad, was peering at something in a closed tank of gently swirling liquid. There was a porthole arrangement for viewing the interior. Prahalad's concentration was such that he did not notice the security guard enter the room. The guard observed the scientist quietly for a few moments then coughed.

Prahalad whirled round. The guard was wearing a dark blue uniform with the Falcon logo on the breast pocket. His cap carried the same insignia. He was one of the least thuggish of the guards, almost friendly in fact. The scientist wasn't nervous of him.

"Time's getting on, Doctor. Most people have gone home. Don't you feel tired?"

Yes," said Prahalad, "But I need to stay a little longer. Something's not quite right with this experiment." The guard shook his head almost smiled,

"You're becoming a workaholic, Doctor Prahalad. Why not go home and rest? You'll be better able to work in the morning."

"Just another half-hour, Geoff. I have to run a couple more checks."

"Would you like me to bring you a coffee or a tea?"

"Tea please. No milk and a little sugar. Thank you."

"No problem - back soon."

The guard left. Prahalad peered intently at the tank again. Something was visible through the porthole. He began to make notes. There were several screens in a bank behind.

When Geoff returned, Prahalad was still taking notes furiously. He seemed agitated, occasionally checking the screens. He took the tea with a quick word of thanks and returned to his task having already forgotten Geoff. The guard left the room for fifteen minutes and returned quietly. He observed that the scientist was looking sleepy.

Prahalad finally sank into a chair and almost immediately fell into a deep sleep. The guard walked over to the tank and peered through the porthole. Then he walked to the door, opened it and checked the corridor outside. He moved to an array of electronic key-pads located in the corridor, performed the required operations. Then he took out a phone and texted one word -

43

"READY."

*

After the shop closed Humble and Louisa began to prepare for tomorrow's forest trip. Emboldened by their earlier encounter, he suggested going up to his flat above the shop and she agreed. Now she looked around the place with keen interest,

"You have so many amazing things."

"I usually keep anything unusual or special I find. There's a photo collection in the bookcase on the back wall. Would you like coffee or some wine perhaps?"

"Coffee," she said. "I'm driving. Your books are fascinating… The Prehistoric Atlas, The World's Greatest Mysteries; Explaining the Unexplained. Quite a collection! Do you read anything else?"

"Yes. Crime and historical novels as well as classics. I'm also a big fan of Science Fiction."

Louisa nodded. She noted his shelves held books by Phillip K. Dick, Arthur C.Clarke and others.

He showed his concern...

"Do you need to let your family know you're okay? It's past closing time."

"It's fine. I called them. I told them we were checking the stock and cashing up. Besides I'm twenty-six. I don't live at home now. I share a flat with my friends, Kath and Jane. I texted them. Anyway, I've got my car."

He remembered Louisa was an independent girl. She owned a yellow Citroen in keeping with her mercurial character. She carried on talking,

"I like crime fiction as well. I love following the clues and trying to solve the puzzles."

He moved to the computer. The iPad was still downstairs.

"We could have a look on the Net to see if we can get any information. I'll log on then bring the coffee," he said.

He worked at the machine then walked into the small kitchen. She sat at the computer desk and moved the mouse, continuing to talk to him from the living room,

"This is very self-contained. Kitchen, living room, bathroom and study. Is your bedroom up here too?"
He almost dropped the milk,

"Er, yes. Further back."

"I bet you've got lots of interesting books and things there too. Do you have many friends to visit?"

"Yes, quite a few. I have friends in the Town," referring to Cruiksdale. "I belong to a few clubs – photography, local history, walking and so on."

He wondered why she was asking these questions. Her directness slightly unnerved him. She threw him completely with her next question,

"Is there a girl in your life right now, Jim? I haven't noticed any around."

Her intense curiosity was showing. It was a character flaw she sometimes revealed, not always tactfully. He returned to the living room, set down the tray of drinks and biscuits and looked carefully at her. She was still scrolling through websites.

"I'm in-between relationships at the moment if you must know," he said. "The last one was quite a while ago - You?"

"No one special."

45

"I'm surprised."

"Why?"

"Louisa," he said, screwing up his courage. "You're a very attractive girl. Men must be falling over themselves to…"

He left the sentence unfinished.

"Thanks," she said, showing no reaction, "But you're my boss. I didn't know you thought of me in that way."

"Difficult not to. I'm human after all."

"I'm no innocent, you know."

"None of my business."

"True. Sorry to be so nosy. Can't help it sometimes but it's out of order. Better get on with the job in hand."

She took a biscuit and returned to the machine. Humble brought the iPad up and they both continued searching. The atmosphere had subtly changed between them.

*

At a point on the inner perimeter fence around the Falcon complex, two men, a security guard and another dressed in Falcon corporate clothing, checked the message from Geoff. The security guard spoke.

"We're good to go. He's switched off the perimeter alarm system, the electric current and the cameras for fifteen minutes as arranged."

"We'll have to watch the embedded ground alarms and the searchlight sweep," his companion warned.

"I know. Speed is the name of the game. They'll spot something's wrong if we're not quick."

He bent down with the heavy-duty cutter whilst the other person peered into the darkness, eyes looking in all directions. After a few moments they hurried to a nearby building to bring out the escapees.

*

The Lingdale Arms was livening up. Meals were being served in the lounge and the bar was crammed with regular drinkers, male and female. Sticky was drinking himself into alcoholic heaven as usual and some others were approaching that state. It was Saturday night. Samantha Leoch returned,

"Hi, Rock, got any spare time or are you too busy for a lonely, country girl?"

"Not right now, darlin.' There's a couple of things going on I'm not happy with."

He nodded to his right. She followed his gaze. In one corner a man with a head of unruly, light brown hair and a long face, was sitting with his hands wrapped around a beer. A whisky was nearby. He was dressed in thick trousers, outdoor shirt and work boots. Strangely, no one was sitting close to him, despite the crowded conditions. Leoch turned back,

"Oh yes, Bain. He's got a nerve coming in here."

Adam Bain was a forestry manager for Shawland Timber, a company owning most of the local commercial forestry operations on both sides of the border. Craggs leaned on the bar, talking to Leoch in a low voice,

47

"People are beginning to resent his playing away from home, especially if wives or girlfriends are involved. He hasn't tried it on with you has he?"
She expressed outrage,

"Rocky, you know I have eyes only for you. Besides I would never come between a man and his wife. What do you think I am?"

Her protestations were genuine. Leoch could be generous with her favours if the relationship felt right but she was not wanton. Some locals described her as, "A bit of a girl."

She just hadn't found the right man yet. Bain had a long-suffering wife, Colleen, and four children. Colleen's fortitude in the common knowledge of his infidelities, earned her respect from some. Others thought she should have thrown him out long ago.

Bain was a predatory womaniser but he knew better than to make advances to Samantha Leoch. She would have sent him on his way with more than a verbal rebuke. His conquests were lonely wives whose husbands worked away (driving, oil rigs, the armed forces.) Currently he was considered to have gone too far even by the flexible standards of Candywood.

Craggs indicated the evolving scene,

"Oh-oh. It's kicking off. Excuse me."
He came out from behind the bar. The drink-sodden Sticky was beginning to goad Bain,

"Who y're shaggin' these days, Adam, my man?"
His beer slopped in its glass as he waved it towards Bain, who stared at him then looked away.

"Ah hear they're getting' younger", Sticky persisted. "Ye'll have to watch out for jail–bait."

"Girls can look older than they are y'know. You should save it for the wife."

He grinned. People shifted in their seats. Bain's fist bunched,

"Shut your mouth you little shit. You're pissed as usual. Get away home before you fall over."

Craggs moved towards them,

"Come on, guys, cut it out. Pete, you've had enough to drink. Take yourself home and sleep it off. Maybe you'd better leave too, Adam."

Bain stared at Craggs,

"I have a right to a quiet drink if I want to. My money's as good as anyone else's. Just get that mouthy little bastard out of here before I do it myself."

Sticky was not willing to give up. Drink emboldened him,

"S'all right. Adam here won't do anythin' to me. Ah know things about the forest he won't want anyone else to know, 'specially about that Falcon place. Come to that, so do you pal, don't ye?"

This was directed to Craggs who suddenly looked uncomfortable.

"Ah've got spies out there, "Sticky continued, digging a hole for himself. " People give me a little money now an' then to help keep me mouth closed - y'know – a few pressies. This bugger won't though."

He indicated Bain,

"Tight as a duck's arse. Free wi' the women but not wi' money."

Bain rose from his seat, his face twisted with anger. Craggs moved to restrain him. At that moment the door was vigorously pushed open and two men entered, momentarily freezing the tableau.

The arrivals were Tommy Coates, a broad-shouldered Falcon worker in his thirties and Charlie Swatte, the local haulage contractor and Tommy's uncle. Without a word they shoved their way over to Bain, grabbed him and began hustling him out of the door, regardless of his struggles; their anger apparent.

Bain was protesting his innocence. A punch to the head, below one ear shut him up. Craggs hurried over,

"What's going on, Charlie?"

"Stay out of it, Rocky. You're a big guy but there are more of us outside. We're goin' to give this bastard the hammerin' he's deserved for a long time. He's been tryin' to have his way wi' Tina."

The room went silent. Even Sticky paid attention. Tina was Tommy's younger sister.

Craggs was shocked,

"That's seriously out of order, Charlie. She's only fifteen isn't she?"

Swatte gave him a bleak look…

"Correct, Rocky, quite correct."

Five

Louisa and Humble heard the commotion from across the street. They had completed their preparations for tomorrow's trip. He tidied away the maps, logged off.

"I'll make some coffee."

"Any more of those biscuits? It's past my tea-time"

"Better than that. You can have some of my home-made cake?"

"Impressive. Where did you learn to do that?"

"I've always had an interest in cooking. Now I'm on my own I have no choice - can't live on takeaways in Candy. There's a distinct absence of Macdonald's and Subway, you'll notice, and *The Heart's Content* is too full of the 'Ladies who Lunch' set."

She laughed. He was referring to a local café with pretensions to become a smart bistro.

"Get the coffee and cake then, before I die of starvation."

They suddenly became aware of the noise outside. He moved to a window and looked down into the street,

"Rocky's place is livelier than usual tonight. Wonder what's going on?"

She joined him,

"Looks like somebody is being escorted from the pub. There's a bunch of men standing around outside."

People were spilling out from the Lingdale. Louisa and Humble could make out Rocky Craggs and Samantha Leoch.

The riding-instructor had made a few meaningful comments when she had caught them together in the shop but they had refused to bite.

None of her business, Louisa had thought. *Nosy cow.*

"I think I can see Adam Bain," Louisa said moving the curtain further aside. "Those guys are taking him somewhere. Everybody seems to be getting agitated, whatever it is."

"Candywood retribution," he said. "You know what he's like."

"Yes, the local stud. Well he'd like to think he is. - maybe gone too far this time."

"It was inevitable," he said. "He's put too many backs up."

"Too right," she agreed. "A total swine."

"Remember that business at the school?"

"Oh yes," she said. "A couple of years ago…the School Secretary."

"Melissa Jarney. She and Bain had an affair. She had a key to the school and she knew the security code. They used to sneak into the school at night. Melissa would tell her husband she was out with friends or working a bit of overtime."

Louisa giggled,

"Well I suppose she was in a way."

Humble pretended to be shocked,

"No need to be coarse, Louisa."

She looked thoughtful,

"But remember the details when they were made public?"

"Do I? It was pure tabloid. They used to do it in the school gym, in the staff-room and even on the floor of the school office - must have been a tad uncomfortable."
Louisa giggled again. It was a nervous habit. She lightly pinched his left arm.

"Ow!"

"Now who's being coarse?"

He was suddenly serious,

"You know those two caused a great deal of unhappiness when the story broke. The whole of Candy knew about it."
She nodded,

"But they kept their heads down."

"Not everybody. It came out eventually. There are some decent people here you know, who run the committees, support charities or help their neighbours. They tend to keep low profiles until they have to stand up and be counted."

"I know, I know. Candy produces some really excellent people as well as a few who could do with personality-bypass operations," Louisa said.
Humble considered her remark,

"People are very flawed. You notice it more in a place like this."

"Actually," she said, "He tried to come on to me once, but I let him know there was no chance. He didn't even get a sniff. Adam Bain is a sleaze-ball. Besides he's married with kids. I may be a bit of a lapsed Catholic but I draw the line at that kind of thing. It only leads to misery for all concerned,"

"I'm glad," he said. "The thought of you with him…"
He shook his head.

She looked at him quizzically,

"You're not getting over-protective, Mr. Humble are you?" A smile tweaked the corners of her mouth. He blinked,

"Course not. It's just that you're a temptation for any man, Miss Moscadini and he has a reputation for being hard to resist."

"Thanks for the compliment but I'm too wise to give in to the likes of him."

They returned to their observation of the street, opening the window for a better view.

"They'll be taking him up an alley to give him a kicking," he commented grimly. "He must have pissed somebody off big time. It's Candy law – far enough away from the real law. Maybe he'll learn his lesson at last."

"That's Sticky Hagg down there isn't it?"

"Drunk out of his skull as usual. Rocky seems to be leading him away. He's swaying all over the place. He'll be lucky to make it home."

Sticky began a retreat from the pub walking with the deliberate care of the truly inebriated. Craggs watched him. The crowd dispersed. Bain and his captors had disappeared. As Louisa and Humble looked down at the scene they could see Craggs walk down the street a little and take out a phone. Signals in Candywood depended on where you happened to be. Craggs frowned and walked on, pressing the keypad as he went. Humble registered the fact vaguely then turned back to Louisa,

"Time's getting on. I'd better contact Kirk if I'm going to."

"Okay. I'm kicking keen to get out there and nose around."

54

He called Andrews, who readily agreed to meet at the shop at eleven the next morning. Humble knew him well and the Local Council Area Manager revealed he had already suspected there was something odd about Falcon. He was happy to help. Louisa looked at her watch. It was nine p.m,

"It's later than I thought. I've had a text from Jane. She's worried about me. See you tomorrow."

He saw her to her car. She gave him a brief kiss on one cheek before sliding into the driver's seat. Across the street, Samantha Leoch standing near the smokers, waited for Craggs to return. She smirked as she watched Louisa drive away.

At The Falcon Centre, Geoff and his colleague were finished. It had been a struggle against the clock to get the objects of the exercise through the fence without being detected. They restored the cut section as best they could but they knew it would be spotted eventually.

By that time, Falcon may have more urgent concerns to deal with. It was a risk for them, but driven by their ideals, they had good reason to take it.

Bain was bundled into an alley near the fire station by Coates and Swatte along with three other men who had waited outside. He continued to protest,

"I didn't touch the girl, just spoke to her a few times that's all."

"Aye, right," said Coates. "Too late for that now y' slimy bastard."

The beating was comprehensive and efficient. Two men kept watch at either end of the narrow alley as the others got to work. Before Bain fell into unconsciousness, Coates gave him a verbal message,

"We're leavin' you outside yer house so yer Missus and neighbours can see what Candy justice is about. We want you out o' the place by Monday y' piece of shite. If we see you again around here you'll get more of the same, only worse – understand?"

A kick provided a useful prompt to Bain's reluctant tongue. He nodded, blood filling his mouth. His head and most of his body was a mass of unbearable pain. They bundled him into one of Swatte's vans and drove to Bain's house, rolling him out and onto the pavement. A few final kicks slammed into his ribs and they were gone. Bain gratefully drifted into blackness.

*

Humble woke at five-thirty a.m, an ingrained habit resulting from years as a shop-owner. It was Sunday. He languished in bed, thoughts of Louisa swimming through his brain. He shook his head to clear them and stumbled to the bathroom to shower and shave.

As he had explained to Louisa, he enjoyed cooking. Normally he applied his skills to evening meals, eating a quick breakfast each morning then a hurried lunch. On busy days, there wasn't even time for that. He might grab soup and a roll from the Heart's Content, eating them in the back shop.

On Sundays he opened until eleven a.m for newspapers and other requirements of the local population. The shop was a retail goldmine, a mini-mart and general caterer to diverse needs. The only competition was the post office, which doubled as a stationery and gift shop. They co-existed amicably, aware there was custom for both as long as they differentiated sufficiently from each other.

There were supermarkets in Cruiksdale but there was a tendency to travel to Carlisle for serious shopping. A car was almost essential. The few buses could easily disappear if subsidies were withdrawn.

He made fresh coffee, croissants and toast, wondering what Kirk would make of his plan to investigate Falcon. Kirk Andrews was a tall, slightly stooped, bespectacled man in his forties. A supporter of community interest groups, Andrews had a learned, intellectual look about him. He walked with short energetic steps, his feet slightly outwards.

Some of the local 'tweenagers' made quacking noises when he passed. He ignored them.

With his wife, Grace, he ran the local history society and the couple were considered to be highly respectable. Andrews also wrote crime fiction, using a nom-de-plume. A good mystery always intrigued him, which was why he had responded so quickly to Humble's text.

The Council official had readily taken the opportunity to apply for his current post when it became vacant. He ran the local Council office. It was essentially an outpost covering the township and the area down to the border.

He was known as 'The District Officer' by his colleagues at Headquarters, who regarded Candywood as the Outback. This meant he was usually left to his own devices with few visits from H.Q. Most communication was now electronic.

Andrews understood the baffling culture of Candywood, so was perfect for the job. He wasn't going anywhere else. His personal suspicions about Falcon were founded upon observation and tuning in to gossip, the facts turned over by a nimble brain capable of reasoned deduction. He was the man to help.

Humble finished his breakfast, cleared up and prepared for the morning's business. He had walking boots ready for the trip as well as an Ordnance Survey map, food and drink, a camera and binoculars. At eight-thirty a.m. Louisa drove up and entered the shop. The street was quiet.

She was wearing outdoor trousers, light boots, and a sweatshirt and had a small rucksack. She smiled,

"How are you this morning, Jim? Ready for an adventure?"

"Ready for anything, Louisa."

"Tempting fate?"

"Who dares wins," he said.

"Okay, we'll dare and hope to win. Kirk on his way?"

"Later. Oh, here's the first customer. Early birds around here."

He readied himself to look business-like.

The morning's trade was unusually brisk and both Louisa and Humble kept their ears open, listening to the gossip. And gossip there was, especially about the scene in the Lingdale.

At about ten a.m Samantha Leoch dropped in for Sunday papers and some minor items. She looked pointedly at Louisa and Humble, noticing Louisa's outdoor clothing,

"Off for a ramble in the woods are we?"
They pretended indifference.

"Your Sunday order is ready for you, Ms. Leoch," Louisa said coolly.

Leoch was not to be put off,

"I'd be careful, Louisa, if I were you. Our Jim here used to be a boy scout. He might want to show you his woggle."

There was a burst of laughter quickly choked off from somewhere amongst the waiting queue. Other customers in the shop controlled themselves with difficulty. Leoch's voice carried well.

"That'll be three-nineteen please," said Louisa, showing remarkable forbearance although her face was slightly flushed.

"Thanks. Well, you'll be okay with Jim. If things get a little hot I'm sure he'll rise to the occasion."

She left, the habitual smirk adorning her face. Louisa walked calmly into the back shop. Humble heard her banging about in there before she emerged again, tight-lipped. She spoke *sotto voce…*

"One day I'll give that supercilious cow a good slapping."

"Don't blame you. You did well not to react. What does she know anyway? Come to think of it what business is it of hers?"

59

"Sour grapes. She's not getting any younger. If she doesn't trap Rocky soon she'll be left with her four-legged friends. Like many people here, she jumps to conclusions."

"I don't give a toss about Sam Leoch's opinions," he said.

The bell rang again. It was Andrews. The time was ten forty-five. Humble quickly shut up shop and they moved to the flat upstairs. Andrews had some disturbing news for them.

Six

"Did you see any of the trouble at the Lingdale last night? Andrews asked. "The shop is almost directly opposite it. "

"Yes, we…er…I heard the noise and looked out. I saw Bain being led away by a couple of guys and Sticky wandering off. I don't know what it was about. Some difference of opinion probably."

"I'm surprised no one mentioned it at the shop this morning. I suppose the news has just broken within the last hour. I met some people on the way here who told me."

"Told you what?"

"Sticky Hagg was found in the Candy River this morning. He's dead."

"What happened?"

"Not sure. Maybe he fell into the river whilst drunk and couldn't get out. It's happened to others in Candywood."

"I know," said Humble. "Poor Sticky."

There was a short silence then Humble told him about his encounter in the forest. Andrew's perceptive mind worked overtime as they explained their thoughts about Falcon,

"You think the police are not to be trusted on this?"

"They may genuinely be convinced that Falcon is kosher," Humble said, "I just have a gut feeling that there's something wrong out there, something big they're hiding from us mere mortals."

"Any ideas?"

"Not a Scooby," said Humble. "Apart from the lush plants and weird animals."

"You know that's the second Hagg brother to die unexpectedly," said Andrews.

They looked puzzled then Humble remembered,

"Oh yes," he said. "Sticky's brother, Ronnie was an alcoholic too. Got a job as a janitor at the school when Willie Moss was sacked."

"I remember," said Andrews. "For nicking money from the school tuck shop."

"Pathetic." Humble shook his head. "But he was desperate. In debt up to his eyeballs to a loan shark in Carlisle. But Sticky had another brother didn't he?"

"Still has," said Andrews." Lives in a shack in the forest. Bit of a recluse really. His name is George as far as I remember."

"Geordie Hagg," Humble said. "The only one left now. Ronnie died of drink inevitably. He couldn't keep the job down – always drunk. Not a good idea when you work in proximity to children. The Council booted him out tout de suite once his problem became apparent. His feet never touched the ground. I'm surprised they hired him in the first place."

"Alcoholics are usually very skilled at hiding their addiction, but it reveals itself eventually. Still, not a nice way to go," said Andrews. "Must have left its mark on Geordie. No wonder he prefers to be on his own."

"As far as I know, Geordie doesn't have a drink problem, no addictions at all. Just doesn't like people. Who can blame him?"

He folded his arms, remembering the events.

Louisa made a suggestion,

"Maybe we could ask him if he's seen or heard anything in the forest."

"We could try," agreed Andrews. "If he'll talk to us."

"There was another incident last night," said Andrews unexpectedly.

They turned to him. He moved to the sofa and sat down,

"You saw Bain being taken away?"

"Yes," they answered together.

"He was found severely beaten outside his house by somebody taking his dog out for a late night walk. It seems to have been Tommy Coates, Charlie Swatte and a few others. They had re-arranged his face very efficiently. The rest of him was not so good either. One or two of the neighbours got him on his feet and took him into the house. They left his wife to clean him up. He was offered a lift to the hospital but Colleen said she would see to him."

Louisa grimaced.

Andrews continued,

"That's not all. Colleen and the children took off for the town this morning without Bain. She has friends there. Seems she's left him at last. Maybe she'll head back home to Newcastle eventually. By the time most people were out and about, Bain was nowhere to be seen."

"Did anyone call the police?" asked Louisa.

"Are you kidding? Nobody around here would grass on those guys. With Bain having gone off somewhere there's nothing the police can do except run a search and rescue operation if he's reported as missing. He wasn't exactly the most popular person in the community."

"I know," said Humble. "He made a lot of enemies."

There was another short silence.

"Well, we'd better go if we're going," said Andrews. "Which is the best route I wonder?" He spread out the O.S map.

*

Although it was Sunday, Prahalad was working. He had a habit of working any hours provided it got the work done – almost a martyr to the job. His worries about the experiments were not resolved. Meticulously he worked through the information on his iPad, searched databases on a computer and occasionally consulted the Internet. He decided to inform Falcon senior management on Monday.

The scientist was pleased to find that a colleague, Senior Agronomist Doctor Lance Bowman, was in the building. A tall, mild-mannered Londoner, Bowman was just as focussed as Prahalad but his speciality was plants. He was part of the team running the hydroponic farm complex as well as the experimental agricultural work – a remit in keeping with Falcon's official raison d'etre.

Bowman's East London social housing background had not helped him to rise to the level he now occupied. He had worked hard to accomplish that himself – an example of social mobility. Despite his status he retained a certain street-wise demeanour. He had concerns of his own. They met in the staff restaurant manned by a skeleton staff on double time. Bowman opened the conversation,

"You look worried, Aashish. I suspect you're overdoing it as always. What's the problem? Tell Uncle Lance."

He used levity to try to lift Prahalad's mood, realising that things were weighing heavily on his colleague. Prahalad sipped at his tea, toying with a breakfast roll,

"Lance, the strain of always working in secrecy is getting to me. In some countries all this security wouldn't be necessary. We're doing important things here and we shouldn't have to work in a cage."

"Just the way things are. The Public are sensitive about certain technologies and this country has a free press. Think of what they could do if they knew about some of the stuff we're working on. It may be worth it one day when the benefits of our research are appreciated, but for now we're obliged to be discreet."
Prahalad stared into his tea thoughtfully.

"But there's something else isn't there?" Bowman persisted.

Prahalad looked up,

"There are anomalies with some of the live specimens. The process has some kind of flaw but I can't find it. Not all the bioengineered life forms are stable. I think I will have to inform senior management. We may have to shut down the process until we can isolate the problem. I've also come to realise that I'm not happy with the way Falcon uses its labour force, the people from outside the country. Now and then there is an influx and I wonder about their origins. Most of them speak no English apart from a few words and they all seem pathetic, cowed. I think Falcon has some hold over them."

"I'm told that the long-term serving prisoners here have volunteered to take part in experiments rather than rot in prison. I don't know how true that is but they seem to receive reasonable treatment. Then there are ones who appear to be virtual slaves. You know the ones I mean – we see them now and again doing the dirtier jobs. They're kept separate from the local workers who only see the conventional stuff Falcon does. Every now and then a few of them disappear. It's becoming a moral issue for me. What's happening to them?"

Bowman was sympathetic,

"Actually I've been wondering the same thing, though my department doesn't use them much. It's a worry I agree, a bit of a moral dilemma. Changing the subject slightly, some of the plants and crops my team have been working on have exhibited weird growth spurts and may be getting out of control. I'm not best pleased with the way it's going right now."

"What do you think we should do?"

At that moment the Falcon interdepartmental communications system suddenly engaged and an official-sounding voice began making an announcement…

"Attention all research staff. An incident has occurred at the perimeter fence. Please report to the main hall at once. Thank you. Attention all research staff…"

The two scientists exchanged looks.

*

Humble, Louisa and Andrews walked past two houses and Lamb's butcher's shop before turning left into

66

Archibald Street. On the corner was *The Three Valleys Hotel*, often used by visitors. Archibald Street was mostly private houses but also contained a bakery and a unisex hairdressers, 'Cuts and Trims.' The remnants of yesterday's baking smells competed with the cloying odour of permanent wave lotion. There were a few people about who greeted them in a familiar way but all three wisely resisted being drawn into conversation. A small park and recreation ground was on their left before they walked down a winding lane into Candyside, the street running parallel to the river.

"We'll be away from most of the houses if we keep to the back lanes," said Humble.

"It's Sunday. Should be quiet," Andrews said. "Which is the best way into the forest do you think?"

"How about along the old railway?" suggested Humble. "From there we can climb up Watchman Hill and be able to look down on part of the Falcon place. It's so big we may have to get closer eventually if we're to find out anything."

"The line's pretty overgrown," Andrews said. "Tough going in places."

"We're all fit enough aren't we?" Louisa said, dodging a large pothole. "I know you guys do a lot of walking."

"We do our best," said Humble. "But we can't match you at swimming and running."

"Got to keep in shape."

He said nothing.

Candyside led into a gravel path down to the track of the old Carlisle railway line, lifted in the sixties during the railway closures.

On the left were allotments and areas of land rented or owned by people who kept horses, goats, hens or rabbits.

There were vegetable gardens and some flocks of sheep bred for showing. A heavy porcine smell came from a piggery, thickening the air as they passed. On the right rolled the Candy on its way to join the River Ling. They slowed automatically as they came to the river, remembering that Sticky had met his end there.

"Oh, shit," said Humble then caught himself, wondering if he had caused offence. "Look who's ahead."

Louisa did not react. She was too busy trying to control her anger. Samantha Leoch was riding slowly towards them, keeping her horse to a walk. She slowed as she approached and brought the horse to a stop,

"Ah, the intrepid explorers. Louisa, dear, you do get around. Two men today? What stamina you must have."

Humble held Louisa's arm gently. He could feel her seething. He kept his face expressionless,

"Hi, Samantha. Out for a trot? Good day for it."

"Heading for the forest, folks?" said Leoch, continuing. "Watch out if you are. You never know what you might find."

She gave her usual smirk,

"You have to know where you're going if you head into Caithland. I know you guys are savvy about the wild but be careful, Louisa. Even with respectable gentlemen like these, going down to the woods with them may not be a teddy bear's picnic. I wouldn't let them penetrate too deeply."

There was no reaction. Leoch leaned down and spoke to the horse,

"Walk on, Freya."

She dug in her heels. Waving her riding-stick, she rode off along the riverside path…

"Enjoy."

"Bitch!" hissed Louisa.

"Leave it, Louisa. We've got an investigation to do. Forget Samantha Leoch."

There was a narrow, arched stone bridge over the Candy. They stopped for a few moments looking down at the toffee coloured water. Humble wondered if Sticky had really fallen in.

Or was pushed, he found himself thinking.

At the other side the path became a track. Ahead was the line of the railway, overgrown with plants in the carbon rich ground. Forcing their way through the thick growth they climbed up to the railway line and looked west. The recent dry spell was about to give way to rain if the massed clouds were any indication.

"Watchman Hill," said Andrews pointing ahead. A rounded peak showed above the trees. It had a small cairn at its summit.

"A bit to go before we get there," said Humble as he set off along the black, stony track. The others followed.

The lumps of flinty gravel were large and made for hard walking even with their boots. Occasionally they had to fight their way through thick trees and bushes as well as splash though puddles. The line snaked ahead. Trees crowded in from the left side. On the right the ground fell away to marshy land. The river wound to the southwest and out of sight. Objects began to appear at the side of the line nearest the woods.

"The place where machinery comes to die," said Andrews.

The track was lined with an eclectic collection of cars, vans, motorbikes, farm-machinery, oil drums and assorted detritus of all kinds. The oldest and most rusted dated from at least forty years ago. The latest were indicative of the twenty-first century: old computers, pre-digital TVs; 'e–waste'…a technology graveyard.

"I'd forgotten about all this," Humble said. "Stretches for about two miles. I don't normally walk along here because it makes me angry. Don't know why it can't be sorted. "

"No one will take responsibility," said Andrews, "The Community Council has tried to do something and there have been clean-up campaigns as you'll remember. The stuff seems to just accumulate again afterwards. The oldest vehicles are so overgrown that it's hard to prise them out. Candy tolerates it these days."

"A problem for someone to tackle eventually, "Humble said.

"Some of these things belong in a museum," said Louisa, examining a car from the fifties era, which had been pushed well into the bushes fringing the path. It was rusted and smelled of damp plastic upholstery.

"This must be a veteran vehicle – could be worth something."

"Maybe too far gone," said Humble.

"You collect things," she reminded him. "You could open a museum as a sideline. You know, get a grant from the Tourist Board and charge for entry. You could run a café as an extra. A lot of people would be glad to see all this cleaned up."

"If I had the space I might consider that."

"I could help. I know about catering."
She took his arm…

"Might be worth thinking about in the future – I've studied marketing. We'd make a good partnership." Andrews broke the spell,

"Some of these cars and vans still have maps and personal items in them. It's like *Flannan Isle* - you know the abandoned lighthouse story. As if the owners had just walked away."

"Strange," said Humble. "Look at this old Jaguar - two-litre engine at least. Comfy seats and walnut dash."

The big car was almost obscured by thick vegetation. He moved branches aside,

"Check this out. Someone's been sleeping in here I'd guess."

There was a damp sleeping-bag in the car, together with parts of car seats for pillows. The items were disarranged but did not look old. They had not deteriorated much. Whoever had slept in there had used it recently.

"Look," said Louisa. "Bits of left over food. Who would want to eat and sleep in here? It's horrible."

"Someone desperate maybe," suggested Andrews, "Someone on the run."

"From what?" Louisa asked.

"Who knows," said Andrews. "There are no prisons round here."

"I think I can make out footprints," Humble said. "Leading from the car. There's a trail through the undergrowth into the woods."

"Should we follow it?" said Louisa excitedly.

"We shouldn't be sidetracked," Andrews cautioned. "Let's stick to the main objective for the day. We could have rain soon. It's important we get to Falcon as soon as we can."

71

Humble took photo-shots of the abandoned car.

They continued along the line, passing more vehicles and machinery until the discarded items petered out and they approached a small footbridge, crossing a feeder stream for the Candy. An information board had been erected just off the exact centre of the bridge. They stopped.

"Welcome to England," Humble said, smiling, "Got your passports ready?"

"The border," Louisa said, reading the information about the history of the region. "Without this notice I wouldn't have known. I've walked and cycled around here with friends but I didn't know about this."

"The Community Council and Tourist Board put it up a few years ago," explained Andrews. "The stream runs into the Candy where the river makes a curve before joining the Ling. The location of the actual border is not always clear. This gives information to visitors. Not that it matters really – nobody bothers about such things around here unless they're historians or have a particular interest."

"The line runs directly ahead for a while then crosses the main river for the run towards Carlisle," said Humble, "We leave it at the Marchland Stone and head into the woods. A small bridge takes the track back into Scotland."

The path remained mainly black in colour and very muddy. They were glad they were wearing boots. In ten minutes they reached a huge natural outcrop of rock, freestanding and tapering to a rounded narrow top. It was to the left of the track, which had now become pleasantly grassy.

"The Marchland Stone," said Andrews.

"What was it for?" asked Louisa, tracing the words etched into the roughly shaped monolith.

"To mark the frontier as it was then."

"Cattle and other stock were brought through here from England to Scotland and vice versa," said Humble, "The writing you see is the names of the two countries and the landowners. It dates back to before the Union of the Crowns."

"Very old," agreed Louisa. "I can hardly make out the words."

She took a picture of the rock.

"It's said to have magical properties," added Andrews. "There are lots of stories about the Marchland Stone and its mysterious energy."

Louisa looked at him with dark, round eyes,

"Magical?"

"Yes. Do you know the story of Hugh of Highwater?"

"Oh, the one who was murdered by a jealous rival and flung into the Candy?"

"Yes, seventeenth century. He was also reputed to be a wizard. It's said he used to walk around the stone at certain times of the year and perform magical ceremonies here with a gang of like-minded followers. The story says he must have been a black wizard because he walked widdershins around the stone."

"Widdershins?"

"Counter-clockwise. It's supposed to invoke powerful magic from the netherworld."

"It feels cold here," said Louisa. "Do you think some of the old magic is still around?" She shivered, hugging herself.

"Well," said Humble, "Highwater House isn't far away. They're a very ancient family. The Estate owns most of the land around here. Lady Helen is known for her strong-minded temperament but some of her husband's relatives are very highly strung if not totally out to lunch."

"A bit unkind," said Andrews. "They're just products of their upbringing and education. But you'll both know about *An Bile Buada*?"

"I've heard Mr. Parke mention it, "Louisa said.

"They're the pagan group in Candywood," said Humble. "The name means *The Tree of Victories*. They use the stone sometimes I've heard, although their main focus is sacred trees, like the oak, the ash and the yew. They gather here from time to time, as well as other spiritual sites," said Andrews, "To perform their rituals."
Louisa was horrified,

"Sacrificing animals, drinking blood and all that?" she asked.

"No," he said. "They're not that kind of pagan but they do dance around the stone to mark the wheel of the Celtic year."

"In the nude?" she asked, stepping back from the monolith.

For a moment he had a delicious mental picture of Louisa drifting naked over the grass like some dark, voluptuous Eve…the *Temptress*.

"Rumour has it," he said, "Could just be gossip of course."

"History lesson over," said Andrews. "We go that way."
He pointed north-east. The track forked in that direction and led into the forest proper. They moved on.

74

*

The management team in Falcon had convened a meeting with senior scientists and security officers. Most were working despite it being Sunday. Falcon was largely indifferent to the outside world when it came to work practices. Prahalad and Bowman were present as well as representatives of other departments.

The proceedings were chaired by the Director, Campbell ("Cammy") Dallas. He was not in a good mood. He glowered at the seated rows in the hall, toying with his pen. He had a large head with very little hair. His manner was brisk and managerial.

Dallas was a bully. An intelligent man with reasonably good qualifications, he had worked his way to his present position through a mixture of ruthlessness and guile. He insisted on being addressed as, *Sir*, or *Director*, which annoyed some of the senior staff.

At either side of him sat Kenneth Savage, Head of Security; Senior Administrator, Lucinda McQuade; Dawn Barclay, P.A to Dallas, and a slightly tubby middle-aged man with thin sandy hair and grey-blue eyes...Nathan Hardisty.

"There's been another breach of security," announced Dallas. "At the fence. Someone switched the electricity off for a few minutes and a small group went A.W.O.L. It was discovered only recently. Guard squads are out in the forest looking for them. This meeting was convened as soon as we knew."

"I need to be made aware if anyone saw or heard anything."

"Please remember you must report anything unusual or suspicious to Mr. Savage or me, no matter how trivial it may seem. Has anyone got any information right now?"

Bowman nudged Prahalad. The scientist raised a hand.

"Doctor Prahalad. What can you tell us?"

Prahalad related the same story he had told Bowman. Dallas drummed his fingers on his desk. Savage looked – well – savage. His pale eyes swept the room. McQuade looked concerned and Hardisty stared at the ceiling. Dallas spoke to the Security Chief,

"Has this guard, Geoff Mulligan, appeared yet?"

"He didn't report for his shift today, Sir. No one's seen him. Speculation is he's done a runner. If he's responsible for the breaches, then he's admitted his guilt by running away."

"It's not the first time," Dallas said. "I doubt he was acting alone. We have to find out who else is involved and why they're doing it."

"Some of the bioengineered life-forms and cybrids have escaped into the forest," said Dallas. "They must have been helped to do that. Does anyone else have anything to report?"

Some other personnel spoke up and voiced suspicions about incidents they had seen or heard about. Dawn Barclay wrote furiously. The group at the top table looked increasingly worried. Bowman decided this was the time he should voice his concerns about the unexpected growth spurts in plants. Prahalad kept quiet at that point. He was not yet sure if his particular worries were founded on reality. There were more tests to conduct before he could be certain.

Dallas concluded by urging them all to be vigilant, aware that the full workforce was not present. He would meet the others tomorrow and issue memos to all staff. All except Dallas, Savage, McQuade and Hardisty left the room. Savage spoke,

"If this was an inside job who else may be involved?"

"And why?" asked Dallas.

"Do you have any suspicions, Sir?" asked Lucinda McQuade. A slim, neatly dressed woman with an athletic poise, she spoke with a slight Glaswegian accent. As Senior Administrator, she was included in top management decisions.

"No, not yet. We do have rivals in the field of course. Other countries might want to get their hands on our technology. The point is that all staff should have been carefully vetted. That's your job, Kenneth, as well as Lucinda's."

"You haven't slipped up I hope. If so I'll have your heads on platters."

Savage and McQuade looked alarmed.

"I'm going to have to conduct a thorough security review," said Savage hurriedly. "There are those who could bear a grudge against us. A few of the experimental life forms and animal specimens must have escaped before the new fences were built. We had some teething trouble with security in the early days. I suppose they may have bred. The most recent escapes must have been with assistance – someone else as well as Mulligan."

They looked at each other, searching their memories.

"Incidentally I believe there is at least one curious person in Candywood who is taking an interest in Falcon," said Hardisty in a measured voice, "My sources tell me he'd been investigating near the perimeter fence and may have witnessed the unfortunate occurrence on Friday. He was caught on camera."

"The man on the fence incident," said Savage.

"I hope there haven't been any more," growled Dallas. "I need to know about any escape attempts amongst that particular group of workers. Do we know who the person on camera is?"

"Yes," said Hardisty. "A shop-owner in Candywood and amateur nature writer. He has previously tried to draw attention to over-large felines. It's a nuisance that he got to the site just before our security guards. He probably saw things he shouldn't have. Those guards are not known for their gentle handling of people."

"Bloody thugs. Hard to get competent staff these days," said Dallas.

"Some of them are ex-military. Remember the atrocities in Iraq?" said Savage.

"I do," said Dallas. "The deaths and injuries are still being investigated but the perpetrators were not typical of the armed forces. Most did a great job and took a lot of punishment. We should not forget their sacrifice. You always get a few rogue elements, however. One or two seem to have found their way into our security force."

"We're not wholly responsible for the military arm," Hardisty reminded him. "This is a joint venture and our colleagues within the Defence Ministry can't use regular guys."

Savage and Dallas were silent.

Hardisty continued,

"We may have to do something to head off any further attempts by amateur sleuths to poke their noses into our business."

"What do you suggest?" asked Dallas.

"I'll try a little subtle persuasion in the first instance if I may, Sir," said Hardisty. "With a gentle warning."

"And if that doesn't work?" said Savage.

"We'll cross that bridge if and when we come to it, Kenneth," said Dallas. To Hardisty he added,

"See what you can do."

Humble, Louisa and Andrews crossed back into Scotland and headed along a path climbing into the forest. The path was way-marked as a designated walking-area. The trees eventually thinned out as they arrived at the foot of Watchman Hill. A branch of the path contoured up the slope then wound towards the summit. The other continued deeper into the woods. They broke off for a drink, sitting in a grove of Scots pine and larch. The air held the threat of rain. Andrews looked around,

"I can see how healthy the plants are, despite the generally dry weather."

"Rain is on the way I think," Louisa said. "Good job we brought waterproofs."

"Rain will be welcome anyway," said Humble. "The farmers are crying out for it. This dry spell is wonderful but not really normal. If rain comes, the forest growth will become even richer."

"What do you think is really going on out here?" said Louisa, sipping coffee.

"Hard to say. It's something they're not keen for the rest of us to know. There must be a reason why Falcon is so cagey about its operations."

"A secret bio-warfare factory," said Louisa. "Or they're making clones. Like in that film, *The Island* – you know, Scarlet Johannsen and Ewan McGregor."

"Steady," Andrews said. "Could be nothing more than research into plant and animal genetics. They may be looking for a way to feed the famine prone areas of the world. If this country achieved a breakthrough we could be word leaders in the field – a potential new source of jobs and revenue."

"In the field," laughed Humble – "Nicely put. But joking apart it's badly needed. The latest economic meltdown came as a shock."

"Maybe it's G.M research," said Louisa.

"Could well be," agreed Andrews. "But what about the outsize animals?"

"And who was using that old car to sleep in?" added Humble, "Whatever. We'd better get going if we're to stand any chance of finding out."

He threw the dregs of his coffee into the bushes and they began to make their way to the top of Watchman Hill.

Seven

Samantha Leoch finished her riding session and invigorated, drove into Candywood in her 4x4. The Lingdale was quiet as was the street outside. The community was digesting the events of the previous evening. Morton Parke's church was disgorging its congregation. He stood by the door shaking hands, his expression hardening as he watched Leoch drive past.

She was another woman he disapproved of – far too bumptious as well as flighty. To his mind her conduct verged on the promiscuous, although this was an exaggeration. In reality she had taken few lovers. She lived in hope of finding a permanent one. Her goal was to net Rocky Craggs. He let her in by the back door. She tossed her car keys on to a table and pulled the pub owner towards her,

"I've just had a long ride on Freya. It's energised me and I need my fires putting out. What do you say, big man? Is there anyone else in the place?"

"Just the two of us. The place is quiet, as it usually is before lunch-time."

"Then what are we waiting for?"

She led him on, tugging at his hands. He smiled, pretending to resist. It was a game they sometimes played.

Afterwards, Craggs sat up reaching for a cigarette,

"There's something we have to discuss. Falcon is getting stressed out about security. They want us to help sort it. I got a text earlier."

"Hardisty their Public Relations Officer is heading into Candy tomorrow. We're expected to meet him."
She made a face,
"Okay, where and what time?"

*

The climb to the top of Watchman Hill was short but testing. They rested for a while taking in the view. Below they could make out the cluster of buildings forming part of the Falcon complex.

Trees densely surrounded it apart from the swathe cut by the perimeter fences. Andrews lifted his binoculars. Humble took some distant photo shots with one of his more sophisticated cameras. Louisa began to unpack her lunch.

"See anything interesting?" Humble asked as he took out his flask. Andrews gave him the binoculars.

"Vehicles parked up – they look a bit military. There's some vans and trucks too as well as minibuses. Quite a lot of activity for a Sunday and there seem to be gangs of people moving about, some in uniform as far as I can tell from this distance."

Humble peered through the binoculars,

"There's a variety of buildings. One looks like some sort of assembly hall. There are rows of identical ones like barracks, and there's a tall chimney."

"Like the ones you see near hospitals," said Andrews. "For burning various surgical items or amputated limbs."

"Ugh," Louisa said. "Can I have a look please?"

"The place is huge, "she said, "The fences seem very high."

"They are," said Humble. "The outer one can be climbed if you're careful. It's like a deer fence. Only the inner one is electrified and alarmed. I think they run patrols with dogs between the two of them."

"They're determined to keep people out," she said, handing the binoculars to Andrews.

"Or in," said Humble. He extracted a sandwich from his bag.

After lunch they followed a rough track through thick bracken, which led gradually down to the forest. As expected they saw the lush vegetation begin to appear as they neared the perimeter barrier. The distinctive sharp smell of crushed fern became strong as they walked through chest high bracken. Their passing threw up a few midges and horseflies.

"Forgot to put insect repellent on," said Humble, swatting at a flying tormentor. "Although I've noticed there's not so many this year. Some areas have none at all."

"Fearsome little bastards," Andrews said. Louisa reached into a pocket and handed him a repellent roll–on. Next she ministered to Humble, her cool hands running over his face and wrists.

"There…" she said, giving him a gentle slap. Their eyes briefly locked and she smiled. "A girl needs to be prepared out here."

Andrews strode onwards indicating the way,

"The fences. We're here."

"Now we need to be very careful," said Humble.

The fences ran far into the forest. Trees, bushes and thick grass crowded up to the outer fence and reached through the mesh. Andrews and Humble took more photo shots. Louisa took some with her phone. The inner barrier was formidable with rolls of razor wire on top, electrical conductors, alarms and the warning notices Humble had seen previously.

A path was visible between the fences. It looked as if it had been made by the action of feet. Apart from a slight breeze, signalling the possible approach of rain, all was still. They stood together to talk…

"We can follow the outer fence for a while and observe the place from there," said Humble. "From my experience I can tell you it runs for a long way. The going will be rough but we can take our time. If anyone gets tired we'll just stop and decide what to do next."

"Remember we have to get back," Louisa reminded him. "However far we walk we'll have the same distance on the return trip."

"I was thinking we'll eventually emerge on to one of the forest tracks," he said. "If we walk on a compass bearing approximately south–west we should come out by an old ruined cottage called *Sweetshaw*. From there I know how to get back to the main track."

"You're the man who knows the woods," said Andrews.

"Lead on," said Louisa.

*

Security at Falcon had been stepped up following the recent meeting with senior management. Prahalad and Bowman did not concern themselves with this but agreed to work closely together after Bowman explained his concerns to his colleague. They had decided to confide in Eva Capilus, a Lithuanian scientist, resident at Falcon.

She was renowned for her expertise in the fields of information-technology and computer applications. Capilus had worked in Australia and the U.S.A and had been headhunted by Falcon two years ago. Prahalad had spoken to her and learned she also had reservations about Falcon's methods and the controversial research. She was a serious-minded woman with a dedicated approach to her work.

Capilus had hair the colour of ripe corn, usually arranged in braids piled on top of her head. Wearing a white lab coat she joined the two men in a corner of the staff canteen. Bowman spoke first,

"Aashish, Eva, you know I've been working on G.M crops?"

They nodded.

"Some events have taken place that I hadn't anticipated."

"Go on," prompted Prahalad.

"G.M research is controversial and we have to be scrupulous about avoiding any contamination of domestic crops or wild plants. Well a few weeks ago there was an incident of contamination – a mistake by one of the lab staff. Some G.M plant material escaped into the wild."

They stared at him.

"That's not all," he continued. "The nutrients we have developed to enhance the growth and strength of existing food plants, turned out to be stronger than we expected. Some of them, in liquid form were accidentally diverted to the outside from the hydroponic farm complex."

"The results of both of those blunders are the over-sized plants growing in the woods. Some are now mature and have gone through their reproductive cycle. The wind has blown seeds into the forest and resulted in more contamination. The various species have also become intermixed. It's only a matter of time before local commercial crops are affected."

"Does Dallas know about this?" said Eva.

"Of course. It's impossible to hide. The errant staff members were dismissed but the damage is done. I got a terrific bollocking but they can't do without me so they couldn't give me the bullet. I'm too valuable to them. I've had a yellow card and have to watch my step these days."

Although she spoke excellent English, Capilus was having difficulty following Bowman's expressions. She hoped she had grasped the general idea from his tone,

"Yes, I remember a couple of lab staff suddenly left. They must have been the ones," she said.
Bowman nodded.

"Can it be repaired?" asked Prahalad worriedly.

"Falcon is right now undertaking a damage limitation exercise, including spraying and eventually burning. The jury's out as to whether it will work or not."

"They will have to be careful," said Capilus. "It may draw too much attention if anyone sees all this happening in the forest."

"Tell me about it," said Bowman grimly. "All that research gone to waste."

"What about the lab staff?" asked Prahalad, "Won't they bear grudges against Falcon? Whistle-blowing happens a lot these days. Many organisations actually have a whistle blowing policy."

"My understanding is that they were given generous pay-offs and told to keep quiet. They were warned that they would be under surveillance for the foreseeable future and should be careful," said Bowman."

"Phone-hacking," his colleague said. "We now know that telephone conversations are not necessarily safe after all that business with the tabloids. Falcon may have scared them into keeping their mouths firmly shut."

"I believe email intercepts are also possible," said Bowman.

"Falcon has links with Government," added Capilus.

"And the military," said Bowman.

They sat with their drinks for a while. Prahalad eventually spoke up,

"My problem is with the transgenic creations."
They waited…

"We've been manipulating D.N.A, itself a highly controversial technique as well as doing stem cell research," he said. "The two are linked. The aim is to produce inter-species hybrids, which can absorb pollutants in the atmosphere thus helping the environment."

"There are also medical possibilities, such as dealing with inherited disorders and slowing the ageing process. It was originally at the level of simple life forms but Falcon has been demanding more so we're looking at cloning and an artificial genome – a machine, which can design animals and plants and grow them to order."

"Ground-breaking stuff," said Bowman. "But very controversial as you say. Runs counter to the values held by many societies and religions. No wonder Falcon is paranoid about security. What are you trying to say?"

"I'm worried that the process is going off the rails. We are producing some strange creatures…cross-species forms. The cloning experiments are top secret but also carry risks. The mixes of various species produce 'chimeras', the inter-species hybrids. Some of them are unstable, potentially dangerous and I'm concerned that some may escape or be released intentionally."

"Monsters?" asked Eva Capilus.

"The Island of Doctor Moreau," said Bowman.

"What?" Prahalad said.

He and Capilus looked thoroughly puzzled. He remembered that it would probably be outside their cultures.

"A novel by H.G Wells," he said. "About vivisection. At the time it too was a controversial science and in the story a mad genius living on a remote island creates hybrid animals through surgical operations. For example, a gorilla/man or a bear/lion, some with human characteristics. It all unravelled of course as the Doctor was totally insane. His bizarre creations finally turned on him."

"It's just a story," he added when he saw their horrified expressions.

"Is management aware of this?" said Capilus, echoing her previous question.

"Not yet. I'm unsure whether I'm correct about it anyway. I need to run more checks."

He rubbed his eyes.

"You need to rest for a while," said Bowman. "Before you do any more work. Tired people make mistakes."

"He is right," said Capilus.

She herself was uncomfortable about stem-cell research and cloning. Some politicians and religious leaders had set themselves against the technology.

"We can meet again tomorrow," said Bowman. "When we've had time to think about these things. There is no immediate concern is there? No chance any creations might escape?"

"I would anticipate security would prevent that," said Prahalad. "Many of the other staff here are not even fully aware of what my team is involved with. But I've heard that escapes have indeed taken place, whether deliberately or otherwise. It means that some cybrids are out there now. If they are encountered by the public, who knows what will happen?"

"And we thought security was tight," said Bowman soberly.

"If they were released by dissidents inside Falcon then it can only be to draw attention to the experiments," Prahalad said. "Reckless behaviour by activists could result in dangerous entities at large out there."

"F…" Bowman began to say then remembered Capilus.

She did not appear to notice.

*

Humble, Louisa and Andrews felt as if they were in a rain forest. They plunged through tangled

89

undergrowth and lank grass. Humble and Andrews kept checking their compasses as they followed the fences. The going was tough. At length Humble called a halt,

"Let's stop for a break in this thinner bit of woodland. We can carry on in a few minutes."
He pulled out his water bottle and drank gratefully.

"Brings on a thirst doesn't it?" said Andrews following suit.

"What's that noise?" said Louisa suddenly.

"Patrol," said Humble in an urgent whisper. "Get well away from the fences and stay absolutely silent."

They drew back into the woods to what they hoped was a safe distance. They heard the patrol approaching from the west and crouched as far down into cover as they could.

It was four armed men and a German shepherd dog. The animal stopped when it drew near to where they been a few seconds before and sniffed the air. The guards waited. Humble and the others tried not to breathe.

"Anything?" asked a guard, clearly the one in charge. His cap badge was different to the others.

"No, don't think so. Probably an animal," his companion said.

They looked around carefully, moved to the edge of the fence and peered into the forest. The space between the fences was worn into a track along which they had been travelling. They wore guns at their waists and had communication devices on their belts. Their uniform resembled military fatigues. The forage caps on their heads, like their jackets, carried a Falcon logo.

"Let's go," said one of the guards. "Nothing to worry about."

Abruptly, the dog barked. The guards stopped and the three in the forest hunkered down even further, frozen into immobility. A noise of breaking branches was heard.

"Over there," said a guard, pointing. A group was emerging from the forest.

It was two South Asian or Middle-Eastern men and an African, dressed in drab, filthy clothes, exhausted and stressed. Their eyes looked about wildly. Then they saw the guards and the dog. One of the guards began to reach for his gun. The fugitives saw the movement and instantly crashed into the forest running as hard as they could through the thick bushes. The guard fired once into the trees before the man in charge stopped him,

"No point. They've gone. Don't want to draw attention. There may be rangers or such-like going about. Let's get back to the Centre and report this."
They moved away and were quickly out of sight, yanking the dog away from the scene.

"I never thought I'd see anything like that," said Louisa.

"I think we're dealing with really serious people here," said Andrews.

Highwater House sat near a promontory above the Candy River. The water flowed swiftly below running over exposed layers of stone known as *Candy Linns*, famous for its layered rock formations and visited by amateur and professional geologists.

White-water canoeing on that stretch of the river was also growing as a high adrenalin activity for city-dwellers looking for a buzz. Candy Linns was now well publicised on specialist websites, receiving a considerable number of hits.

The three-storey house, home of the family since the thirteenth century, was a spectacular grey-stone building in extensive mature woodland. Wings had been added through the centuries and it included a pillared entrance porch, numerous rooms and a turret complete with flagpole. It was occasionally used in film-making and the family were considering developing it into a tourist attraction. The walled gardens were particularly fine.

The family hosted shooting parties and rented their portion of the Candy for fishing. The estate included several working farms and reared pheasants for the shoots. A lake stocked with brown and rainbow trout was situated in the grounds near the house. Stately swans glided in their dignified way across the water. The acres of mixed woodland gave way to commercial forestry and the firm had a stake in Shawland Timber as part of its investment portfolio.

As a family, they had endured rises and falls in fortune, both politically and financially. More than a few ancestors of the current incumbent had lost their heads as a result of being on the losing side in internal conflicts. There had also been casualties through the long-running border wars before the Union of the Crowns.

During the period of border anarchy it was expected that the male head of the household would lead his men in battle – a risky undertaking. Many had not returned from the field.

The Highwaters were also a little inbred and had their share of family eccentrics as well as those who were more or less insane. Bloodlines ensured that disorders, physical and mental, tended to resurface now and again. The family had endured, however.

The current Earl, Sir Alexander, a sixty-seven year-old baronet, lived there with Lady Helen, sixty-two. Their children were in business elsewhere or at University. The marriage had become a notional one in recent years and they occupied adjacent but separate areas of the house coming together for meals and to entertain their frequent guests.

Sir Alexander had succumbed to the family weakness and was now under treatment for severe neurosis, including paranoia. He had become increasingly delusional.

Lady Helen, in contrast was a Garelette, a robust family of venerable French origin, generally untroubled by mental weakness. She took effective control of the estate and its extensive holdings leaving her husband to his fantasies. Lady Helen had strong business acumen and a ruthless streak. She was described by some of the estate workers as "Tough but fair." Her assumed responsibilities had at times led her to take risky business decisions. One such decision had been the leasing of a large acreage of land in that portion of Caithland Forest owned by the family. They had leased the tract to Falcon Organic Research. She had a directorship on the Board of Management.

Whilst Humble and his friends were pursuing their investigations she was in Highwater House, having returned from Church with her husband. Holding a position in the community meant there were certain obligations and duties. Church attendance was one of them. Personal beliefs did not matter in this regard.

93

Seated at her desk after lunch, Alexander having retired to his rooms, she was engrossed in administration work when there was a knock on the door.

"Come!" she called. It was her housekeeper, Belinda Anfield.

"Telephone call for you, My Lady – a Mr. Dallas from Falcon Research."

"Bring the phone in, Belinda," said Lady Helen, moving away from the computer keyboard. "I'll take it in here."

After Mrs. Anfield had left, she answered the caller,

"Helen Highwater."

"I'm sorry to disturb you on a Sunday, Lady Highwater," came the harsh voice of Dallas, "We are planning to convene an extraordinary meeting of the Board and I thought I would inform you in good time. The official papers will arrive by special delivery within the next three days."

"Is there a problem, Mr. Dallas?" asked Lady Helen testily. She hated to be disturbed when working.

"We hope not, My Lady," continued Dallas obsequiously, "But we felt it could not wait for too long and we need to bring it to the attention of the whole Board of Management. It's not something all the staff here need to know about but as you are a director I considered it important to keep you in the picture, so to speak."

"Can you give me an idea of the nature of this difficulty?" she asked.

"It's a question of security as well as our future relations with the surrounding area," he said evasively. "The details will be in the papers we will send you. After

94

the meeting they will be shredded as usual. We are working on next Monday as the meeting date - six p.m in our office in town. Would that be suitable for you?"

"Yes, I shall attend. I happen to have several appointments in town that day anyway. I will lunch there and be at the meeting at the specified time."

"Thank you. The papers will be in the post tomorrow. Goodbye for now."

"Goodbye, Mr. Dallas, until Monday."

She pressed the end call button. Returning to her desk she thought for a few moments then began to call a number.

In his office in the Falcon Research Centre, Dallas was also thinking,

We have to keep her in the picture to an extent. She's one of our major investors and a useful front. But we can't tell her everything – too risky. Better she doesn't know the whole truth about Falcon.

He pursed his lips and rose to visit Savage in his lair.

*

They heard the noise before catching sight of the workers. Halting near the fences, Humble and his friends heard and saw a group of men in helmets, goggles, jackets and boots, directing a fine liquid from powerful backpack spraying equipment.

The three assumed the spray was heavy-duty, industrial weed killer judging by the stinging fumes blowing towards them. Once more they hunkered down in the long grass.

"Trying to reduce the over-active growth everywhere," said Humble.

"Then it must be G.M," said Louisa. "Maybe it's got out of hand."

"Mistakes," agreed Andrews. "Causing contamination amongst crops and wild plants."

"It certainly fits," said Humble. "The activists in the early days of G.M pointed out that a blunder was likely to happen at some stage. They saw the technology as unsafe."

"I remember," said Andrews. "Those guys are likely to be here for a while so what do we do?"

"We'll have to move further into the forest," suggested Humble. "If the compass bearings are correct, we should find a forest track soon and we can follow that until we bypass the sprayers."

"Two o' clock," said Louisa. "How soon do we need to think about heading back?"

"Plenty of daylight," Humble said. "We should start the return trip at about three. Might be able to pick up more information before we have to call it a day."

They pushed through the forest, the two men making a path for Louisa by shoving aside grass and bushes. After some twenty minutes Humble pointed ahead,

"The track. I don't think it parallels the barrier exactly. It curves round towards Sweetshaw and then we can begin to turn towards home. We'll be pretty tired by then but we can have drinks or something at the cottage."

"We can always make another visit," said Andrews, "Although tomorrow is Monday and I'm working."

"And I'm at Uni," said Louisa. "Flexi Study Time but I have to put in an appearance."

"I'll be manning the shop," said Humble," with Stella."

Louisa stopped to wipe her face.

"What's that?" said Andrews suddenly. They looked at where he was indicating.

"I don't like this," said Humble. "Back off."

They moved closer together. Louisa grabbed Humble's arm. A group of four entities was emerging from the undergrowth. They had grey, hooded tops with the Falcon logo and were taller than average. Their genders were difficult to determine, the clothing obscuring any obvious body features. They wore close-fitting grey trousers and boots. Their flesh was smooth with a slight coppery tinge and pale, prominent eyes.

Moving slowly they looked around, scanning the area. It was difficult to identify what they were. They looked human but there was something weirdly unfamiliar about them. The three friends stood, motionless. There was a brief impasse. Humble reached for his phone and managed to squeeze off two shots before the tableau changed. One who was apparently the leader, indicated to the others. All four moved back into the woods. They were gone in a few seconds.

"What were they?" said Andrews, exhaling breath.

"I'm not happy with this," Louisa said. "Can we go on now?"

"Of course," said Humble. "But what did we see?"

"Hard to say," Andrews answered. "Nothing I've ever seen before."

"Androids," said Humble suddenly.

"What?" Louisa exclaimed.

"Artificially created beings."

"Impossible," Andrews said shaking his head. "Not here. That's just in movies."

"You're right. I don't think so either. There's no proof that such things exist. The thought just came into my head for some reason but I don't think it's what we saw. I've probably read too many Science-Fiction stories."

"What then?" asked Andrews, "They looked like something out of a novel, as you said...they're not making a film around here are they?"

"Who knows?" said Humble. "But Louisa's right. We've had enough for one day. Let's move on."

They made for the forest track, vigilant for other sightings. In five minutes they arrived at the track itself and could see the cottage ahead. Deciding not to stop but to turn for home immediately, the small group passed the semi-ruined cottage and began to make their way back south in the direction of Candywood.

In ten minutes they had reached a broader track and could make better time. Trees, mostly beech, birch and conifers, grew thickly on both sides and the track twisted and turned, running up and down short slopes, following the topography of the land. When they rounded a corner and encountered the group of men, their shock was profound.

It was another three guards from Falcon, they guessed. They had no dogs but had shotguns broken and held loosely against their arms. Both groups halted.

"Well, out for a little country walk are we?" asked one of the men. "Do you know you're on private land?"

Disgustingly, the man spat out a stream of saliva. He looked about forty. He spoke with a North Cumbrian accent and had a Falcon logo on his breast pocket as well as the usual military–style cap. He stood with legs apart, as did the others. They blocked the track. Humble decided to play ignorant,

"Er no, we didn't know. Just out for a hike and a look at the forest. We're interested in the wildlife."

He attempted to look innocent. Andrews and Louisa watched him, waiting to see how the men reacted. Not well…the tallest of the three – an older man with a heavy-jowelled face, spoke,

"You need to be out of here now. This is a private estate and we're authorised to keep a look out for intruders. We're telling you to leave."

His speech was not local. It sounded vaguely South of England.

"There's no law of trespass in Scotland," Andrews said, "Not in the criminal sense. We're on our way back to Candywood anyway but we're not doing any damage."

"That's not for you to say. We're the law around here so don't give me any bloody clever-dick stuff. Just get out of here and don't think about coming back. Go on, fuck off."

He hefted his gun. Their attitude was aggressive and Humble feared for the welfare of his friends. He tried to placate the men,

"We're going. We didn't know this area was out-of-bounds. No harm intended, okay?"

The guards parted, allowing them to move on.

The three walked on as quickly as they could, putting distance between themselves and the guards. Risking a glance back Andrews could see the men had not moved and were still watching them. He was relieved they had not tried to take their phones – an oversight.

"Charming," he said in a low voice.

"They're a bit far from the barrier," said Humble. "Shows that Falcon must be worried about security. They must be enforcing a quarantine zone."

"Outrageous really," Andrews said. "The law is clear on the right to roam."

"Tell that to them," said Louisa, looking shocked. Humble showed concern,

"The sooner we get back the better. This is turning out to be a very difficult day."

"Sorry, "said Andrews. "Comfort stop. I need to go into the trees for a few moments – too much coffee and excitement, I suppose. Give me a minute will you? I won't be long."

They nodded. He shoved his way into the tree cover and disappeared. Louisa took Humble's arm,

"It's been the weirdest day I've ever had, Jim."

"Yes. Who'd have thought we'd encounter so much on our first trip into the forest?"

They remained like that for a minute or two before hearing Andrews returning. Humble stiffened. Kirk Andrews' face was ghastly – he was obviously shocked. Emerging from the woods at speed he almost fell as he struggled through the thick vegetation.

"What…?" Humble asked. Andrews just pointed,

"See for yourself. I have to sit down for a minute." He sat down heavily on a tussock of grass, shaking his head. Louisa guessed he must have seen something awful.

"What's wrong, Kirk?"

Andrews gave no answer - just put his head down trying not to throw up. Humble made his way into the forest and saw what Andrews had encountered. Amongst the lower branches of a pine tree the body of a man hung, gently swaying. A thick cloud of flies circled around the head, crawled over the face. There was the nauseating smell of decomposition. The tongue was blue and protruded from the mouth. One remaining eye bulged. The crows had been at the face but it was still recognisable. It was Adam Bain.

Eight

Rain began to fall before they returned to Candywood – a steady, persistent downpour accompanied by a freshening wind. Their waterproofs protected them but they were glad to reach the sanctuary of the shop and sit with hot drinks and biscuits. They felt drained, exhausted by their encounters. Humble offered something stronger but Louisa reminded him she was driving and Andrews declared he would bring up his lunch if he drank anything more robust than weak tea.

"We wanted to discover things and we certainly did that," he said.

"The police will have to know about Bain," Andrews pointed out.

"I feel really stressed about what we saw today," said Louisa. "But I'm glad we went. No sense in bottling out if we're serious about investigating Falcon."

She had insisted on seeing the corpse. After ejecting the contents of her stomach she had slowly recovered her composure. Now the sight was swirling around in her mind – a hideous vision.

"It must have been too much for him – the beating, his family leaving - all of that stuff. Suicide may have seemed the only option."

"If it was suicide," said Humble.

"What else? You can't be inferring he was murdered."

"It's possible, "said Andrews. "He had a lot of enemies that's for sure."

Louisa continued,

"But why go to all that trouble? Why not just beat him up and throw him in the Candy?"

"Two bodies in the Candy in one night would be a bit suspicious," said Humble. "This way it looks like suicide. Who would challenge that assumption?"

"You for a start," she said. "Wait a minute – two bodies – you're not implying Bain and Sticky were both murdered?"

"I'm not implying anything. All I know is that there's some bizarre things going on and they all seem to be connected with Falcon."

"Those men were clear that they wanted people to keep away and would take steps to enforce that prohibition if necessary. Bain was a forestry manager. If anyone had a handle on what Falcon is about it would have been him."

"Geordie Hagg lives in the forest too," said Andrews. "He must know things. He might have passed his knowledge on to his brother, Sticky."

"Who was notoriously loose-tongued when he'd had a drink, "said Humble.

"We might be seeing a conspiracy where there isn't one," said Andrews. "We need to let Marcus Burn know about this in the first instance. It's the law to report the finding of a body to the police."

"I'll ring the police in town," agreed Humble. "Burn isn't on duty today."

"They'll have to take Bain's body down anyway," said Andrews. "The crows will pick the flesh off the bones if he's left there."

Louisa looked nauseous again. Humble glanced at her but she waved him away…

"I'll be okay. Better make that call."

103

She filled a glass with water and drank it slowly.

The police station in Cruiksdale said they would send a team out to recover the body within two hours, and some officers to conduct interviews. Humble explained that Louisa would be at the University but he and Andrews would be in Candywood, working. A sergeant was then asked to come to the phone. Following a discussion, it was agreed that they would all travel into the town after five p.m on Monday to be interviewed, but officers would come out with the retrieval team to get a few details. He ended the call. The police would be there in less than an hour.

"More gossip for Candy to make a meal of," said Louisa grimly."

"We'll weather it. Two police visits to the shop will certainly cause a sensation though. It will either boost trade or reduce it," said Humble.

"A two-day wonder," Andrews said. "Before they find something else to talk about. Don't worry about the shop. Candywood needs it."

"Anyway we haven't done anything wrong, just taken a walk in the woods. You may well find business increases. People love to be near the source of a perceived scandal, even if there isn't one."

"He's right. We haven't done anything wrong," added Louisa, recovering. "We've reported it to the police. It's up to them now."

"It will go to the Procurator-Fiscal anyway," said Humble. "The body was found in Scotland."

"Only just," said Andrews. "But it's enough. I presume Sticky's death went to the Fiscal?"

"Certainly. It's automatic. I imagine there will be a fatal accident enquiry in both cases."

"Two in the course of as many days," Andrews said. "And in the same area. They'll probably assume Sticky's death was an accident and Bain's was suicide. The Fiscal doesn't have to order an enquiry if he thinks it isn't necessary."

"Candy will make a big deal of this when it comes out," said Louisa. She finished her water,

"Can I brush my teeth? My mouth feels like a budgie's cage."

"Of course," said Humble. "Come up and I'll show you where the bathroom is."

They walked through his first floor flat to the bathroom and he opened the door for her. She smiled gratefully. He motioned with his hand,

"I'll be downstairs with Kirk. If there's anything else you want, give me a shout, okay?"
She nodded and closed the door.

"Do you think there's a conspiracy, Kirk?" Humble asked when he was seated with another mug of tea. He seemed to have an unquenchable thirst – the result of the dry mouth he developed after seeing the body.

"It could be. I suppose it's something we should really leave to the police."

"How would you feel about going back to the forest? Perhaps to talk to Geordie Hagg as Louisa suggested? I have an idea where his place is."

"I'm game," said Andrews, "We can ask Louisa when she comes back."

When Louisa returned they discussed what they would say to the police.

"The truth is usually best," said Andrews. "They can usually tell if anyone is lying."

"We have no need to lie," Humble said. "We went for a walk in the woods and found a dead man. Unusual but it can happen."

"I've never seen a dead body before," said Louisa, her hands round her knees, legs up under her on the armchair. She was still in shock.

"It was horrific," agreed Andrews. "Especially seeing him like that."

"How do you think the police will react?"

"Just routine for them I suppose. But I'm just not sure about their attitude. Dalveen and Marcus Burn seem to have an agenda of their own."

"Maybe they're genuinely supportive of Falcon as an employer in the area," said Andrews. "When more people are working there is usually less crime. You know, 'The Devil makes work for idle hands to do.' They won't want any more mini-riots would they?"

He was referring to a short period of disorder when a disaffected group broke windows in Candywood, spray-painted buildings and set fire to bus shelters during the long, dark, winter nights.

"Our own version of the 2011 urban unrest," said Humble.

"Not so much theft, though," Louisa reminded him. "More arson and criminal damage."

"Just feral behaviour," said Andrews.

"Ah," said Humble. "Our visitors have arrived."

*

Dalveen accompanied Marcus Burn. They asked questions and took notes. They were non-committal but critical of the activities of Humble and friends.

"Tell me again what you were doing in the forest, Mr. Humble," asked Dalveen.

"Just out for a hike with my friends, Sergeant," he said, indicating Louisa and Andrews.

"So close to the Falcon Centre? I thought I advised you to stay away from the place? Were you not concerned for everyone's safety?"

"We're not afraid of the forest," said Louisa, sticking out her chin, "We were all brought up in this part of the world."

The Sergeant frowned,

"But it's a secure area. That's why it's fenced. There are hundreds of hectares of woodland out there in which to walk – marked tracks, picnic areas, all that. No need to go so close to Falcon. The going can't have been easy. Why didn't you stay on the usual routes if you were looking for a day's walking?"

"We've done the regular paths already," said Humble. "We like to explore a bit, nothing more. How were we to know we'd find a body? Nobody would expect to come across that in the course of a country walk. There are forest tracks quite close to Falcon in places, and they're not out-of-bounds officially. We haven't done anything wrong or damaged property. I happen to possess a sense of adventure, shared with my friends and we deviated from the usual paths. Is that a crime? We reported what we found as soon as we got back."

Louisa was impressed with Humble's ability to make their case.

He in turn was impressed with her ability to remain calm. Dalveen closed his notebook, a signal that the interview was over. Burn stood up in his turn. The sergeant spoke,

"Tomorrow's interviews in Cruiksdale will be at five-thirty in the police station. Please be there on time. If there is anything you haven't told us, be sure to remember it then. You'll be a little traumatised after today. Your memories might improve after a night's sleep."

"I would like you to say nothing about this until the body has been removed. The Procurator-Fiscal will decide on the next course of action. Good evening."

He moved to the door. The rain had stopped and the expected curious locals had found reasons to linger in the street near the shop. The door closed on the departing officers. Louisa looked tired. Humble guided her to a chair and they all flopped with exhaustion.

"I'll have to get back, said Andrews after about ten minutes of recovery. "Work tomorrow."

"Me too," said Louisa, standing up. "I'm shattered."

"If we all meet here at five p.m tomorrow I'll drive us into town," offered Humble. He was feeling a little guilty about involving them in his amateur investigations.

"See you then," called Andrews from the doorway. "Tomorrow at five."

They watched his figure walking away down to the south end of Lingdale Street. Louisa turned to Humble…

"Today was really awful."

"You handled it well," he said.

"Thanks. Do you mean that?"

"Believe it, Louisa. I don't think any of us could have been prepared for what we saw."

"My mind's still racing. I'm going to have to wind down emotionally before I go."

"I know what you mean. Would you like to stay a little longer."

"I think that would be good. How are you at consoling people by the way?"

"I'll give it a try."

She smiled and reached for his hand.

Lady Highwater's telephone call had been brief but useful. The person she had called agreed to travel to the estate house for a discussion. She returned to the spreadsheet she had been working on before the call from Dallas.

Just after five she walked to the French windows and looked out over the green manicured lawns rolling down to the fringe of mixed woodland. Bats were beginning their nightly swooping, catching insects. The trees waved in a gentle movement she always found soothing at this season of the year. She thought for a moment then left to visit Alexander's rooms. It was time for his evening medication.

Louisa and Humble talked over the day's horrors. She began to relax and they planned what they might do next. She was adamant that she would not give up on their quest,

"I'm a woman of twenty-six. This is scary but it's exciting too. I know the risks. I'm not some brainless bimbo. I know what I'm capable of and I want to see it through."

"I've never thought of you as a bimbo. I love having you with me on this and I don't doubt your ability to cope with whatever comes next. I just don't want any harm to come to you that's all."

"You say such nice things, not like other men I've encountered."

"Oh?"

"Most of the men and boys I've met just wanted to get into me into bed from the kick off. You seem less driven by that, more inclined to treat me as a person."

"I don't take you for granted," he said. "By all means stay with me on this Falcon business if it's what you want. I'm concerned about Kirk too as it happens."

"I know. I think you feel responsible because it was your idea."

"Got it in one."

She stood up decisively,

"Have to go. See you tomorrow – I'll call you."

"Are you sure you're okay?"

"Of course. I'm a Moscadini. We endure."

He saw her to her car and watched her drive away. The taillights faded into the encroaching night. He locked up and walked into the kitchen to pour a steadying drink. On the other side of the street someone lit a cigarette and observed their parting.

*

Louisa drove out of Candywood and headed west. Gillerston was only another five miles. The rain had stopped but the roads still glistened. There was very little traffic. Her mind was filled with the events of the day. She needed to reach home and settle for the night, maybe watch something mindless on T.V to wind down. Jane was at her parent's house tonight and Kath would be out with her boyfriend.

Louisa was used to driving this route. Negotiating the bends in the road with practised skill, she let her thoughts drift. She was getting into something dangerous with the Falcon affair, she thought.

Was she also getting into something with James Humble?

There was excitement in both, she realised. There was also uncertainty. It was the buzz she had been looking for. Fatigue hit her as the lights of Gillerston came into view. They had rarely seemed more welcoming.

Nine

The three men had experienced a difficult night in the ruin of Sweetshaw cottage, enduring rain then the early morning chill. They had eaten the food they had brought with them and drunk most of the water. They needed to move on. The only language they had in common were a few English words picked up since their arrival in the U.K, their incarceration and subsequent move to Falcon.

By six a.m they were ready to go, hoping to reach a road, a house or a village. The forest was endless, alien and empty of people. The track near the cottage was a hopeful sign. They decided to follow it, hoping it would lead them to some kind of assistance. They knew that others had escaped before them. Wearily, they began to tramp along the muddy path.

When they saw the old caravan parked in the lee of a tiny stone cottage, their spirits lifted. Smoke was rising from a cracked metal chimney protruding from the structure. There was a cleared space, which had been made into a garden. Rows of vegetables and fruit bushes were visible. Hens pecked about in a fenced off area and goats grazed in another enclosure. A former railway carriage formed part of the eccentric conglomerate. There were smells of smoke, animals and damp wood. The men stopped.

A figure emerged from the cottage. It was dressed in what had once been a coat, trousers and a sweater but were barely recognisable as such now. The figure was a man of about sixty with a grey-black tangled beard and a woollen hat. His hair was too long for his age and his face was weathered deep red. He narrowed his eyes,

"More of you lot. Must be hundreds in that place. You'll want to be fed and watered. Wait there and I'll see what I have."

He pointed to a decaying garden seat and some large, upturned logs to the right of the dwelling. They looked at each other but had caught his meaning. They sat. Geordie Hagg disappeared into the habitation and returned in a few moments with plates on which were bread, cheese, boiled potatoes and slices of goat meat.

There was no cutlery. Chipped mugs held fresh goat's milk. He distributed the items and watched the men shoving the food down as if their lives depended on it, which of course they did. He spoke to them, explaining what they could do but they only understood a little,

"You boys can't stay here but I can show you how to get out o' the forest. The last ones headed for the old railway line. Don't know where they went from there. None of my business. There's some queer things goin' on in that place but they leave me alone so I keep quiet. Enjoy your food then I'll help you on your way."

He pulled an old chair forward and sat with them. A smell of sweat and unwashed skin rolled from him but it was no worse than they smelled themselves. They were not entirely sure what he was saying but caught some of the sense of it. They munched on with concentration. When they finished, Geordie took away the plates then led them back to the track.

*

Humble began work at six a.m as usual, with the morning papers, milk and rolls. He had forgotten to order fresh ones from the bakery. This was noticed by some of the regulars when he opened at seven. There were quips, such as,

"Not quite on the ball today, Jim. Rolls from the freezer? Too busy with the old love-life, eh?"

The comments depended on how well he knew the wisecracking local concerned or how tactless the speaker happened to be. Humble was polite but calm, resisting the goading. He knew what to expect. Stella kept her counsel, serving customers efficiently. Morton Parke was an early visitor,

"Jim, we need to talk. The place is full of stories about Sticky and Bain. It's only a matter of time before they get round to you. You know how it is."

"I know, but they can think what they like as far as I'm concerned. Most of it will be made up anyway. I can have a chat later if you want, say about lunch time when I close for an hour?"

"Okay, boy," said Parke. "Pop over to my house. I'll ask Margaret to organise some lunch."

The shop received more than the usual number of customers for a Monday. Humble resisted being drawn into conversations about recent events. Just after ten a.m a plump middle-aged man with thinning hair entered the shop. He wore a neat suit with a striped tie and black shoes,

"Mr. Humble?"

"Who wants to know?"

"Nathan Hardisty. I represent the Falcon Research Centre. May we have a little talk?"

114

He exhibited a business card on which the legend, *Nathan Hardisty, Public Relations Officer, Falcon Agricultural Research Ltd.* was inscribed. Hardisty spoke in clear precise tones, annunciating each word like a newsreader. There were no customers currently in the shop and Humble was curious to find out what this visit was about,

"Go ahead, Mr. Hardisty, I'm all ears. Could you look after things for a few minutes Stella while I take this gentleman into the back shop?"

Stella nodded. In the back Humble cautioned his visitor,

"I would ask you to be brief. It can be difficult to talk in a shop like this."

"Quite," said Hardisty. "Then I'll get straight to the point."

"Please do."

Hardisty placed his hands on the table. They were small and well cared for. The man himself was dapper in appearance but had an air of quiet authority.

"Your interest in Falcon – purely academic is it?"

"I'm enthusiastic about many things. I enjoy walking and I know the forest well. When something unusual occurs I like to investigate it. You may know I write a column for the local paper."

"Ah yes, *Country Cousin*. You're a man of many talents but you must know the facility has been in this area for some time now."

"Yes."

"So why the sudden interest?"

"It's not sudden. I just happened to walk in that direction and found I had to satisfy my curiosity. It's my nature as an enthusiastic amateur so to speak. I've noticed odd things in the forest on previous occasions."

"You know what curiosity did to the cat, don't you?"

"What are you trying to say? That I can't walk in the woods I've known most of my life?"

"No, just that it would be best, in your own interest, to respect our privacy and not venture too close to the facility."

"The police have already mentioned that to me."

"And don't you find that speaks for itself?"

"Perhaps, but it begs the question, what are you hiding?"

"That would be too strong a way of putting it. Think of us as like a military zone. You know there's a huge military area in the Cheviots not too far from here. There are restrictions there for reasons of safety and security as I'm sure you know."

"Yes I know the place you mean. Anyone who wishes to enter the zone must report to the Military Commandant for permission. No one may enter when a red flag is flying."

"Correct, "said Hardisty. "Well that area is far larger than ours yet people respect the restrictions and get on with their lives. They never dispute the reasons for the security."

"That's because it's military and it brings revenue into the area."

"So does Falcon. Much of the workforce is from Candywood and the surrounding region. We are an established provider of much needed employment and our remunerations are well above minimum wage."

"But why the tight security for an agricultural research station? Are you anticipating attempts to steal your data or sabotage the place?"

116

"That's exactly it. It could happen. You'd be surprised how many organisations, not to mention countries, would like to get their hands on the fruits of our research. It can provide an edge in the area of food production."

"But armed guards?"

"That's the nature of the world these days," Hardisty said. "It seems to be quite easy to obtain dangerous materials these days. Remember London? Norway? Boston?"

"Who could forget?"

"Precisely. Then there was the man in Sweden."

"The one who tried to make a nuclear device in his apartment?"

"Indeed. He got almost all that he needed from the Internet. So you see anything is possible. We have to work in a secure facility."

"Okay," said Humble. "I buy what you're saying about needing some sort of security but I still think it's way over the top for the kind of work you do. Maybe you should arrange for guided tours like they do at nuclear power stations? That would reassure the public."

"It may be worth considering in future when we're in a position to do that. We have not felt the need for it up to now. The public around here do not seem to need reassurance at present. Meanwhile I have to ask you to leave us in peace and avoid any amateur investigations as well as speculative magazine articles. Can I have your assurance on that?"

"I'll have to think about it," said Humble, "And discuss it with my friends."

"Ah yes, Mr. Andrews and Miss Moscadini," said Hardisty.

Humble was taken aback,

How does he know?

"Yes," he said, recovering quickly. "Others may want to do some investigating too of.course. We can't be the only curious people in Candywood."

The shop bell rang. Hardisty broke off and leaned away from the table. He turned for the door,

"You'll think about it at least?" he asked.

"Yes. Will that be all for now?"

Three customers were entering the shop, antennae at the alert.

"Nice talking to you, Mr. Humble," said Hardisty as he left. Take care."

At eleven a.m his mobile rang. He was serving customers but took the call quickly in one of the empty aisles while Stella took over. It was Louisa,

"Can you speak?"

"Not easily. There are people in at the minute. Can I call you back?"

"Okay, don't make it too long."

She sounded anxious. He waited until it was quiet and Stella could manage the shop. He swiftly made the call, looking around in case he was interrupted. She answered,

"I'm at Uni but I can get some time off later. I'd like to see you before we go into town."

"I'm happy to see you anytime. What time were you thinking?"

"I can get in by three p.m."

"I'll still be working but I can let you into the flat and you can make yourself at home. Stella can do the last hour before closing and we'll talk before we meet Kirk."

"Fine, see you later."

118

He floated back to the main shop. Stella smiled to herself, noticing the expression decorating his face.

*

Craggs and Leoch met Nathan Hardisty in a quiet room in the back of the Lingdale. It was not yet opening time and he asked Anne-Marie to keep an eye on things. Bridget was noisily getting on with her daily cleaning. The whir of her vacuum cleaner could faintly be heard. The new carpet Craggs had arranged to be fitted, still had its fresh shop smell, mingling uneasily with the odour of the previous night's beer and food. Hardisty related how his talk with Humble had proceeded.

"Do you think they'll give up their investigation now, Mr. Hardisty?" asked Craggs.

"Probably not," said Hardisty. "In my estimation our curious friend, Humble will not be able to resist trying to find out more. Remember he's tried previously. He is not above asking Falcon employees if they know anything and many of them use his shop. I'm not sure about his two friends. What do you think?"

"You might be right," agreed Rocky. "He's like a ferret down a rabbit hole once he gets an idea in his head. He's a bit of a journalist too."

"There are more and more magazines devoted to unexplained occurrences. He could bring some unwelcome attention as he's done before. He may well have taken photographs," said Hardisty.

"So what can we do?" asked Leoch, "And more to the point – what can the three of them realistically find out? Falcon's security is very good."

119

"Not good enough, it appears," said Hardisty soberly. He frowned then spoke again,

"You both know most of what Falcon is trying to do. It's not being clandestine for the sake of it. We're carrying out research, which will ultimately benefit the nation, perhaps the wider world."

"You were both recruited to be the eyes and ears of Falcon in Candywood. We also pay you very well for your services. Our concern is that information will leak into the public domain before the appropriate time. You know the community. Can you come up with ways in which this group can be dissuaded from their investigations? What we don't want are others following their example."

"I know you pay us well," said Craggs. "It's meant that Sam here has been able to refurbish her riding school, hire staff and buy more thoroughbred horses and ponies. I've been able to improve the pub and add a restaurant. Falcon wins too of course. You get a substantial profit from the Government contract."

"Arms-length companies are the norm these days," said Hardisty, his fingers briefly pressing the surface of the table at which they were sitting. "They provide business expertise and take the risk whilst Government ultimately gets the credit when it goes right. We can't afford to let it go pear-shaped."

He lifted a hand, finger pointing upwards as he continued,

"Now we have this crisis, it's time for you to earn your money."

*

120

When the three men neared the old railway line they paused for a moment, trying to decide what to do next. They had hoped when they arrived in the country to find a way to a large town or city and go to ground amongst the general population, perhaps London. Their futures were now more uncertain.

Cities were good places in which to disappear and work could be found for those who were not particular. That had been their original aim before they were scooped up by the Falcon organisation. With only a rudimentary working knowledge of English, however it was always going to be a challenge.

As they rested, trying to communicate with each other, they gradually became aware of the group of armed guards closing in, forming a circle around them. There were six of the men and they were tightening their pincer-movement. The escapees looked around in panic but there was nowhere to run. One man still made the attempt. There was the crack of a gunshot as he tried to dodge through the circle. He dropped to the ground.

"You see," continued Hardisty, "We have another problem. There have been some escapes recently. From the captive workforce, as it were."

"The slaves," said Leoch, her mouth turning down in a frown. "I had no idea that was going on at the beginning when I signed up for this or I wouldn't have gone along with it."

"Come now," said Hardisty without smiling. "That is an emotive word to use. They have work, food, shelter – everything they hoped to find when they set out to enter the U.K illegally."

"They were trafficked," said Leoch. "Let's not mess about."
Hardisty's voice was velvet,

"If you wish to use that term it's your prerogative. The point is you are both now fully involved with Falcon operations and it's too late to back out. You know too much."

Samantha Leoch's blood began to boil like a hornet's nest. She fixed Hardisty with a steady look,

"Are you threatening us, Mr. Public Relations Man?"

"Sam," said Craggs. "Just leave it will you? He's right. We're in it for the long haul - might as well accept it."

"Good advice," said Hardisty briskly. "If you think about it you would agree that a safe environment in Falcon is better than working illegally and running the risk of being deported. Now we should turn our attention to what we can do about Mr. Humble and his friends."

"I won't go along with violence," insisted Leoch. "No way, I'd rather take my chances with the law."

"Not necessary, Sam," said Craggs. "There are other ways. I think it's time I paid a call on Shannon."
Leoch stared at him…

"That Guffock tart you have a child with? What can she do?"

"You'd be surprised," said Craggs. "She's very manipulative when she wants to be. Humble won't stand a chance."

"I know she's pretty indiscriminate about whom she goes with," said Leoch. "But how are you going to persuade her to seduce Jim Humble?"

Craggs reached for his wallet and revealed the contents,

"The usual way – money is tight these days."
She looked at him in disgust,

"You'd ask the mother of your child to whore for you?"

"Now, Sam, you know Shannon. We haven't had a relationship for a long time. There've been others since me. She'd enjoy the challenge. This will just sweeten things a little."

She shook her head and stared at the ceiling,

"I wonder about you sometimes. Just when I think I know you, a stunt like this emerges from your devious mind."

"I've always had an understanding with Shannon and her family. I was never the only one. I help with most of their needs and I visit the little boy now and then. I'll see him okay for school and whatever. That's another thing I can do, thanks to Falcon."

"Oh yes," she said, bite in her voice, "Uncle Vince."

Hardisty intervened in what was building into a lover's tiff,

"I have had some other thoughts," he said, "To make the Candywood gossip industry work for us. Tell me if you think my ideas would work."
They listened carefully to his plan, Leoch with some reluctance, Craggs with nodding acquiescence.

The guard patrol hastily dragged the body into the undergrowth intending to return later for more efficient disposal. The remaining two, an Eritrean and a Kurd, were grabbed and handcuffed before being taken on their way back to Falcon. Demoralised and afraid, they submitted meekly, knowing their future was uncertain.

"After we get these guys back to the Station we need to start looking for the escaped freaks," said the leader.

"How many are there, Sir?" asked one of the men as they pushed their captives ahead along the track.

"We're not entirely sure but there's some fucking weird things out there and the bosses want them back."

"Or incapacitated," said the man who had asked the question.

"If necessary," agreed the Leader. "We can't let them wander out of the forest."

"How freaky are they?" asked another man.

"Pretty strange, some of them," the Leader said. "I've only seen a few but I can see why Falcon doesn't want them out there. The publicity would kill the place. Remember, boys we're being paid extra for this work. Don't be squeamish now, think of the cash."
There were grins all round. They moved on.

*

Helen Highwater toyed with her coffee cup and looked at the man sitting opposite her. He was in his fifties, tall with short grey hair, grey-clothed to match.

He wore a light grey shirt and a grey tie with faint white stripes - a grey man altogether. Even his skin looked grey. He was a city dweller from the dense centre of that vast behemoth, London. He had judged her call to be important enough to take an overnight flight to Newcastle and had travelled from there in a hire car with driver.

"My family have invested a great deal in this Falcon place, Mr. Galliard."

"I know, and our arrangement with the company means your connection remains discreet. It is nevertheless greatly appreciated."

"When am I likely to see a substantial return?"

"Soon, I hope. The prognosis looks very good. We expect the innovative work being developed at Falcon will enable the country to gain a huge advantage in smart technology and in many other fields such as new agricultural techniques and eco-friendly industries. We have been trailing behind India, China, India and Brazil for too long. Even Angola is forging ahead these days. The country needs an economic boost equivalent to the original industrial revolution."

"Angola?"

"Yes, former Portuguese colony in South West Africa."

"I know where it is," she said acidly. "I'm just astounded you should bracket it along with the Asian tigers."

"My apologies, I was merely pointing out the seriousness of our economic situation."

Roland Galliard was a senior civil servant at the new Technology Futures Agency set up by the current administration in London.

His brief was to drive forward any advantages the country might gain in new science and technological fields. He had been instructed to reveal whatever was appropriate whilst refraining from giving offence, in order to keep this important investor on board. He knew it was important not to insult her intelligence.

She continued,

"I'm not keen on that Director man, you know – Dallas, nor his security chief, Savage. I wonder what their backgrounds are. Are they qualified for their jobs?"

"Yes. Savage has experience in the Military Police and Dallas has held high positions in utility companies. They may not be very refined people but they're efficient."

"I'm due to attend a meeting tonight of the Falcon Board in Cruiksdale at short notice," she said. "Will you be there too?"

"That would not be appropriate, I fear," said Galliard, removing an imaginary thread from his trouser leg. "I'm more of a background person and should not be involved with purely operational matters. Might I ask the reason for such a quickly convened meeting?"

"Dallas just said something about security. Frankly there are aspects of Falcon, which I suspect may verge on the controversial. I have a feeling that some questionable methods are being used. Do you know anything about this?"

Sharp old dame, thought Galliard...*mind like a bloody power-saw."*

"We have no reason to suspect anything like that, although the technology is admittedly very cutting edge."

"Please define, "Cutting edge."

126

Galliard decided he would tell her about the bioengineering and the genetic research but emphasise the benevolent side such as medical advances. He reasoned she would identify with smart technology for the common good and research into ways to slow down the ageing process, a sideline Falcon was investigating. He had to work hard to convince her that Falcon was well intentioned.

In the end she seemed satisfied and he left, having secured her compliance, promising her she would be given a tour of the Falcon operations in the near future. Travelling away from her house, he decided it would be worth paying a visit to the facility. He leaned forward to instruct the driver and reached for his phone. Making the connection, he spoke to Dallas,

"Why did you feel the need to invite her ladyship to the meeting tonight, Campbell?"

"We need her permission to expand Falcon further on to her land, Mr. Galliard," said Dallas. "We also need to keep her on side if any problems arise here."

"What kind of problems?"

Dallas briefly explained the events of recent days. Galliard thought for a few moments then spoke,

"I'm on my way to Falcon now. Please instruct the staff on gate security to allow me in. We need to talk about this whilst I'm in the area."

He stared out of the window at the passing landscape. The car rolled on smoothly.

*

Humble received a call from Andrews just before noon,

"Can we meet for lunch? I'd like a chat before we go into town."

"I'm meeting Morton at the Church House. Why not come too during your lunch hour? I'll close the shop but ask Stella to stay on to re-open in case I'm late getting back. Louisa's coming in at three, by the way."

"Okay," said Andrews. "See you soon."

At Parke's house they talked over one of Margaret's hearty lunches.

"I don't usually eat as well as this during my working day," said Andrews. "Hope I don't fall asleep when I get back."

"'You're not very busy on Mondays are you, Kirk?" said Humble, attacking a plate of sandwiches enthusiastically while his home-made soup cooled. There were delicious odours from the kitchen. They indicated that a batch of Margaret's renowned scones were emerging fresh from the oven.

"Good job," Andrews said. "But what did your visitor ask you about this morning?"

"You're well-informed," said Humble. He explained about the visit from Hardisty. They were intrigued when he repeated what the Public Relations Officer had said.

"He basically warned us off doing any further investigating. I have to say he made a very good case for Falcon's tight security and seemed to be saying their work was crucial as well as benevolent," Humble said.

"Maybe you'd be better to go along with that advice," said Parke. "Remember that Falcon is an important employer for the people around here."

"I know," said Humble. "You've said that before - the Cash Cow. But if they're hiding something dodgy they have to be exposed." He spooned soup into his mouth, "Didn't realise how hungry I was."

"We saw some strange things yesterday, you know," said Andrews, "Things which didn't quite fit with the notion of Falcon being the golden goose with the welfare of Candy and district at heart."

He related everything they had experienced during their visit to the forest. Parke listened without interruption then gave his opinion,

"It is puzzlin', I admit. I wonder if what they're doin', is against the natural way of things. If so it may also be contrary to the Will of God and I would then have an interest."

"Quite," Andrews said. "So do we carry on or what?"

"After you reported finding Bain's body," said Parke, "The police will have taken over. It will go to the Fiscal, in which case you'd be advised to stay well out of it in case you are seen to be obstructing legal proceedings. There may be no need for you to take any further part. You don't want to push Falcon into a corner."

"I don't," Humble said. "But I still have a gut feeling there's something else."

"You and your gut feelings...don't you trust the police on this?"

"Yes and no. Let's see how they react when Louisa, Kirk and I attend the interview later today."

He explained about the visit to the police station in town scheduled for five-thirty.

"Bain's death is all over Candy, this morning." said Andrews. "It's assumed he topped himself."

129

"The Candy justice boys who gave him a hammering are keeping low profiles."

"Gossip about you three will probably start doin' the rounds," said Parke, "In due course."

"So what?" Humble said, "Nothing to do with anybody else is it? What do they know anyway? You know the old saying is true."

"What old saying?" Andrews asked.

"Life's a bed of roses," said Humble, "But you've got to watch out for the pricks."
He bit into one of Margaret's cheese scones as if he wanted to bite someone's leg off.

"Of course," Parke said soothingly, not in the least offended. "I was just worried that Louisa's involvement with your investigative activities might place her in danger."
He looked embarrassed – an unusual state for Parke. He regretted his earlier assumptions about Louisa.

"Well," said Andrews. "Let's just enjoy this wonderful lunch then we'll talk."

After lunch, Andrews looked at his watch,

"Got to get back soon," he said. "I'm supposed to be managing the office until five o'clock."

"I'll have to get back to the shop too," Humble said. "So what have we decided?"

"Do you have half-day closing tomorrow?" asked Andrews.

"Yes, usually do on a Tuesday. What are you suggesting?"

"I've got some 'T.O.I.L' coming to me – time off in lieu. I can meet at this time tomorrow and we can take another trip into the forest, this time for a different purpose."

"What purpose?" Humble asked.

"We can visit Geordie Hagg. He's Sticky's brother and he needs to know what's happened."

"I don't know if anyone has thought of telling him, but if and when the funeral takes place he may want to be there. He might also be able to tell us what he knows about the forest and Falcon."

"Good thought," said Humble. "I know where his place is. It's that little cottage in Whiteside Woods – part of Caithland. Rough as a badger's arse - oh sorry, Morton."

Parke did not react.

"There's an old caravan parked right next to it," continued Humble. "Geordie uses it as part of his home. There's also a carriage from the railway after it was axed. He does actually have title to the land and cottage, you know. It was inherited from one of his uncles. It's been in the family for years."

"How does he make a living?" said Parke. "I've often wondered."

"He does a little poaching, some fishing, grows vegetables and fruit. He keeps goats and hens and chops firewood. He exchanges it for food from farmers and people who have holiday homes. He's not above doing an odd job now and again - gardening, farm-work and so on."

"Not a complete isolate then?" said Parke.

"No but he rarely comes into Candy."

"He'll have to, for the funeral," Andrews said. "Were they close?"

"Not especially, but blood is thicker than water. He should be told what's happened if he doesn't already know."

"I'd like to come along," said Parke. "I can make time for it."

"No problem. You're very welcome."

"At least Falcon can't claim we're interfering with their work," said Andrews.

"No," Humble said, "Just paying a visit. As we'll have a Minister with us it could be described as a pastoral one."

"Someone's got to keep you boys on the straight and narrow," said Parke.

"Thank Margaret for us please, Morton. We'll let you know what happened at the police interviews."

Parke waved his acknowledgement as they stood up to leave. He saw them to the door,

"See you tomorrow, boys. What time?"

"One-thirty at the shop - bring your phones. You never know – we might get some interesting pictures. Okay with you, Kirk?"

Andrews raised his thumb as he moved off towards the council building. Humble crossed the road. A figure pulled on a cigarette, watching the shop-keeper return to his place of business.

Ten

The two scientists and Capilus met as they had planned, comparing notes.

"The security side is becoming more active," said Bowman.

"They're obviously worried," Bowman said. "What do you think, Eva?"

"I have had more security visits to my part of the complex than I can remember," she said. "Are you two still concerned about problems with the procedures and research you are involved with?"

She spoke quietly although they were seated in one of the lounges, well away from anyone else.

"Yes," said Prahalad. "I've been very careful to monitor the work and instruct my staff to treble-check everything they do. It has improved things I think."

"Would you mind if I brought someone else into our group?" asked Capilus.

"No," Prahald said. "If you think it would help."

Bowman was more wary,

"Who were you thinking of?" he asked.

"A colleague - Dos Santos."

"Who?"

"Antonio Dos Santos. He is Brazilian. He has been involved with bio-fuel research as well as bioengineering," she said, "His country has introduced ethanol–fuelled vehicles extensively. He too has concerns about what is going on here. He could be a useful ally. I have already sounded him out."

"Have you now?" said Bowman, a little irritated, "We shouldn't make this group too big, you know. Are you sure he's not a management stooge?"

Capilus was momentarily disarmed by the expression before she understood,

"Oh I see. No, Antonio is okay. I can vouch for him."

"Right. Well, if you think so. We should be very careful in future, however. That's all I'm saying."

*

Dallas and Savage instigated a comprehensive investigation into possible internal sabotage, stimulated by the imminent arrival of Galliard. They wanted to show they were on top of the problem. Theoretically, McQuade was doing the same, searching her electronic records.

"Check all staff databases for anything out of the ordinary, Kenneth," Dallas said. "Have your people interview everybody around the clock as far as possible until we've spoken to them all. Report progress to me every three hours. I want these renegades caught and I want to know who's supporting them."

"Yes, Sir," answered Savage. "What do we say to the shift workers and those who do only day work?" he asked. "People from Candywood - cleaners, office staff, drivers and so on. They'll leave the building at the end of their working day. Are they also under suspicion?"

"Everybody is," said Dallas. "But we can tell those workers that it's just routine security and there's no emergency, if they should ask. Handle them carefully and without fuss so that no reports of over-reaction get back to Candywood and the community gets the idea there's a crisis. Are the patrols still searching for runaways and so on?"

"Yes, Sir. Two escaped prisoners have been captured. The patrol reported that one was shot dead whilst trying to run away."

"Oh shit, shit, shit. Give me strength. Where's the body?"

"Still in the forest. The men have not had time to retrieve it and carry out a full disposal."

"Bloody stupid ex-squaddies. Hardly a brain cell between them. Tell them to get on with it at once. If they do anything like that again I'll have them out of here before they can break wind. We can't leave any evidence out there especially with these nosy locals snooping around. Any reports about this man, Humble and his pals?"

"Gone quiet, Sir. I believe Mr. Hardisty paid him a visit today. No sign of any activity near the fences."

"Good. Then after bringing in the body and getting rid of it in the crematorium you need to organise more patrols to round up the freak accidents of those experiments."

"Yes, Sir. I'll see to it as soon as possible. Will that be all, Sir?"

"Yes. Keep me informed will you?"

"Of course."

Savage left the room. Dallas moved the mouse and gazed at his computer screen. Angry thoughts were whizzing around in his head,

Bloody scientists....incompetent eggheads – and those fucking ex-squaddies. You just can't get the staff.

*

Louisa arrived in Candywood just after three and drove into one of the side streets, turning left into Long Lane, parking as close to the back of Humble's shop as possible. She phoned him and he promptly squeezed through the stacked crates and boxes, signalling non-verbally to Stella who nodded, a smile playing on her mouth. He met Louisa at the back door,

"Are you okay? You sounded worried on the phone."

"I'm fine. I just wanted to talk to you for a while before we go to the police station. Are you very busy right now?"

"Stella's holding the fort but I can't stay away too long."

He led her up to the apartment and helped her off with her coat.

"You'd better get back to the shop," she said. I'll make myself at home here. It's been hectic at Uni today so I've brought my laptop to do a bit of work in peace before we go out. See you in a while."

"Help yourself to anything you need," he said. "You know where the kitchen is. I'll be back up as soon as I can. I saw Kirk today and we made some arrangements, which I'll tell you about later."

He closed the door quietly and headed down the stairs back to the shop, returning to his customers with reduced concentration. The next hour seemed to pass before his eyes without registering. At four-thirty the number of customers tailed off.

Stella winked at him,

"Go on up, Jim. You know you want to. I'll manage here then I'll put the closed sign up and slip away. Don't worry about the shop."

"Thanks, Stella. You're the best."

She grinned and waved him off. He took the stairs two at a time. Louisa was sitting at a small table with a mug of coffee and a sandwich,

"Back early?"

"Couldn't keep away."

"Tell me about your day."

Humble moved to the sofa and indicated the place next to him. He gave her an account of his meetings with Hardisty, Andrews and Parke and the arrangements for the following day. She frowned,

"Falcon is going to extraordinary lengths to prevent us from learning their secrets. We can't be the only curious people around here. I wonder if anyone else has tried to investigate there."

"They must have, but nobody ever talks about it. Do you think they were warned off?"

"Or bought off."

"I hadn't thought of that. It explains the shroud of silence around the place."

"Remember it's a Cash Cow. People don't want to lose it."

"I wondered about asking a few discreet questions. You know, when I meet people in the street or the shop, maybe in the pubs or the café. What do you think?"

"Be careful who you ask. You don't really know who to trust."

"You're right. It's time to go anyway. Kirk will be here soon. Before we meet him however, I need to ask you something."

"Yes, what is it?"

"Will you come to dinner with me? Tonight?"

"Hmmm, moving things on a bit, Mr. Humble? Okay, where?"

"How about the Italian place in Gillerston? I could book us a table and we could go there after we drop Kirk off. What do you say? Do you like Italian food? Oh I forgot."

He hit his forehead with the palm of one hand.

She laughed,

"I'm a hot-blooded Neapolitan girl, remember?"

"Sorry, of course you must be well used to it. We could go somewhere else. What about that Chinese place in town - *the Golden Pagoda?* Do you like Chinese?"

"Do I? I love it. Makes a change from pizzas and pasta. But that means we'll have to drive all the way back to town after we drop Kirk off. Then back again. There's another place in Gillerston, *The Forest Inn* – good food and a quiet location by the river. What do you think?"

"Right. I'll phone and make a booking."

"Should I pop into the flat and change before dinner?"

"You don't have to change for me. You'd look fabulous in an old sack."

He made the call as she digested the backhanded compliment.

*

Galliard arrived at Falcon twenty minutes after leaving Highwater House. The security was very efficient at the entrance gate, he noted approvingly. His car nosed along a narrow drive and stopped at a cluster of functional looking buildings. Dallas met him and shook hands so firmly that Galliard thought his hand would be permanently crushed. Galliard's handshake was a little more polite, smooth and long-fingered. He walked with an elegant stride up the steps into the main reception area. Savage was waiting there. Another crushing handshake,

What is it with these career managerial types?

They walked along carpeted corridors past rooms with glass - panelled doors and a laboratory section. There was an air of quiet purpose about the place and everywhere there was the smell of air freshener masking the chemical odours permeating the building. Employees moved past them nodding respectfully to Dallas, calling him *Sir* or *Director*. Galliard was impressed.

He had asked to see the hydroponic farm complex and Bowman had been dragooned into showing him round. There was no mention of any glitches at this stage. Bowman left Dallas to reveal the problems to Galliard later. The experimental labs were also visited and Galliard viewed the staff and worker accommodation. Prisoner blocks were tucked out of sight amongst thick screens of trees. They completed the tour and moved to Dallas' office where coffee was served.

"Thank you, Campbell," Galliard said. "Very impressive set-up. If we continue to make progress with all this then we should be able to achieve our aim to get an edge over other economies through innovative research and methods. Now tell me about these difficulties you've been experiencing."

Dallas explained the recent incidents and mistakes with some of the technology. Galliard listened without interruption then said,

"How serious is this?"

"If we can round up all the escapees we can contain it. The same applies to G.M contamination. Otherwise we could have some difficult issues to deal with. The public are not yet ready to accept what we're doing here. Apart from some local people who are aware of the extent of our activities and the means by which we are pursuing the research, the outside world thinks we are developing new food sciences or eco-friendly applications and mechanisms," Dallas said.

"Of course we're actually doing this. That's not just a front. Those specialists in the classified sections are scientists from around the world and live on-site. They are sworn to secrecy and are in any case motivated to achieving breakthroughs and ultimate recognition for their work. It keeps them on side, together with generous remuneration, medical provision and living conditions." Their contracts are time-limited. They are not encouraged to visit Candywood or the other towns and villages in the immediate area."

"I see. How are the captives faring under the regime you have in place?"

"Well, as you know, we use long-serving prisoners who initially volunteer to test medicinal drugs in exchange for a more comfortable existence and reduced sentences with full rehabilitation. A proportion of them are terrorist suspects or actual convicted terrorists. Falcon functions as our Guantanamo Bay. Once here they can be used for experiments of greater risk."

"And if they refuse?"

140

"We keep them locked up until they comply. In most cases we can use certain drugs to ensure their compliance. We have space to accommodate a large number of prisoners although this is becoming limited. Our secure accommodation blocks are now pretty densely populated. That's one reason why we need more land for building, hence the need to keep Lady Highwater on board. Of course some subjects of experimentation inevitably fail to survive due to the rigorous nature of the processes."

Galliard was slightly uneasy about this aspect of Falcon's work but knew it had been sanctioned at the highest level. He sipped his coffee and said,

"There was a bit of a sea-change in political opinion when the economy nose-dived after 2010 and bottomed out. Not helped by the rolling crisis in the Eurozone, the competition from emerging economies and the shift of global economic dominance to the East. A more desperate climate emerged. Tell me about the foreign workers."

"Again it helps to solve a perceived national problem. Immigration is an emotive issue in many countries and we have seen the rise of extreme right wing politics across Europe," said Dallas. "Huge numbers of people at any given time were being trafficked from the former Soviet Union, Asia and Africa as well as those who struggle to get here themselves by fair means or foul."

Galliard nodded,

"It's amazing to see the lengths some people go to in order to reach the U.K."

"For sure," said Dallas. "Many are stranded across the Channel for years living in limbo."

"Many more disappear into London and other major cities and live illegally there for considerable lengths of time. We have helped to relieve some of the pressure by bringing a proportion of them here."

"To be used for…?" asked Galliard.

"Labour mostly, sometimes experiments, testing, organ-harvesting. They have no rights you see," said Dallas. "Technically they don't exist."

A look of distaste passed fleetingly over Galliard's face but he collected himself,

The end justifies the means, he thought.

He couldn't remember who in the past had said that - possibly Lenin.

"Remind me of the new research you are pursuing here, Campbell."

Dallas had been slightly phased at first by the use of his first name. It felt like a Rubicon had been passed,

"Well as I mentioned earlier, we have already made substantial progress with new agricultural techniques and food production…"

Galliard interrupted,

"G.M?"

"Mainly," said Dallas. "And other forms of bioengineering. If we can sell the technology to the hungry countries of the world we can get ahead of the field. I anticipate we will approach that stage in the very near future."

"Excellent," said Galliard, approvingly. "Go on."

"Then we have our research into parasites which effect animals and plants. Our scientists are developing ways in which to eliminate them, even those which effect humans."

"Oh?"

"Yes, Toxoplasma Gondii and Plasmodium, to give two examples."

Galliard pretended interest although he was completely out of his depth. Dallas continued,

"We think some parasites or pathogens interfere with the brain's ability to produce dopamine, a chemical messenger between nerve cells. This may cause mental illnesses in some more receptive people. If we can develop an antidote it would be a tremendous boost to our pharmaceutical industry. Some of our other research is already pointing towards new products. If we can produce a range of new medicines we can become world leaders."

"It's gratifying to know you have the commercial possibilities in the forefront of your work," said Galliard smoothly. He glanced at his watch,

"I'm getting pushed for time. Can you sum up the range of your current research in as short a time as possible, please? I know the general approach but things change regularly. An update would be helpful."

"Certainly," said Dallas and proceeded to list the technologies Falcon was currently working on,

"In addition to those I mentioned we are also looking at the use of surgical transplant technology to create blends of machine-humans and an artificial genome - new animals and plants designed on a computer and grown to order. We are developing a machine that prints organs using 3.D bio-printers for manufacturing human tissue – regenerative medicine."

"It works by producing simple human tissue using samples of living flesh, from which a new organ can be grown using precursor cells. Stem cells are extracted from adult bone marrow and fat."

143

"Printing heads like those in an inkjet printer are used to deposit scaffolding (a sugar-based hydro-gel) into a pre-built structure similar to that of the organ being replaced or replicated. A laser-based calibration system, together with a computer graphics system, allows cross-sections of body parts to be created."

"We are also working on a medical means by which human life can be prolonged for much further lengths of time (We call it "The Life Extension Project"). We're using flatworms for that."

"Flatworms?" Galliard echoed.

"Yes," replied Dallas. "Planarian worms to be exact. It's known they can repeatedly regenerate their cells and replace lost or damaged tissue."

"They possess tiny sections of D.N.A called *telemeres* that cap any damage and loss of cell function linked to ageing. Each time a cell divides the protective telemere cap gets shorter. When they get too short they divide and a new worm is formed. On this basis the cells of such an animal should to be able to divide indefinitely so that they would continue to replicate."

"One type of flatworm actually reproduces like that instead of sexually. If we could harness that mechanism and transfer it to humans it would be theoretically possible to achieve immortality through the process. We are also experimenting with transgenic creations – the use of genetically modified life forms to perform various functions."

He paused. Galliard looked bemused,

"But this is pure Science-Fiction. The concept of immortality and machine-assisted humans, for example. Are these things really possible?

144

"Perfectly possible. Computers for example are inexorably getting faster and smarter. They are approaching the time when they are capable of becoming as intelligent as us. Like cloning, it cannot be stopped. We don't know for sure about smarter-than-human machines. It's important to be cautious. Too many mistakes and we would have serious problems. The same applies to immortality – think of the effect that would have on the world."

"One of the scenarios we are working on, is that eventually we will blend with them and become cyborgs - to use a quaintly inaccurate expression, linking with computers to extend our intelligence. A better term may be what we like to call, *bio forms*...bio-engineered humans. Perhaps the artificial intelligences will help us overcome the effects of ageing and prolong our life-spans indefinitely – an alternative to the medical approach I mentioned earlier. Cybernetic organisms have existed for a long time actually – think of artificial hearts, prosthetic limbs, heart pacemakers and insulin pumps for diabetics."

"It is already possible to use a direct path of communication from brain to external device. It won't be long before we have cochlear implants, which can be placed in the human ear to cure deafness, even in children. Cybernetic bugs are now a reality. Implants are placed in insects during the pupa stage and the resulting life-form can be programmed and controlled to perform certain functions as required. This can also be extended to such organisms as slow-worms, eels, salamanders and others."

"We are investigating the possibility of creating a human exoskeleton, which supports a machine inside but looks human on the outside."

"It could just keep on renewing itself when its parts begin to wear out. This would be a boon for space exploration or for the military."

"We can even posit a future where biotechnology will give us the means to manipulate our bodies as we wish. It's not Science-Fiction any more. It could eventually lead to the post-human era and a new age in which we are no longer alone. We will share the world with new creations, made here first, in our experimental facility."

Galliard was amazed. He had not known the full extent of Falcon's research,

"Do you know if any other countries are working on these things?"

"Undoubtedly. But not on a single site and not all these technologies at once. There is potential for further development in other areas too, such as nanotechnology. If we were to expand we could be the greatest single innovative research centre in the world."

"*Academgorodok*," said Galliard suddenly.

"I'm sorry…I…?" Dallas said, puzzled.

"In the old Soviet Union, a centre for research was established deep in Siberia, somewhere near Novosibirsk," said Galliard. "It was called Academgorodok – The City of Sciences. The idea was to gather the best brains in the U.S.S.R and beyond to work on new technologies and ground-breaking science, which would make the country a world leader. They had everything they needed on site and money was no object. What they asked for they got."

"Falcon is our Academgorodok. We actually used that model to form the basis of this facility. Our idea seems to be paying off."

146

"Yes I see what you mean, Mr. Galliard," said Dallas.

"Please, call me Roland."

Galliard held up his hands.

Dallas was suitably flattered,

"You may know…er, Roland that we have already released genetically modified life-forms into the wild."

"What?" Galliard was momentarily alarmed.

"The common midge and the mosquito can be curses in northern latitudes," explained Dallas. "Northern England, Scotland, Scandinavia and Russia for example. To say nothing of the horsefly, known in Scotland as the cleg."

Galliard nodded. He had experienced the midge problem around the Falcon complex on previous visits. He knew it was worse the further north and west in the world you travelled, culminating in the potentially lethal Siberian mosquito, which could cause encephalitis of the brain.

"What we did was to breed large numbers of the target pest, sterilised them and released the males. When they mated with wild females the resulting eggs were non-viable. Theoretically we could exterminate entire wild populations."

The senior official was astonished,

"Can this technique be used for any insect pest?"

"In principal yes, said Dallas. "Think of the potential for eliminating sheep tick, the malaria mosquito, the tsetse fly and many other disease carrying insects. We use doses of radiation to do the job and it could also apply to other parasitic species."

"Great work," said Galliard. "Are there other innovations Falcon can consider in the future?"

"Oh yes. There are no limits apart from religious or ethical ones. Success breeds success. In a closed environment such as this we can see fiction become fact. In terms of bio-forms we have already produced prototypes which are up and running."

"What? You've manufactured some?"

"Yes. At the moment we're still testing and experimenting and it's not clear if the prototypes we have are suitable. They have flaws. The technology still has some way to go. That's why we have experienced some of the problems I mentioned earlier. But you can't make an omelette without breaking eggs."

"What do you use to provide the human element for these cybernetic hybrids, the bio-forms?" asked Galliard although queasily, he was fairly sure what Dallas' answer would be.

"Prisoners, illegals and so on," replied the Falcon Director calmly.

"Volunteers?"

"Not always. Sometimes it is necessary to use er…persuasion."

"I see," said Galliard, digesting the implications.

"We're doing pioneering work here. It means taking tough decisions at times. I'm sure you understand. Our original brief was wide-ranging and we were given a great deal of autonomy."

Galliard stared at Director Dallas but the other seemed perfectly serious. He rubbed his eyes and took a gulp of coffee suddenly wishing it had brandy in it.

This is too much to take in. The risks are enormous but we are committed now.

"The ethical and religious constraints are an issue for both Governments of course," he said.

"We in the political arena are treading on eggshells with this. It's further complicated because two countries are involved. Although close to the border, Falcon is in Scotland, which has considerable autonomy these days."

"I understand the Scottish Government is happy to see Falcon become a generator for new technology," said Dallas. "We are expecting a visit from some of their ministerial team in due course. Like the Government in London, they have been kept in the dark about some of our more controversial techniques as well as the research pursued... cloning, stem cell research and so on. There is also the use of prisoners and captive labour."

"I represent a small group operating at a high level in London", said Galliard.

"Few people are fully aware of the inner workings of Falcon. It has to stay that way. When we reach take-off point and begin to harvest the economic benefits of our gamble we can tough it out then. We will in effect present the wider world with a fait accompli."

Dallas felt privileged to be part of all this and was inwardly congratulating himself when Galliard continued,

"These glitches you've been experiencing – are you making any progress in recapturing any escapees?"

"The security team are rounding up the escaped workers as we speak," said Dallas. "We're on top of it and will soon identify the cause of the problem and stop any further breaches of security."

"Good. Could there be saboteurs amongst the staff, do you think?"

"It's possible. If so we will deal with them accordingly. There's no way they can hide in a closed complex such as this."

149

Dallas did not mention the shooting of the prisoner or the unauthorised release of cybrids and bio-forms from Falcon. Too much for Galliard to swallow, he decided.

"Deal with them? In what way?"

"If we sack them they'll talk to the media – whistle blowing," said Dallas. "They'll simply join the ranks of the prisoners and be held for as long as necessary. They'll not be allowed to communicate with the outside world."

"What's motivating them, do you think?"

"We had to dismiss some operatives for incompetence some time ago," said Dallas.

"They may have sympathisers on the inside. It's also possible that *sleepers* have infiltrated into the complex even though our screening procedure is very robust. They may be animal rights activists or be motivated by ideals of a religious or ethical nature, but we'll find them eventually. You need not worry on that score."

"Good. Well, keep me informed. I have to get back. You're doing excellent work here, Campbell. One day you'll be recognised for your efforts."

Galliard stood up. He felt overwhelmed. Inwardly pleased, Dallas showed him to his car and watched as his political boss drove away. He returned to his office to check on progress with the security situation.

*

At five p.m Stella closed the shop just as Andrews arrived. Humble and Louisa met him and they drove off together towards Cruiksdale.

The journey would take twenty-five minutes along a meandering, country road long overdue for upgrading. They passed small farms and cottages, but mostly ran through deserted countryside.

"What do you think we saw in the forest yesterday?" asked Humble.

"Nothing I've ever encountered before. If they were anything to do with Falcon the question arises – why were they there in the first place?" Andrews said.

"Escaped, presumably," said Humble. "Either somebody got careless or they were deliberately released. Remember the giant rats I told you about? Then there were the other over-large animals, not to mention the vegetation. The whole thing's very weird. I just don't know what to make of it."

"Falcon could be doing something that's really out of order, even illegal," said Louisa.

"It's looking like it," said Humble. "Sooner or later we'll have to tell somebody about those strange entities we saw. I can't understand why they haven't been spotted or reported before now."

"Maybe they have," said Andrews. "People may be too wary to say anything or they're afraid of being ridiculed. On the other hand they may not have been in the forest long. We could have been the first to see them properly."

"Louisa, said Humble, "Kirk, Morton and I are going to visit Geordie Hagg tomorrow, as you suggested. He may know more about Falcon than we do."

"I'm at Uni all day tomorrow. But you can call or text me."

"We should all share phone numbers and email addresses," said Andrews,

"But what you said made me think. Sticky may have known more about Falcon than he let on. But as he was unreliable when drunk, it's possible someone decided to get rid of him in case he said too much."

"If you're right about Sticky," Humble said, "Could Bain have been seen off for the same reason? He must have known about Falcon as his work took him into the forest most days."

"We found him. It looked like suicide. He'd hung himself."

Andrews frowned at the memory. Louisa looked out of the window, swallowing.

"He was also very badly beaten the day before. In his weak state could he have put up much of a fight if a few strong guys decided to make it look like suicide?"

"Perhaps not, but we're jumping to conclusions. Bain had good reasons to top himself."

"True, he was increasingly out of order with his extra-marital activities. That would have left him open to blackmail. Falcon may have decided it was too big a risk to take."

"Or someone acting unilaterally thinking it would benefit Falcon – someone linked to the facility, perhaps an employee," said Louisa.

"Now we're really just speculating," Andrews said. "We're here anyway. Let's concentrate on getting these interviews over with then we can think again."

They had arrived at Police H.Q in Cruiksdale.

The interviews were conducted by Dalveen, a W.P.C Harland, and Marcus Burn. They were seen separately but as they had agreed, stuck to their original stories, omitting only the sighting of the strange people.

They had decided not to mention the incident, as they were in any event, not sure what they had actually encountered. Harland took notes.

Their instincts told them to avoid anything smacking of Science-Fiction, aware that they were unlikely to be taken seriously – the *Hicks from the Sticks* syndrome. Eventually it was over. They left with the usual warning – to give Falcon a wide berth. Humble had tried to hint that Bain might not have died by his own hand, but Dalveen had brushed this aside,

"The Fiscal will decide about that, Mr. Humble," he had said. "As well as about the death of Mr. Hagg. It's out of our hands now."

Humble knew how the Scottish system worked but nevertheless pushed a little further…

"Two deaths in a short space of time are more than just a coincidence, Sergeant, don't you think?"

Dalveen had been visibly irritated,

"Mr. Humble, it's not for you or for any other members of the public to openly speculate on these matters. As I've already said, the Procurator-Fiscal will examine the evidence and make a decision accordingly. If there is a case to answer we will know in due course."

Humble was more respectful after this reprimand.

Following the interviews, they were all less inclined to be talkative. The daylight was going on the return journey and Humble concentrated on the road.

"Did the police quiz either of you two about Bain's death?" he asked, slowing down for a logging lorry.

"No," they both replied.

"I didn't speculate on it," said Andrews.

"Just told them what we saw, including the armed men we met and the incident with the three foreign guys. I didn't mention the android-looking things, as agreed."

"Me too," Louisa said. "They asked me a lot of questions about the three men and I told them they were shot at. They were very interested in that."

"Good, our stories were the same then," said Humble. "They didn't like me trying to link Sticky's death with that of Bain. I felt they were taking us for country simpletons at first but they sat up when I mentioned the encounter with the Falcon guards."

"I thought they were implying Falcon has permission to deploy armed men but were genuinely surprised that a shot had actually been fired," Andrews said. "You know – outside the complex itself, technically."

"Those scary guards we met seem to think they owned all the woods anyway," Louisa said, shivering at the memory.

"Arrogant bastards," Andrews growled in an undertone.

They were silent for a while. The road had emptied again.

"What time are you heading into the forest tomorrow?" asked Louisa.

"One-thirty. I'm meeting Kirk here and Morton outside the shop."

"I'd love to go with you but I'm not free during the day until Friday."

"If we don't find anything tomorrow we can always go back another time," said Humble, "If you're up for it."

"I'm up for it. You can't keep a Moscadini down."

"I can get off early, depending which day," said Andrews, "Morton can be more flexible as he manages his own hours to an extent."

"Okay. We'll talk about this some more," Humble said, "It's only Monday after all."

"It feels as if we've been doing this for weeks," said Louisa.

They passed the sign proclaiming the beginning of Candywood.

"We're back," Humble said. "Can I drop you off at your house, Kirk?"

"Perfect. We'll talk again tomorrow."

They exchanged email addresses and phone numbers. Andrews cautioned them as they prepared to drive off,

"Mind how you go."

"He's a nice man," said Louisa as they drove away.

"Yes, good to have as a friend in a situation like this. Now are you going to drive home? We're booked up for eight. Where shall I meet you?"

"Do you know Fir Hill Drive in Gillerston?"

"By the park? Yes."

"I live at number twenty-four. Meet me there at seven-thirty. We can drive to the restaurant."

Humble drew up at the shop and jumped out to open the door for Louisa.

"You're very polite."

"My pleasure."

He walked with her to her car. Louisa took his arm. She briefly kissed him, got into the Citroen and drove off.

He stood, thinking for a few moments, mulling over the day's events then opened the door and mounted the stairs to his flat, suddenly immensely tired.

*

Meanwhile, the meeting of the Falcon Board of Management, Lady Highwater, various Board officials and Falcon departmental managers, was taking place. After routine Board business the matters of security and the possible expansion of the site came up.

"We're currently dealing successfully with the issues we have encountered," reported Dallas. "I'd like to ask Mr. Savage to comment from an operational standpoint."

"Yes," said Savage. "The G.M contaminations are now more or less under control and the small amount of sabotage we detected has been repaired. My operatives are interviewing the workforce in order to identify those who have attempted to undermine the research. We should be able to bring it to a conclusion soon."

He did not elaborate on the actual incidents, hoping the Board would not ask for detailed written reports.

"You used the term, "More or less" Mr. Savage," said the Scottish Government representative, George Tinto. "Does this mean there is still work to do in order to contain the contamination?"

"That is correct," said Savage smoothly. "But we are confident the problem can be sorted out in due course."

Tinto continued,

"But even a small amount of contamination could spread beyond the forest and into agricultural land. If that happens there'll be hell to pay."

"If I may interrupt," said Dallas, "Caithland Forest is vast and our facility is located deep inside it. Our teams are working round the clock to check the contamination before it can spread out of the forest. Time and distance are on our side."

"What about the trees and plants inside the forest itself?" asked another member, "They'll be affected won't they? I understand a local amateur naturalist has already identified variants amongst wild flora?"

"The chemicals we are using will deal with problems of that nature," said Savage.

"It's true however," Dallas said. "That some changes in the wild vegetation have occurred but these were minimal and will not have a serious effect. The individual in question was exaggerating and we are informed he has a reputation for making wild, unsubstantiated claims. He was told by the local newspaper that they would not accept articles about that kind of thing in future."

Good job we got to the Editor of the local rag, Dallas thought - *Had to lean on him a bit though. A nice, fat bundle of cash helped the process. Some of these provincial papers struggle to keep going.*

"And the sabotage," asked Lady Highwater, "Do you know why it took place?"

"We surmise it may have been former employees who were dismissed for incompetence and could bear a grudge against us,"

"We followed agreed disciplinary procedure in their cases and their offences were judged to be serious enough to justify their dismissal at the time." "The Board will recall the offences concerned. Our workers are instructed to observe a high level of vigilance at all times and to be mindful of the need for 100% security."

"Does that include computer-hacking?" she persisted, "For example do you have adequate firewalls in place to prevent viruses or Trojan horses infecting your computer systems?"

How the hell does she know about that stuff at her age? Dallas thought. Smoothly, he said,

"Certainly, we have an excellent I.T. team at Falcon."

"That's gratifying. These animal rights people can be more than just a nuisance at times. Could they be behind the attempted sabotage too?"

She had herself encountered problems with animal rights activists over the Falcon Centre. They believed that experiments on animals were being conducted there. She had experienced the same resistance during the debate surrounding the anti-fox hunting bill.

"It's possible," said Dallas. "It's one of the lines of enquiry we will pursue. It will be placed in the hands of the police if that is the case. We have good links with them. Anything else we can deal with internally. We have a healthy relationship with the community as a whole. Most people are behind us and appreciate the economic benefits of having Falcon in the area, not least as a generous employer."

The meeting continued and Dallas and Savage were relieved when the Board moved on from the issue of security.

In due course, the Board decided in principle to allow the future expansion of the Falcon Centre. Lady Highwater agreed to the lease of more land in exchange for a satisfactory price and the Board moved to discuss other matters. During the break for refreshments, Dallas conferred with Savage in a low voice,

"Glad that's over and done with. Now we have to finish sorting out those fucking amateur snoops."

Savage nodded.

*

Humble arrived at Louisa's flat early and was shown in by Kath, a tall girl in her twenties. Louisa's other friend, Jane, was not at home. He spent a few moments making small talk with Kath before Louisa arrived in the living room. She was dressed in a pale yellow outfit, complementing her dark colouring. He felt he had to say something,

"You look wonderful."

She smiled, acknowledging the compliment,

"You've met Kath I see. Shall we go now? I'm starved after all that stress with the interviews. See you later, Kath."

She let him help her on with her coat.

As Louisa had said, the Forest Inn was tucked away in a quiet part of Gillerston. The location allowed them to discretely talk over their recent experiences. Humble had driven them to the restaurant and would be driving home afterwards.

"So much seems to have happened recently," she said, "Yet it's only been three and a half days really."

159

"And this is our first date," he said. "Not the most conventional way to begin a relationship."

"Is that what we're doing?"

"I'd like to think so - if you want that."

"Maybe I do, James, maybe I do."

He was encouraged…

"Then let's drink to us - the best team of amateur detectives in the district."

"You're a funny guy you know," she laughed. "But I think I'll keep you on."

Afterwards he drove her home. Kath had discretely gone to her room. Louisa made coffee and they relaxed together on the sofa. Humble did not expect too much at first but as the evening progressed they gradually became closer. Suddenly she moved away and vigorously shook her head,

"I can't do this. Not with Kath in the house and Jane due back any time. It doesn't feel right."

He was jolted back to reality,

"It's okay. I understand."

"Do you?" she said. "Thanks."

"Not a problem. I just like being with you. Anything else is a bonus."

She looked at him,

"Really?"

He nodded, keeping his expression neutral.

Eleven

An early mist hung over Caithland Forest as Falcon Research Centre geared up for the first shift of the day. Smoky wisps trailed above the thick stands of larch, spruce and birch. The air had a fresh tang, sharp and cool, after the recent rain. The group of saboteurs knew the vice was closing on them. To avoid capture they had to escape. They had planned this for several weeks.

As many captives as possible would be freed and the created entities would show the outside world what Falcon was doing. The activists imagined they would be able to keep control of events. It was a mistake.

Stationing themselves at various points around the complex, they waited for a signal from their organisers. Those who were outside had manoeuvred two bulldozers up to the fences during the previous day, taking care to position them out of sight but with short enough distance to quickly drive up and break the barriers. They were camouflaged with branches and foliage. The plant-hire company had assumed their customers were working on a building-project. The false paperwork was sufficiently convincing.

So far the roving patrols had not found them. Being close to the facility, paradoxically gave them more cover. The old forest trail, which Humble and his friends had used, ran quite near to the perimeter fences at one point. There was only a small area of woodland to negotiate before the barrier was reached.

The machines had S.U combination blades and rippers on the back, with steel alloy tips, stump- busters and brush-rake blades. Phones were used to co-ordinate the operation but the risk was extremely high. At any time the security personnel could find them.

The saboteurs were animal liberation activists, religious idealists and political activists. Those working for rival companies or governments had not immediately made themselves known to the main group – only to each other. This changed when the first escapes occurred. They formed an alliance and succeeded in gradually infiltrating the organisation, most keeping a low profile until the time came for them to act. That time had arrived. Recent releases of small groups and individuals meant that they had revealed their presence. Savage was looking for them.

*

Ruth Bromirski and Colin Evan had supposedly been security cleared to work at Falcon. They were laboratory technicians in deep cover and in reality worked for a company named 'I.B.A.C' ('International Bio-Applications Consortium'). Together with their fellow conspirators, they were now actively engineering the mass breakout. Bromirski was a slightly built, Jewish girl. Evan was originally from Belfast.

The breakout was an attempt to alert the outside world to what was happening in Falcon as well as sabotage the company so that I.B.A.C could hoover up the juicy bits later.

162

The consequences of any release of Falcon captives were not seriously considered – a reckless approach. The saboteurs did not succeed with all their plans, but the audacious release of fifteen prisoners, five bio-forms and a considerable number of cybrids was accomplished.

The alarms sounded as soon as the bulldozers began their work and security personnel, led by Savage, pounded to the breaches in the barrier. The air was shrill with the rending of metal as the machines smashed down the fences at two pre-selected points.

Some of those inside had closed off the power to the inner fence. Smells of broken branches, crushed plants; exhaust fumes and mud filled the atmosphere. Shouting and swearing was heard as saboteurs urged the escapees to quickly make their way out. The security guards were unable to use their weapons close to the facility for fear of alerting the local workforce. Dallas was white with rage.

"What the fuck is going on, Kenneth?" he yelled down the phone to Savage.

"Sabotage attempt, Sir. We're dealing with it now."

Bromirski and Evan were operating under the orders of co-ordinators within Falcon who intended to stay on unless their carefully manufactured covers were broken.

As those being released made their escape, the security guards, assisted by special ex-military personnel, attacked the saboteurs with rifle butts, truncheons and tasers. Some fell and were dragged back for later interrogation. The badly injured would be treated in Falcon's on-site clinic until they were fit to be questioned.

"We have to go now," yelled Bromirski. "Most of them have got away. We have to follow on, okay?"

"Just a few seconds more," said Evan.

Bromirski screamed as a truncheon hit her hard on the shoulder. Evan turned to help her and received a blow to the head for his trouble. She crawled into the bushes and lay flat as the man who had struck Evan dragged him backwards over the barrier. Evan was unconscious, blood oozing from his wound.

The bulldozers were reversing away. The operation was virtually over. Bromirski had gone unnoticed in the melee. She shrank further down into a tangle of ferns and thick grass. There was a raw earth smell all around her. She felt overcome with nausea and fainted with the pain in her shoulder. In the forest, guards chased the escapees and their helpers, shooting to disable and bring them down. Several escapees and a saboteur fell. Dallas arrived, as the carnage was still raging. He issued orders.

"Get out there and get those bastards but avoid killing any. Bring them back if you can but don't hesitate to use your weapons to take them down. We're not letting all the work we've done here be destroyed."

"Yes, Sir," replied the guard commander. "Come on boys."

"Go with them, Kenneth," ordered Dallas, anger still marking his face.

"Sir," said Savage and climbed over the broken barrier. Repair teams moved up to begin restoring the fences. In the distance the rumble of the retreating bulldozers could be heard.

*

Humble had to open the shop and appear his normal self to the customers. It was difficult but he had a shower and a substantial breakfast before putting on his business face and venturing down from the flat. The world seemed to have changed.

Despite his raging thoughts he remembered to ask a few discreet questions of those customers whom he knew were also Falcon workers. His enquiries centred round any unusual incidents they may have witnessed or any weird people they may have seen.

One of the customers was Shannon Guffock who had a brother and a cousin working on the site,

"What's makin' you ask these questions, Jim? Are you worried about the place for some reason?" she said, when he casually brought up Falcon activities with her.

"A bit," he said, walking straight into the trap,

"I've noticed a few weird things when I've been out in the woods near Falcon and I wondered what was going on. It's so big you know they could be doing anything there and we'd never know."

"What kind of things?" she asked, picking some items from the grocery section and dropping them into her basket. She was wearing a short, tight skirt. A wave of strong perfume rolled from her. She fluttered her eyelashes unconvincingly.

Shannon had applied make-up generously and her hair was carefully arranged, framing a sweet-tough face, still retaining some of its earlier prettiness. Her smile was as false as her hair colouring. Dark roots were faintly visible below the blonde waves.

"Um, guys going about wearing military-style clothing and some really big animals and plants. There seems to be a lot of vehicles going in and out as well," he said, the words spilling out. He failed to spot Stella's non-verbal signals to close his mouth and get Shannon out of the shop.

"Oh they're just the security men. It's a busy place so there's always a lot of vans and cars movin' about. We've had a really warm summer. Maybe that's what's makin' the plants and animals grow bigger, eh? Have you been walkin' out there a lot then?"

She favoured him with a friendly smile. Her right hand reached out and rested on his left arm. Stella made urgent cut-throat signals, which he suddenly picked up.

"Well I always need material for my column you know," he said, a little flustered.

"Aye, you're a clever man. I always thought that. An' good-lookin' too," she said, squeezing his arm. Customers were beginning to queue up. With an effort he completed the transaction, politely but firmly ushering her out of the shop.

"I'll pop back again if I think of anything," she said as a parting shot.

Later when there was a gap between customers, Stella said,

"What's wrong with you? Don't you know that Guffock slapper is bad news? She's after something that's clear enough. Be careful. You don't want to give anything away to a low-life tart do you?

"Thanks. You're right. My head's all over the place today. I must pull myself together."

He straightened up and gave his attention to arranging a display of loss-leader items on the counter.

"Love can do that," she said. "It takes away the ability to concentrate but you still need your wits about you in Candy."

*

The clean-up and repairs at Falcon got under way quickly. The morning mist gave way to mellow sunshine for a short while then light rain returned. Patrols continued to roam the forest, capturing escapees where possible. Where capture was resisted they were shot in the legs to bring them down.

Dallas was professionally calm after the shock of the incident but it had shaken him. Savage had returned from the forest.

Dallas said,

"When those bastards are ready for questioning, use robust methods and get the truth out of them. I want to know whom they're working for and if there are any others in the place. Our screening procedures will need to be reviewed so we don't harbour any damned cuckoos in the nest in future. How they managed to do this I don't know. We have to keep this from London and Edinburgh at all costs."

"Yes, Sir. I've organised a more rigorous patrol regime and improvements to the perimeter fences. My staff will be more high profile in future as regards scrutiny of staff."

"The ordinary workers need to remain in the dark about this, Kenneth. We use a softly, softly approach to security as far as they're concerned. We don't want to alarm the Candywood people."

167

"Yes, Sir. What about the military?"

"They can help with security and rounding up the escapees."

"Their Commander is fully aware of the sensitive nature of our work and is under orders from a covert group within the Ministry of Defence. Galliard has assured me that there are Defence personnel on our side...members of the group of cross-ministry people secretly committed to Falcon. This is a seriously worrying incident. Our opponents are obviously more organised than we thought"

"I realise there was no way you could have anticipated this but it's important to be more alert in future. I hope you're not slipping."

"Yes, Sir. I understand. My apologies. It won't happen again."

Savage accepted the reprimand and went about his task of damage-limitation.

*

Being persistent if not inherently stubborn, Humble continued with his discreet questioning of anyone he knew had Falcon connections, as they visited his shop. Stella tried to suggest that he might be making himself too obvious,

"I know you're interested in the place, Jim, but be careful. You need to be wary in case people start to smell a rat. I don't know what you're up to and its better I don't but I'm a bit worried about you."

"Yes, Mum," he said to the older woman, gently teasing.

"Just trying to help. I'd hate to see the business suffer. I know it's just a job but I wouldn't want to work for anyone else or anywhere else. I'm quite fond of the place you know and you pay well."

"Point taken, Stella. You're a wise person and I'm lucky to have you here. I'll settle down."

One of his customers that day was Samantha Leoch. She wandered around the shop gathering a large quantity of items together, before approaching the checkout whilst Stella was dealing with someone else.

Humble served her in a business-like way, helping her to pack bags and attempting a few pleasant remarks,

"Still kind of wet I see, Samantha. Will that mean the lessons will have to be in the indoor school today?"

"Probably. It's a good forecast for later though. We're really busy in the afternoon so we might be able to get some of them out on the hill. Are you planning any more country walks with the lovely Louisa? I see she's not gracing the shop today."

Stella shot him a warning glance. He registered it and replied,

"Louisa is at Uni during the week. She likes walking I believe but it depends on the weather and her studies. Now, is that everything?"

"Yes, thanks. If you're out doing your research, do drop by at the equestrian centre. We'd be pleased to see you and can offer you a coffee or something. Nothing more exciting than that of course."

She winked,

"You two could always consider taking up riding," Leoch said. "It's very healthy you know."

"Better than traipsing around the forest chasing myths and mysteries. You wouldn't want your girlfriend to come to a sticky end would you?"

He said nothing.

She strode out of the shop, carrying the laden bags without difficulty, the usual smirk playing on her lips. Stella shook her head and Humble nodded in understanding.

Morton Parke entered the shop around ten a.m,

"All right?"

"Fine. That Leoch woman's been passing comments again but who cares?"

"A dangerous hussy. You need to be careful."

"Everyone keeps telling me that. I'm beginning to think the whole of Candy wants to be my guardian angel."

"Not all of Candy. Just your friends. We wouldn't bother if we didn't like you."

"I know. I'm grateful. Are you still okay about visiting the 'Old Man of the Woods' after lunch?"

Parke glanced around. There was no one within earshot,

"Of course – with Kirk. I'll bring my camera. I only have a basic phone I'm afraid, not the kind that takes pictures. I can bring a bit of spiritual strength however, if that's needed."

He smiled,

"You know where he lives, do you?"

"Oh yes. He may not be in of course but if we can hang around a bit he'll turn up. He only strays from his home if he has to."

"See you later. I'll let you get on."

Customers were coming into the shop as Parke left. The last in the queue was Shannon Guffock,

170

"It's me again. Something I forgot to get."

She set off down one of the aisles. Stella looked at Humble,

"I'll serve this customer. You have some stock to check in the back shop don't you?"

She spoke the last words in a slightly louder voice, indicating with her head. Humble got the hint and disappeared. He emerged as Shannon left and heard her say to Stella,

"Tell Jim I'll be back later. I've got things I need to ask him."

*

Bromirski woke up with an intense pain in her right shoulder. For a moment she was disorientated but when she heard the sounds of workers repairing the fences, she remembered the escapes. Rolling over, she had the presence of mind to keep low and very quiet as the repair work proceeded. They hadn't seen her yet but she knew she had to get out of there as quickly as possible. Her mouth felt full of acid and she was smeared with mud. Grass stains were on her jeans. There were leaves in her tangled hair. She was suddenly violently sick, heaving up her breakfast with great gut-wrenching spasms, eyes watering. It began to rain.

Crawling very slowly and carefully away from the barrier, she put as much distance between the fences and herself as she could before cautiously rising into a semi crouch, still keeping her hands on the ground. No one had heard. The sounds of power tools and blowtorches had covered up her exit.

Bromirski was filthy, thirsty, in pain and afraid. There was no sign of any of her co-conspirators. She was alone. A thick-legged spider scuttled over her right hand where it rested on the forest floor and she resisted the urge to scream. There was a smell of damp moss and fungi. She stood up and made her way shakily through the thickets, hoping to find a path. The light rain began to ease.

*

The escapees from Falcon spread through the forest, exploring their new surroundings and beginning the search for food. Some were dangerous, especially the rats and outsize cats. A few were combinations of species – Falcon's bizarre creations – the cybrids. They had little interest in each other at the moment, just in the need to survive.

In small groups the released slaves who had originated from the clandestine trafficking routes through Asia and Africa, as well as parts of Europe, moved in a bewildered way through the woods, uncertain of their destinations. Their guides were the activists who had organised the breakout from the outside. The bulldozer drivers, also activists, were returning the machines.

The former slaves had picked up some English whilst in Falcon and they were able to communicate and support each other. Most were men but there were a small number of women. Some had been the subjects of testing and experiments. Ultimately if they had remained in the Falcon Centre, some of their organs would have been harvested.

The bio-forms were different. The technology was not yet perfected so they were flawed.

Being machine-enhanced entities meant that they tended to be emotionless for the most part and quite deliberate in their actions. The result was an eerie combination, which was as yet untested in the outside world. Their behaviour was therefore highly unpredictable. They had been released by the idealistic, but not fully aware activists before receiving all their faculties.

Theoretically the bio-forms could live off any protein available, ingesting juices from the source or host as spiders do. The activists tried to keep up with their ground-eating strides but eventually found they could not keep pace. They called ahead to warn the others. The plan was to keep the escaped slaves together and transport them away from the area, to safe houses where they could be looked after until the time came for them to tell their stories, thus bringing Falcon down.

The outside activists were few in number and some were biased whistle-blowers. The newly freed prisoners, the terrorist suspects in particular, decided they should head for the cities. The cybrids and bio-forms were beyond the ability of the activists to control. It became clear that naive decisions based on soft-headed ideals had resulted in an unpredictable situation.

Bromirski stumbled upon the old forest track and began to follow it. She had a vague idea she should head south but had no real concept of where that was. She was a city girl. Her feet were throbbing painfully. She was wearing lightweight shoes unsuitable for walking in rugged terrain. Her shoulder throbbed agonisingly and she suspected it was badly damaged or broken.

Another hour passed and the track showed no sign of ending. It looped and curved through the trees, vegetation encroaching on it in places. It was obviously no longer in regular use. At least the rain had stopped completely. Tired, hungry, thirsty and on the verge of tears, Bromirski was feeling desperate when she suddenly saw the cottage ahead. Smoke came from a chimney and there was a caravan parked up close and a former railway carriage behind. It was a little settlement in the middle of nowhere. There was no one around as far as she could tell.

All was silent except for the scratching of hens and the sound of goats munching the grass in a fenced area. She sat on an upturned log wondering what to do next. The track led away to the south-east. She felt intense pain again and the nausea returned.

"Another wanderer? A girl this time. Don't usually see them out here. You'll want something to eat and drink like they all do, eh?"

Bromirski stood up when she saw the man and began to back away. Images of rape or worse flitted before her eyes. She felt too weak to take on a determined assailant and paused, ready to run.

"No need to be scared, lass," said Geordie Hagg. "Sit there and I'll bring you somethin' then I'll show you the way out."

He disappeared into the cottage. She looked around wildly, wondering if she should take the chance to run off down the track. Hagg re-appeared with the food and drink he had promised, guessing her intention,

174

"Run away if you like, dear. Saves me feedin' you. You'll get somewhere eventually if you follow the track but you'll fare better on a full stomach. Still, it's up to you."

He sat down opposite her and waited. She decided he was just an old recluse – harmlessly eccentric and quite grubby, but she was desperate. The food, which had been rejected by her stomach earlier, needed to be replaced. She would take a chance,

"I'm from the Falcon place," she said hesitantly, "My name's Bromirski, er…Ruth Bromirski." Her accent had flat vowel–sounds. She was originally from Manchester.

"There was a breakout and I was hit. I passed out and when I woke up everybody was gone. I've been wandering the woods all morning. Feels like hours. I'd like to get to a town or village."
She carefully touched a hand to her painful shoulder.

"I thought I heard a lot of noise this morning," Hagg said. "There're some queer things runnin' about in the forest as well. More than usual. Knew somethin' big had happened. Go on eat up. I'll not jump you if that's what you're thinkin'. You're hurt I see. I'm used to meetin' folk who've escaped from that place. When you've finished I'll show you the way out like I do wi' all o' them."

She reached for the food. As she ate she listened to him telling her about things he had seen in the forest and escapees he had helped.

175

"Why didn't you report all this to the police?" she asked, drinking deeply from a chipped mug of water. It could have been champagne as far as she was concerned.

"They won't do anythin'. The local ones are in league wi' Falcon as far as I can tell. My brother knew a lot about the place but he was paid to keep his mouth shut. Kept him in drink at least. Not for me to spoil his little business arrangement. It was all he had you see."

Bromirski was not really following him but was at pains to be polite. She stood up when she was finished. She badly needed to pass urine but was not about to do that in front of this old guy, nice as he was. He pointed out the route, urging her to fork right when she came to the place where the track branched.

"You'll reach the old railway line and if you turn left on that you'll come to Candywood. You'll get help there."

"Thank you, Mr..?"

"Hagg," he said, "Geordie Hagg. When you get to Candywood tell somebody in authority, not the local police, about that Falcon place. My brother won't but I think it's time it was known. There's some strange things goin' on in there and I don't think they're good things. You'll know if you've been inside the place. I'm sorry for Pete but it has to be done."

Bromirski agreed and said her farewells, thanking him once again. He waved her off,

"Better get a move on, lass. It's not gettin' any better."

She walked on down the track looking for some privacy to address the urgent need to relieve herself.

Twelve

Humble, Andrews and Parke met outside the shop at one-thirty. They were dressed for the woods, Parke without his clerical collar. Deciding on the most direct route to Hagg's home they set off along Lingdale Street. Rocky Craggs watched them from the pub window. Other locals noted the fact that they were in a purposeful–looking group together.

Craggs called Shannon Guffock after the friends had walked out of sight. He also called Samantha Leoch then Nathan Hardisty at Falcon. Hardisty passed the information on to Savage and subsequently Dallas. As the three made their way out of Candywood, the ring-tone on Humble's phone sounded – Rossini's *William Tell.* He was within range – a pocket where a signal could operate. The caller was Louisa. He moved away from the others slightly,

"Hi."

"Hi, Louisa. Are you okay?"

"Fine. I was just calling to ask if you're coming to see me tonight."

"Try and keep me away."

She laughed,

"Meet me at the flat again and we can go for a drink at a nice place I know in Gillerston High Street. Okay?"

"Okay - Say at eight? We could maybe get a takeaway later if we're hungry or just go back to your place. What do you think?"

"Whatever. Are you busy right now?"

"I'm with Kirk and Morton. We're going to see Geordie."

"Pity I can't come with you as we planned. Be careful. I'll worry."

"There'll be three of us. Not a problem. See you tonight and I'll tell you all about it."

"Okay. See you then."

The others had courteously walked on a short distance so he could talk. They guessed it was Louisa. Now they waited for him to catch up. Andrews pointed ahead,

"Jim, will it be quicker to go in by Hollybank Farm do you think? There's another track into the forest near there."

"Yes we can do that. I've used that route before. There's a couple of ways to get to Geordie's place. The track used to be in better condition at one time – when more workers were employed on the farms. His cottage would have been a shepherd's house once."

Curving away from the farmhouse, the track crossed two fields grazed by sheep and cattle then entered the outskirts of the forest. It became greener, more like a wide path than a former access road. Trees arched overhead, Scots pine, birch and ash - easily recognisable by its black buds. The undergrowth was thick on either side, crammed with lank grass, thistles and fern.

Humble stopped to examine the purple flower head of a knapweed. It was large, almost inflated. He hauled out his phone and took two shots, homing in close to capture the image of a yellow and black striped insect on the flower – startling against the purple.

"Ever the naturalist eh, Jim," said Parke. "Careful that wasp doesn't sting you. They're really bad-tempered at this time of year."

Humble straightened,

"It's not a wasp. It's one of those hover-flies, which mimic wasp markings as a survival technique. Totally harmless but I need its picture for evidence. Like so many other things, it's bigger than it should be."

"Fascinating," Andrews said. "Hate to spoil the fun but we must get on."

"Of course. Sorry. I'm a photo-opportunist you see. Can't help it."

They marched on deeper into the woods. At one point something large and nimble climbed with astonishing speed up a tree trunk, vanishing in the foliage.

"Squirrel?" asked Parke.

"Too big and dark for that," said Humble. "I think it might have been a pine marten."

"Or just an over-sized grey?" the clergyman said.

"Could be," agreed Humble. "It's also possible it's the result of experimentation and is some bizarre creation. Have you noticed how big everything is now we're in deeper?"

"I have," said Andrews. "We passed a huge blackbird a few minutes ago and that pheasant scrabbling in the woods looked more like a heron."

At that moment they heard the unmistakable clack of a carrion crow. It sounded like a sheep coughing.

"Weird," said Andrews.

"There's the cottage," Parke said. "Hope he's in."

They arrived outside Geordie's home. Once the cluttered collection of dwellings, outhouses, pens and garden plots, had possessed a name, *Woodhope*.

179

It was still the case on the O.S map but those who knew it simply called it, "Geordie's Place." The man himself was chopping wood outside when they arrived.

"Hello, Geordie," said Humble.

"It's young Jimmy," answered the bearded, greying-haired man with the axe. "And your friends are?"

"Kirk Andrews and the Reverend Morton Parke."

"Right. You're not here for the good of your health. Have a seat and tell me why you've sought me out. I'm guessing it's that Falcon place."

"Spot on," said Humble. "But before we get to that, do you know about Sti...er Pete?"

"Why, what's he done now?"

"He had an accident. He fell into the river and he...er... drowned. I'm sorry."

Humble and the others felt genuine compassion for the woodland recluse. Geordie sat down on a tree stump and looked away. The others sat on whatever they could find. There was a short silence.

"Oh fuck. Poor old Pete. He'd be pissed I suppose. Had to happen one day," said Geordie at last, "When?"

"Saturday night."

"Nearly three days ago? Shows how often I go into Candy. And no one thought of telling me before now? Not many people remember Pete had a brother of course. They wouldn't bother comin' out here anyway, the bastards. Where is he now?"

"He'll be in the morgue at Cruiksdale Hospital. They'll be waiting for the Fiscal," said Andrews.

"Can we do anything, Geordie?" asked Parke.

"You could pray for him I suppose, Rev. Not that any of us had much time for church stuff. I just hope he's got some peace at last."

180

"He has, he has," the clergyman said.

They commiserated with Geordie for a while listening to the sounds of the forest around them. Then Andrews coughed slightly,

"Er…we wondered if we could ask you if you've seen anything unusual in the woods lately."

"I see strange things all the time. A lot more today mind. Somethin' big happened at that bloody Falcon place."

They were all attention.

Geordie continued,

"People were runnin' through the forest – there was yellin' and guns. Then it was quiet. Later, I went along to see. I know how to move through the woods without bein' seen."

"There were two breaks in the fences an' they were repairin' them. Place was swarmin' wi' security men an' workers. No sign of any bodies, not like the last time."

"The last time?" Humble leaned forward,

"What last time?"

"Just the other day," Geordie said. "I heard a shot an' I went to have a look. There was a body in the bushes. They'd shot one of their prisoners – one of them foreign fellers."

"Good God," Andrews said? "Did you not think of reporting it?"

"Aye, I wondered about that. So I went back later and it was gone. I don't trust the local cops anyway but even I know you have to have a body before you go accusin' folk of a crime like that. Besides how do I know they aren't allowed to do that sort of thing? Some of those men up there are military."

"It looks like a Government place to me an' it's a sort of prison too. Maybe he was dangerous an' they had no choice. A lot of folk get shot these days. More like fuckin' America every day."

"There's always a choice, Geordie, "said Andrews. "They could have just winged him."

"Aye well they didn't. Trigger-happy bastards. Country's goin' to buggery as far as I can see. Politicians lie all the time and do what the fuck they like. When they're not takin' backhanders they're bangin' their secretaries or fiddlin' their expenses. I still have a radio and I see the papers now and then. I know a bit of what's goin' on. Will you have a mug o' tea while you're here, by the way? There's more I can tell you about the place if you're interested?"

"We are," said Parke, "And we'd love some tea, thanks."

He was used to being offered refreshment in all sorts of homes. The others were a little reluctant but knew it was the only way they could learn more. Geordie was glad of the company. Despite his choice of lifestyle, he got lonely at times.

As they drank from the bizarre collection of mugs and cups, Geordie told them about the over-sized and strangely mixed-species creatures he saw from time to time. He also informed them that he had recently given shelter and food to escaped prisoners,

"Started a few weeks ago. Don't know if someone was lettin' them out or they managed to find a way themselves but they came in small groups – three or four at a time. They were all foreigners – could hardly speak any English. I got used to them and showed them the best way out o' the forest."

182

"Most of them were men but one or two were women. Pretty beaten down they were – sort of dispirited, tired."

"You directed them towards the old railway line," said Humble.

"That's right. Where they went from there I don't know. I only helped them as far as that point."

"Some of them slept in the old vehicles down there," Andrews said. "We found evidence of that."

"They must have made their way to Carlisle then further south," said Parke.

"How would they live?" asked Humble.

"Steal food maybe, "said Geordie. "Raid allotments, gardens, hen-houses, poach fish, kill the occasional sheep. Who knows what you would do if you were desperate? In Carlisle they could steal things, even get food from the bins."

"Wait a minute," said the clergyman. "I remember someone in the church saying their hen-house had been robbed a few times. Blamed it on the foxes."

"And Charlie Stout lost a pig or two from his piggery," added Andrews.

"There've been a few reports of missing cats and dogs lately," Humble said. " People place them on the community notice board as well as the shop window. More than the usual number lately."

Who would eat a cat?" said Andrews. "Or a dog for that matter?"

"Good eatin' on a cat," said Geordie absent-mindedly. He did not elaborate. Without inhibition, he released a loud fart. The others looked at each other.

It was an illustration of how far Geordie had moved from civilised behaviour. They pressed their lips together hard, trying not to react.

"Some cultures are quite happy about eating cats and dogs," said Humble at last.

"I had octopus once, "Andrews said. "On holiday. It was like eating bicycle tyres."

"When I was at primary school the teacher read us a story called, *How to Eat Fried Worms*. It was about some boys who bet each other they couldn't eat worms for a week," said Humble.

"What happened?" asked Parke.

"The one who won cooked them in all sorts of ways to make them palatable. In the end he got to like the taste. He couldn't give them up."

"Anyway we've established that these runaways could survive if they had to," said Andrews. "Have you seen anything else?"

"Aye. You're not goin' to believe this but I've seen queer people wi' weird eyes. They walked in twos or threes. Seemed more like machines than people. I'm not windin' you up by the way."

"We know. Did you tell anyone about this?"

"No fear," said Geordie. "I'd be taken for just another crazy Hagg and get carted off to the fuckin' nuthouse. That's the second time I've been asked that question today."

"They don't have nuthouses now," Parke said.

"Well whatever they have now. Do you really think the police or the authorities would take me seriously? Old Geordie Hagg who lives in the woods and had two alkie brothers? No chance."

"We believe you, "said Humble, "Because we've seen them ourselves."

"Hang on," said Andrews. "You said that was the second time you'd been asked the question today. Who asked you the first time?"

"Skinny, dark girl I met after all the carry on at Falcon. About seven-thirty this mornin.' She'd been wanderin' about in the woods and I gave her some food and drink. Showed her how to get out o' the forest like I did the others. Only she wasn't one of the prisoners this time. She'd been helpin' them escape. Been hit on the shoulder by a truncheon she said. She was certainly in pain. Name was Ruth something or other…foreign name…Polish maybe. She went off down the track to the south-east."

"So there are people helping prisoners to escape?" said Humble.

"Oh aye. They guide as many as they can to cars they park on the main forest track. They can't help them all though – too many get let out sometimes. Quite a lot don't want to be helped. They run away before the helpers can round them up. They're the ones who've been living rough and sleepin' in the old vehicles I reckon," said Geordie.

"Geordie," said Andrews. "Other people come into the forest from time to time. They must have noticed things. Jim did after all."

"Well I do see folk about sometimes," said the recluse "Mostly forest rangers, a few walkers. They tend to stick to the main trails. I think some rangers are either in the pay of Falcon or they keep quiet for fear of causing trouble and being given a hard time. Of course the one who would know all about Falcon would be Adam Bain."

185

"He's dead," Andrews said.

"We found him hanging from a tree in the woods," said Humble.

"What?"

"Looked like suicide," Andrews added.

"Wouldn't have thought he was the type," Geordie said.

"Every man has his breaking point."

"Aye, I know that."

*

Bromirski had little innate sense of direction. Although she had tried to remember Geordie Hagg's instructions she had been desperate to pee at the time and in pain. After following the track for twenty minutes she came to a place where it joined two others and stopped.

Left or right?

She turned left – the wrong way. The track snaked and contoured through the woods and she became dispirited and tired once more, realising she had taken a wrong turning. Stopping to rest near an ancient oak tree, she leaned against its massive trunk and looked around. A few metres ahead she could see where a more substantial driveway curved away from the track. She wondered if this could be a way to somewhere inhabited and limped to the entrance. There was a weathered wooden gate, painted in a faded white, closed but not in a way that gave the impression the drive was strictly private.

Feeling she had little to lose, she opened the five barred gate and began walking up the drive.

It turned a corner near a clump of rhododendron bushes and she stopped again.

Before her was a venerable, country house surrounded by clipped lawns and flowerbeds. She continued up the drive, having no thought of anything else she could do and eventually was spotted by a gardener. He approached her,

"Hello, can I help?"

"I'm lost," she said wearily. Her shoulder was throbbing with incessant pain, "Where am I?"

"You're in the grounds of Highwater House," he said.

"Oh," said Bromirski, exhaustion in her voice, "That's nice."

Her eyes rolled upwards. He stepped forward and caught her as she passed into unconsciousness.

Humble and the others left Geordie Hagg with a promise that they would inform him as soon as it was time to make the funeral arrangements. He in turn offered to help them with their investigations.

"That fuckin' place needs sorted. It's all gettin' out o' control. I'll come into Candy when I'm needed and explain about everythin' I've seen but I don't know which of the coppers to trust yet. If you need me to tell what I know, give me a shout."

"Of course," said Andrews. "Thanks for your help and we're sorry about Pete."

"Well, you know what they say - life's a bitch and then you die."

Hagg raised a hand in farewell and returned to his cottage.

"Shame," Humble said as they moved further along the track. "Nice guy, Geordie. I hope they find out the truth about Sticky."

"Do you still think he could have been murdered?" asked Parke.

"Two deaths both connected closely with Falcon and then the news we've heard today. It's getting more and more bizarre the more we find out."

"Where to now?" said Andrews. "It's past three."

"A quick look at the barrier fences then back to Candy I think," Humble suggested. "We've all got things to do later I'm sure and I've got a date."

It was a reasonable hike to the perimeter fences but they never actually reached them. In the distance they could see the repairs being carried out. They had left the track ten minutes ago as it turned away from the barrier. Seeing the intense work still going on they prudently decided to return to the trail and head for home.

Deep in discussion, they were taken by surprise when the encounter took place. Near the forest's western boundary and before the climb up to the old railway track, they were slowing down when five escaped bio-forms approached from behind. The beings matched their speed, stride for stride and were completely silent.

Like the ones Andrews, Louisa and Humble had met previously, they were expressionless and seemed to possess considerable strength and energy, walking tirelessly. Humble and the others looked at each other and stopped, suddenly realising they were being herded.

The bio-forms began to close in.

188

Humble and Andrews reached into pockets to locate their phones. They got off some shots before running out of elbow-room.

"Who are you?" asked Andrews. There was no reply, only a collective swivelling of heads, as they looked at him together, moving closer, tightening the circle.

"Can you speak?" he continued. There was no response.

Then the five bio-forms turned. The friends turned with them. A dark green Toyota pick-up was approaching from the east, bumping along the track. A crew of armed security guards were evident in the vehicle. The beings immediately began running with incredible speed away from the three friends, who instinctively withdrew into the bushes and crouched down.

If the guards in the pick-up had spotted Humble and the others, they gave no indication. The action had been quick and the vehicle some distance away in a dip. The vehicle swept past and continued its pursuit of the quarry. Once everything was quiet again, the friends emerged.

"Right," said Parke decisively. "That's it. We've got to tell someone in authority about this."

"Who?" asked Humble, "Geordie's convinced the police are working with Falcon."

"Morton's right," said Andrews. "This has gone too far now. Let's head back and do what we have to do."

*

Bromirski awoke in a comfortable single bed. The room was high ceilinged, filled with period furniture, paintings and ornamentation. There was a smell of furniture polish. A dignified-looking lady of mature years was sitting in a chair near the bed, watching her. She leaned over and helped her guest to sit up,

"I thought you were stirring. We've sent for a doctor. That shoulder of yours is not in very good condition. Doctor Hunt will arrange for you to go into hospital in Cruiksdale or Carlisle, depending on the seriousness of the injury. Are you hungry?"

"Yeah, a bit," said her guest in a hoarse voice, "More thirsty really. What happened?"

"You passed out. On the back driveway. Luckily, Lamb, my Head Gardener, caught you before you could bash your head on the ground."

"I'm sorry…"

"Lady Helen Highwater. And you are…?"

"Ruth Bromirski. I was trying to get away from the Falcon place. I was a lab technician there. I met an old hermit in the woods but I forgot the directions he gave me and got lost. I ended up here."

She gasped as a sudden stab of pain shot through her shoulder. Lady Highwater helped her to a more comfortable position,

"Yes we all know Geordie Hagg. Harmless old chap. He's on his own land so we can't move him but he isn't any trouble. Takes the odd pheasant or fish now and again but he keeps the rabbits down. We get along quite well."

There was a soft knock on the door.

"Come in," called Lady Highwater.

190

Belinda Anfield entered carrying a tray of sandwiches and a bowl of soup. There was a jug of water, a glass, a pot of tea and a mug. Bromirski realised she was dressed in someone else's pyjamas. They fitted quite well.

"We changed your clothes when you were unconscious," said her hostess. "You were really out for the count and didn't even notice. You must have been overcome with fatigue. We'll have them washed and get you some more. I have some clothes, which once belonged to my daughter. They should fit. Your build is much the same."

"You're very kind," said Bromirski. "You don't even know me. I was on your land where I had no right to be."

"Right has nothing to do with it. You're clearly a stranger round here and in a lot of distress. Whatever brought you here can be dealt with in due course. In the meantime you need to eat and drink what you can then rest. We'll talk later after Doctor Hunt has seen you. If you need to go to hospital, one of my live-in staff can drive you there. Now I'll leave you for a while then come back to see how you're getting on. Enjoy your food."

They were close to the edge of the forest when they almost blundered into another group of five armed men. Being seasoned woodsmen, Humble and Andrews quickly concealed themselves in the thick bushes, pulling Parke in with them.

The track had become a narrow path at this point. The men were heading towards them but had not spotted the three friends. As the group approached however, something else became apparent.

The guards were driving three tired and demoralised prisoners ahead of them and they were not being gentle about it. Prodding the prisoners with rifle buts and administering an occasional kick, they drove their captives stumbling and dragging their steps, with casual brutality. Two walked as flankers, toting Uzi machine-pistols.

Humble sensed Parke's outrage and both he and Andrews placed hands on his arms to caution silence. They held their breaths. The procession passed. Waiting until the group was out of sight, Humble and the others emerged from their hiding place and Parke immediately gave way to his feelings,

"Boys, I wanted to give them fellers a good kickin'. There's no excuse for that kind of treatment whatever those men may have done."

"I agree," said Humble. "This is not North Korea."

"Those heavies behave as if it was," Andrews said. "I think they've enjoyed carte blanche within the isolation of Falcon for some time now. They evidently think they can flout accepted convention and moral values with impunity."

"Power corrupts," observed Humble.

"We've got to do something about this as we agreed," said Parke. "Go as high as we need to. Come on, boys, it's after four. Let's get back as quick as we can and get the ball rollin'."

Thirteen

It was four-fifty when the friends returned to Candywood. Andrews called his wife, locating a signal on a higher spot. The others waited. He and Parke had to go home for their evening meals and Humble had his date. They agreed that Andrews and Parke would share their experiences with their respective wives. Humble would talk it over with Louisa.

They would meet at the Church House at six. Humble planned to leave at six-thirty for Gillerston. In his flat, he set about preparing a quick snack. He felt a little drained but also excited about the prospect of seeing Louisa again.

As he turned the thoughts over in his mind he heard a knock at the shop door. The same one served as the door to the flat, reached by an inside staircase adjacent to the shop itself. He placed his coffee mug down slowly and stood up. The knock was there again, this time more insistent. He made his way to the door,

"Yes, who is it?"

"It's me, Shannon. I said I would come back later with some information. Can I come in?"

He procrastinated. She may genuinely have information for him or she may have some other purpose for coming to the shop. He could not imagine what it could be. If the friends were going to alert someone in high authority to the situation at Falcon however, further knowledge could be useful. He opened the door.

"Thanks. Don't worry I'm on my own. Mind if I go up?"

Without waiting for his answer she set off up the stairs. He was obliged to follow. Shannon was wearing strong perfume and a knee-length red coat. She was also carrying a large carrier bag, one of those supermarkets issue to be re-used over and over. In the flat she turned and smiled brightly at him,

"Hope you don't mind. I've something I need to say to you – after our talk earlier."

Her coat had fallen open. Humble saw she was provocatively dressed, entirely in red. He suddenly remembered Ethel Moans' warning,

"Would you like a coffee, Shannon? I'm afraid I have to go out at six so maybe you'd better make it quick, eh?"

"No problem. I'll hurry up then. Can I pop to your bathroom please?"

He showed her the way, noticing she took the carrier bag with her.

What was she up to? Maybe he should politely but firmly ask her to leave.

Shannon had already disappeared into the bathroom and he was left to make the coffee. She returned with the carrier bag, still wearing the coat – buttoned up this time,

"I'll get straight to it, Jim. Some of my family work at Falcon. We don't want any trouble and we want you and your friends to leave the place alone and let it do its work. I know it's very important and will give us jobs for a long time to come. We know you like findin' out about things and you're good at writin' for newspapers and magazines but we need you to back off this time - for the good of Candy. What do you say?"

194

"I don't think I can. You see I've learned a lot about the place, which worries me and I can't just forget it. I hear what you're saying about Candy and jobs but I have a conscience too. I can't just leave it."

"I can make it worth your while."

"What do you mean?"

She did not answer – simply unbuttoned her coat, let it drop and stepped away. Underneath, she was wearing jewellery, a watch, thigh-length red stockings and red shoes – nothing else. She flashed her bright smile at him again and moved forward.

Refreshed after her meal and further sleep, Bromirski was ready to talk to her benefactor. Doctor Hunt, an efficient medic, confirmed she needed hospital treatment and made the necessary arrangements. Before leaving in one of the estate's cars, she gave as much information as she could to her benefactor,

"I work for a rival company to Falcon. My job was to stay in deep cover and cause as many problems for the facility as possible whilst ferreting out its secrets. What I and my colleagues discovered was much worse than we at first suspected."

"Where are your colleagues now?"

"The outside ones are well away from the forest I should think, having rescued and moved on as many of the captives as they could. I'm the only inside one to escape, as far as I know. The others were caught I think, including Colin, whom I worked closely with. He was knocked down when I got my injury."

"The last I saw of him he was being dragged back into the place by a couple of security guards."

"You are painting a picture of brutality and unconventional behaviour, which I find most disturbing. Falcon is built almost exclusively on my land and I sit on the Board of Management. You have admitted you were engaged in industrial espionage amounting to actual sabotage. Can you really expect me to take you seriously?"

"Yes, I agree I was carrying out industrial espionage and being paid by I.B.A.C to do so but once inside I found others who had higher motives and I came to an understanding with them. My original remit became unimportant compared to the more urgent need to expose the abuses going on in there."

"Strong words and a serious allegation. Can you substantiate your claims?"

"Yes, as soon as the rescued captives have been shown to the public and as many of the bizarre creatures caught. I also have photographs taken on my phone, as do some of the others."

"I'm not following you. What bizarre creatures?"

"How much do you know about Falcon?"

"It's a centre for research into new crops and environmentally-friendly means of food production. I understand it's looking into bio-fuels and new ways to provide water. It's developing all sorts of innovative research to give our country a better chance to compete in the global economy."

"Yes, it's doing all those things. It's also researching into halting the ageing process, artificial intelligence, robotics, bioengineering, stem cell research, cloning and G.M /D.N.A techniques."

"There are possible military implications, which is why some Ministry of Defence people have an interest. Apparently this country can no longer afford large, professional armed forces. Leaner, more efficient, high–tech outfits are the future. I've learned about these things whilst talking to colleagues and keeping my ears and eyes open but I don't know everything Falcon does. It's a huge complex."

"This information has been kept from me. If it's true then Falcon is operating beyond the normal code of ethics."

"It's true, I assure you. I take it you are not aware of the nature of the labour force currently being used at Falcon?"

"A lot of local people have jobs there and I support that. When I released the land for building, I was assured there would be long-term employment for the Candywood area and the job prospects would continue to improve as Falcon expanded. Work is hard to come by out here and I felt it was my duty to assist the process. Of course financial benefits accrue to the estate but we are also an employer and it is important to secure a future for in difficult times."

"I know, and it's good that Falcon is providing work for local people. Those jobs tend to be in the more conventional side of Falcon, in administration, catering, cleaning, driving and work in the hydroponic farm complex. The other activities are known to only a small number of people. In those areas labour is imported."

"From where?" asked the landowner, increasingly uncomfortable.

"Well, the scientists and lab technicians such as myself are brought in from all over the U.K and overseas. Many of the top scientists there are from other countries and receive all the perks you would expect. Falcon pays well in all sectors. Non-locals live on site in high quality housing and have very good facilities for recreation and socialising."

"Go on," said her rescuer. "I can see you have a point to make."

Bromirski took a deep breath,

"For secret research in the experimental fields, a captive and expendable workforce is required. The elements of that are criminals, terrorist-prisoners; illegal immigrants and trafficked labour from various countries of origin. They're a kind of *untermenschen.*"

Helen Highwater was astounded,

"But that, surely, is a form of slavery."

"Correct" agreed Bromirski. "The subjects are also used for controversial experiments and as a source of organs as required. Harvesting takes place when needed."

"I can't believe all this. It's simply not possible in this day and age."

"I'm sorry, but whether you accept what I'm saying or not these things are happening at Falcon."

"But I've been given tours of the site from time-to- time, during the early building stages and since then at regular intervals. All the Board members have. I don't remember seeing anything out of the ordinary."

"They are past masters at concealing controversial aspects of the research there. You would have seen the residential quarters, the social centres, the sports facilities, I'm sure?"

"Yes, more than once."

"And of course they are legitimate," said Bromirski. "The prison accommodation however and the labs where the controversial, secret experiments take place, are very carefully screened. It's a large sprawling site. It's easy to hide things if you want to. Visiting parties are always escorted and staff told to avoid answering questions except in a routine way. Have you ever heard of a place called Theresienstadt, now named Terezin?"

"The second world war concentration camp in Czechoslovakia?"

"The Czech Republic."

"Oh yes, they will keep changing the names of countries these days. How is this relevant? It was a long time ago. Many similar horrors have occurred in other countries since then."

"My family is Jewish," said Bromirski. "My Grandfather was interned in Theresienstadt. It was known as "The Paradise Camp." Visiting Red Cross dignitaries and other officials from neutral countries were shown round it from time to time. It looked beautiful with its gardens, its clean streets; its orchestra playing. But behind the façade it was every bit as murderous as the others and the inmates kept in the same miserable conditions. Only a selected number of well-scrubbed and apparently well-fed inmates were shown to the visitors. I know this from my study of history and the knowledge handed down through my family."

"But the Government and the military are involved with Falcon. Just the other day I had a discussion with a very high level person from London."

"We know only a small number of officials across Government are involved."

199

"We think most of the ruling party is unaware of the exact nature of the research at Falcon. You could say it's an internal conspiracy. If it succeeds then they are gambling that the Government will have to accept it because it will hugely increase the status and influence of the country as well as provide a valuable economic boost."

"Some politicians will do what they have to in order to survive in power or increase their chances of re-election. I guess you will be aware of that yourself. I've only recently learned of the extent of duplicity and double-dealing. Expediency rules the day. If they can gain from this, they will."

Helen Highwater sank back in her chair and was speechless for a time. The shock was clear on her face. She seemed to collect herself eventually and stood up,

"My family have considerable investments in Falcon. It would be hard for me to see those lost. I'm not a young woman and my husband has poor health. I expected the facility would continue to develop as a source of employment and revenue well into the future. If you're accurate about this then I have been duped and so have others who trusted the management there and those above them. It's possible the legitimate side of Falcon could be allowed to continue under a new structure and rigorous inspection but the hidden side is morally reprehensible."

"As I've come to accept," Bromirski said, "It's no longer a case of serving the company I currently work for but to expose the real nature of the place. It's effectively a *Creation Farm*, using questionable technology to play God."

"Falcon is a pie into which many fingers are poking - picking their plums like lots of Little Jack Horners. Political people, powerful people; unscrupulous people."

"What do you intend to do?"

"When I'm discharged from hospital, I will alert the relevant authorities and the press. I can't just forget what I know. I am also aware that the captured saboteurs will receive brutal treatment and will not be allowed to leave Falcon alive. That in itself is good reason to blow the whistle."

"I never did like that Dallas man or his horrible security chief, Savage," said Lady Highwater. "After your treatment you must do what you have to do. One question I need to ask is - why didn't your fellow activists simply go to the police instead of facilitating escapes and breaking down the fences?"

"The answer is we don't know whom to approach in the police. There are rumours that the conspiracy could reach into the local force and may possibly beyond that. We don't really know whom to trust. Rogue Police officers have been known to take bribes. Of course some of the activists prefer direct action anyway. They're young, anarchic; idealistic. It's a kind of adventure for them."

"Yes it was ever the way," Helen Highwater said. "Better get you fixed up now."

Relieved, Bromirski moved from the main room of the house to the lobby and then out to the waiting car. After her unexpected guest left, Helen Highwater stood looking out across the broad lawns of her estate. She was in a dilemma. If Falcon fell, her investments could become worthless and her husband's health was failing.

She was aware of the old adage about speculating in order to accumulate but her moral values were remorselessly tugging at her. She turned away, pondering her options.

*

Humble was at a loss to know how to react. Shannon's lips parted and a pink tongue emerged. It had a small stud inserted in it, like a diamond. She laughed at his expression,

"Don't worry, Jim. I'll be gentle with you."

"Shannon, this is not a good idea. I have to go out shortly."

"Saving it for the luscious, Louisa? You may have to wait a long time."

Humble was quietly angry. His voice was icy,

"Please leave...now."

Suddenly she got the message,

"Okay, if that's the way you want it. Miss Ice-Cream must be something special for you to pass up a chance like this."

He ignored her obvious anger. When she had dressed, Shannon turned to him,

"You might regret this you know. People don't like you nosing into Falcon. I came here to offer you a chance. All you had to do was agree to leave well alone but you blew it. Don't say you haven't been warned."

She swept downstairs and out into the street. As soon as she found a place to receive a signal, she began to text. Humble leaned against a wall and passed a hand over his brow. Time was pressing. He needed to see Andrews and Parke before going on to Gillerston.

*

Lady Highwater had ended her deliberation. She called an old lawyer friend. On his advice she called her financial advisor and on her own initiative she began to make calls to friends and contacts in the Government, the Military and business.

A pre-emptive strike might allow her to salvage something from the forthcoming debacle that would inexorably occur over Falcon. She felt on balance it would be better to support the moral argument than the purely political and business one. It was a difficult decision.

The outcome was uncertain but she knew about risk. She thought about calling Dallas and Galliard but hesitated. It was possible Galliard was part of the plot. Dallas, of course, was at the heart of it – the dark beating heart of a system which remorselessly exploited human beings in the name of progress, if that was what it was.

Greed and ambition were also there. A *Creation Farm*, her recent guest had called it. Inwardly she hoped Bromirski might be wrong. Her thoughts could be clouded by idealism and emotion. Some discreet enquiries would do no harm at present.

Humble hurried over to the Church House where Andrews and Parke were already waiting in the reception room.

"Sorry I'm a bit late. You'll never guess what just happened."

He went on to relate the incident of his attempted seduction by Shannon Guffock, asking his friends not to repeat anything for fear it would leak out into Candywood...

"I promised myself I wouldn't tell anyone but you two should know. So does Louisa. I can't hide it from her."

"Must have been tough," said Andrews. "Weren't you tempted at all?"

"It's not funny," said Humble, "But it shows what lengths they're prepared to go to keep us away from the Falcon place."

"They're one step behind us anyway," said Parke. "We need to decide who we're going to contact about the goings on at Falcon. Clearly they're unaware of how much we already know. Did you say anything to the Guffock girl about it?"

"No fear. I hardly had time to draw breath."

Andrews smiled.

"Well, boys," said Parke. "I think we need to pass on our information to Police H.Q in Edinburgh, the local Council, the Press and our M.S.P at least. What do you say?"

Humble was a little wary,

"Good enough. What are we going to tell them?"

"The truth," said Parke.

"They might think we're just country bumpkins – you know, with one slate missing. Candy has a name for that, rightly or wrongly."

"I'm a Church Minister. They'll believe me surely?"

"Hopefully. Are you going to start tonight?"

"No time like the present. Kirk can help me. Are you off to see Louisa?"

"You bet," Humble said, standing up. Sorry I've got to rush but I didn't expect the encounter I had tonight."

"Who would?" said Andrews.

Humble left the others to their calls and set off on the twenty-minute drive to Gillerston. He drove a dark red Nissan. The watcher was there again as Humble drove off. He waited for a few minutes then walked to a suitable location to make a call. Shortly afterwards a car started up.

The drive to Gillerston was uneventful. The road was quiet as dusk approached. Rain was falling again but it was still mild outside. The temperature reading in the car indicated 16 degrees C. Humble made good time and there were no other vehicles on the road. About two miles from the town, he spotted the lights of a car rapidly approach behind him and stay in that position, without overtaking. He drove into the little town and up into the estate where Louisa lived. The other car continued past and he thought nothing of it. His mind was on other things.

Louisa looked lovely as usual. They walked along the High Street and slipped into a small, stylish bar. As they sipped their drinks, she listened with interest to the morning's events,

"So, Kirk and Morton are going to make some calls?"

"That's the plan. They hope to be taken seriously."

"In that case we may not need to investigate any more. It could be out of our hands."

"Possibly. You have your studies to think of too."

"It's hard to concentrate on them these days."

"What do you say we grab a take-away and go back to your place? Unless your friends are there at the moment."

"No, they're away tonight."

He paid for the drinks and they left. The soft rain had eased and the night was still warm. There was a fast food outlet on the High Street where they bought light suppers. At Louisa's flat they ate their food with coffee then relaxed on the sofa.

Tonight she was less inhibited, quickly warming to him. He suddenly remembered his earlier encounter with Shannon Guffock,

"Louisa, there's something I have to tell you."

"Oh? Nothing wrong is there?"

She straightened her clothing and sat up. He told her about Shannon Guffock's visit and what had transpired,

"I have to be honest and not hide it from you but I swear I resisted. Nothing took place. She tried her best but I wouldn't let it happen. It was a ploy to make me forget about Falcon and about us."

"Thanks for telling me, Jim. I'm impressed with your strength of character. I know men are weak when it comes to offers of that sort."

She kissed him affectionately.

The evening passed too quickly for his liking. Louisa eventually stood up,

"I have to get up early for Uni tomorrow and you have to open the shop."

"I know. I can't stay the night. I didn't expect to anyway."

She took his hands, looking suddenly serious,

"Mi rendi felice. Ti penso sempre."

"I know that's Italian but what does it mean?"

"I'll explain what it means one day but not tonight. I'm not ready for that. I'd like to teach you Italian some time."

"Well as it happens I do know an Italian word that's just right for you."

"What?"

"Bellisimo."

"You're saying nice things again, Mr. Humble. It's getting to be a habit."

"Can't seem to help it *mi amore.*"

His mind was buzzing as he said his goodnights to Louisa. At the main road, he failed to see the car drive up behind him. Only when its headlights startled him, did he break out of his reverie. He was out on the rain-washed road to Candywood by this time,

What was the driver doing? Too many bends for easy overtaking on this road.

Accelerating, he moved ahead hoping to put some distance between them. The car simply moved closer still. The driver had not dipped his lights and Humble was dazzled through the rear view mirror. He tried to make further progress but the vehicle just kept pace and moved so close it became dangerous. There was virtually no space between his car and the one behind.

He couldn't tell what kind of car it was or make out the driver. There were some tight bends ahead. He couldn't go much faster.

He was already going over sixty on a country road. There were no other vehicles in sight. Suddenly the car behind flashed its headlights and tailgated him again. Now he was really worried. After recent events his reserves of strength were low. He felt the grip of panic,

I'm being forced off the fucking road!

Suddenly he remembered the unclassified road to the tiny hamlet of Pennyland. It was a narrow road with passing places but there was another road leading from it into the hills. It looped round, passing several farms and cottages before arriving at Candywood. If he could turn into it at the last moment, he might lose the following vehicle and so escape.

He was sure now the driver of the car behind was trying to cause him to veer off the road, perhaps to kill him. There was some surface water and the road felt a little greasy. He was cold with fear, his stomach churning; sweat on his brow.

The Pennyland road entrance was just ahead. With a supreme effort he accelerated just enough to gain a slight advantage then yanked the steering wheel over hard left. With tyres squealing, he veered into the minor road and had just enough presence of mind to notice the pursuing car shoot past him.

Now it was a race for his life. Hoping not to meet another vehicle coming the other way, Humble took the bends as fast as he dared. No headlights appeared as he decelerated for the corners then speeded up for the straights.

His heart leapt into his mouth when a deer plunged from the verge and shot across the road ahead of him. He slowed, expecting another one then caught sight of headlights in the distance behind him.

The next minor road was ahead and if he turned into it and curved into the loop around Candywood, he could drop down into the township and reach home. Humble set his teeth firmly. There was no way he could get up to any speed but neither could the other car.

The Candywood junction approached. With relief, he gained it and entered the main street. The lights of the pursuing car were not yet visible. He remembered to drop speed as he drove into the township and came to an abrupt halt, parking as near as he could to the shop. Risking a glance through the rear view mirror, he saw no sign of the car behind.

Fumbling for his keys he jumped out, locked the car and looked along the street. There were three vehicles as far as he could see but no indication of which one had pursued him. Reaching the door, he locked it immediately behind him and raced up the stairs. In the kitchen he grabbed a whisky bottle and glass and poured a stiff drink.

Fourteen

Parke and Andrews experienced mixed results from their attempts to alert the authorities about Falcon. The M.S.P's secretary had replied to their initial email and phone call, saying she would inform her boss as soon as he returned from Holyrood. The Council offices were closed but they left a message.

They did better with *Police Scotland* in Edinburgh. At first they were told the matter would be referred to the local officer, Marcus Burn but the friends insisted it needed to go higher. With reluctance, the civilian operator transferred the call to a senior officer at Divisional H.Q.

He promised to investigate and send officers to see them as well as visit Falcon. An unmarked car would be used in deference to the friend's concerns about gossip and speculation. It was unclear if he was taking them seriously but at least they had the promise of the visit on Wednesday afternoon. The officers would come to the Church House. Parke was making good on his determination to support his friends. He and Andrews decided they would contact the Press in the morning when everything opened again.

*

At Falcon, interrogations were under way. Savage was sure his robust methods would yield results. Colin Evan was isolated like the other saboteurs, then the tough questioning procedures began.

It was only a matter of time. With the capture of more and more escapees, Dallas was beginning to think he had turned the corner.

Prahalad, Bowman, Capilus and Dos Santos met again to discuss events. Bowman, who was becoming the unofficial leader of the group said,

"It's all very tense at the moment. Cammy and Savage are rattled."

"We are all implicated if Falcon's activities are exposed," said Dos Santos, not previously a contributor to their talks. We have all used the labour provided by the facility."

He had a strong accent but his annunciation was clear.

"We told ourselves we were governed by higher motives," Capilus said in her slightly inflected English, "But ethical considerations are important too."

"If we suddenly refuse to use the captives, management will suspect something," said Bowman.

"I know," said Prahalad. "Maybe we could just find excuses for a while until we know what the future holds."

"You mean use other methods rather than relying on human subjects?" asked Dos Santos.

"We're all specialists in our fields," Bowman said. "I suggest we procrastinate as long as we can, blinding Management with science until the thing is resolved or until we have no choice but to continue as before."

"All we can do I think," agreed Prahalad. "For now. But we won't be able to fool Lucinda McQuade for long. She is frighteningly intelligent and as sharp as a tack."

Capilus and Dos Santos remained silent.

*

Humble woke early having spent a restless night reliving the attempt on his life. The whisky had helped but the flashbacks kept recurring. It was five-thirty a.m. - too early to contact the others. He rose and began to make breakfast. He didn't know whether to tell Louisa but then realised she might be a target too.

As he munched toast he ran everything through in his mind. There was a day's business to conduct and he dared not let anyone know, apart from his friends.

The shop was opening early as usual for the morning papers. He walked down the stairs, turning on lights and heating, preparing the shop. Unlocking the main door, he peered outside. The street was quiet, beginning to dry out after the recent rain. The sky was clear. A bright star was visible in the east just above the horizon. The sun was emerging and light streamers of cloud filled the sky. There was the sweet smell of peat fires.

Humble glanced idly at his car and was horrified. All the tyres were down and there were long scratches along the bodywork. He drew back when he saw the writing. It was on the driver's side and was scrawled in white spray paint, starkly obvious against the dark red...

"HUMBLE LIKES ITALIAN PUSSY."

Panicking he ran into the shop where vehicle touch-up paint was kept. Finding one that almost matched the dark red colour of his car he rushed outside and began applying it. An approximate match would be enough.

Working furiously, he covered up the words using two cans of paint then frantically looked around to see if there was any other graffiti. There was. Some was on the door of the shop. They proclaimed,

"NOSY BASTARD,"
"ANARCHIST SHITHEAD" and
"HUMBLE IS AN ENEMY OF FALCON."

In the ironmongery section, he knew there were tins of a substance, which would clean it off after several applications. He began to work, grinding his teeth in anger, sweating profusely. Then he noticed the dog excrement on the window and door. The shop window carried the message,

"HUMBLE AND HIS PALS DESTROY JOBS."

Feeling acutely vulnerable, knowing that someone was out to bring him down big-time, he looked around. There were few people about. He had to open the shop, behave as if there was nothing wrong. Stella would arrive soon. Frantically he worked to clean off the worst of the graffiti and the shit, completing the job in time before the first customers turned up.

Humble felt sick, imagining the reaction if the messages had still been there when the street began to fill up with people. He threw several buckets of water over the window. It was a crude job but it would have to suffice. A strong chemical smell remained in the air. He knew someone would be watching his actions. Someone always was.

Dashing into the shop, he cleaned himself just in time to begin the day's business. He was already exhausted. When Stella arrived he would ask the local garage owner to take away his car and let him know when the tyres were replaced. The bodywork could be dealt with whenever possible. After that he would keep it out of sight in an old, wooden building he was aware of near Candyside. The owner was Max McGlimpy, a friend. As far as the writing was concerned, he couldn't work out what to do yet. He had to talk to Andrews and Parke.

The morning passed without incident but Humble felt on edge, expecting further outrages. Stella knew there was something on his mind but reasoned he would tell her if he wanted to. He felt he could trust few people. He tried to read the expressions on customer's faces but knew he was being paranoid. Customers were surprisingly few in number...

Was the shop being boycotted?

Parke called in at eleven a.m and knew immediately there was something wrong,

"Jim, I can see you're upset. You look terrible. Come over for lunch and we'll talk. I can let you know how Kirk and I got on last night, okay?"

"Yes. I'll be over at twelve. See you then."

Stella could contain herself no longer. When the shop was temporarily empty she turned to Humble,

"The outside of the shop smells of paint stripper and cleaning fluid, Jim. There are some streaks on the window and the door and I can see the state of your car. What's happened?"

He told her. She pressed her lips together in anger,

"Right, I'll mind the shop whilst you see to the car and get someone to properly sort out the window and door. Then you can talk to Reverend Parke and anyone else if you need to. Try not to worry about the gossip. You know what it's like."

"What gossip?"
She looked alarmed, biting her lip,

"Oh, you know. Talk about you and Louisa – the usual."

"And..?"
Stella looked away.

"Come on, I need to know."

"You're right. You'll hear it soon enough. It's about you nosing around Falcon and trying to get the place closed down. They're saying you're really a green activist or that you've become an animal rights supporter. The talk is that you, Kirk and Louisa are in it together, that all of you are anarchists and you've persuaded Rev. Parke to help you. I was afraid this would happen."
She paused…

"And what else?"
He guessed there was more.

"Well, some are kind of on your side but say that you're soft in the head and just pursuing another of your crazy ideas. They're comparing you to one of those U.F.O fanatics or weird conspiracy geeks."

"Oh, God, that's all I need."

Stella asked her cousin, Susan to help her in the shop. Susan was younger and had children at school. Her husband was Max McGlimpy. Humble said he would pay Susan for her time. The two women laughed it off but he resolved to make sure she was recompensed, needing all the friends he could get at that moment. He moved to the telephone.

The garage-owner was able to promise he would take the car away within the hour. He owed Humble a favour. The shop had given him a credit line during tough times, when fuel deliveries had dried during a tanker-driver's strike. Humble had not made an issue of it and the man had been grateful. He called some tradesmen friends to see to his window and door then concentrated on what he would say to Louisa and the others.

Walking along Lingdale Street, trying to find a spot for a phone signal, he felt people were staring at him, judging him, giving him hostile looks. It was a dry morning with a strong breeze. The air was cool - a word which could not be applied to all the population of Candywood at that moment. A signal was unattainable so he was grateful to arrive at the Church House. He would ask Parke if he could use his landline. The ebullient Ulsterman greeted him at the door,

"Good to see you, Jim. Glad you could come early. Come away in, boy."

Once inside Humble told the clergyman about the graffiti on his car and the shop. He listened carefully, mouth closed like a trap but eyes smouldering,

"Margaret's got a bit of time free this morning. I'm goin' to ask her to visit Stella and Susan. I haven't kept anythin' from her as you would expect but she's on your side and very discreet. Hang on a moment."
He disappeared into the back of the house. A minute or two later his plump, energetic wife emerged wearing an outdoor coat.

"Margaret, you don't have to…" began Humble.

"Now say no more. Morton's told me all about it. I'm in this with you so don't even bother trying to get me to change my mind. See you both later and please let me know when you've finished so I can get back to my other jobs. Remember the children will be back from High School by five, Morton."

"Yes, dear. We won't take that long."

After Margaret had gone Parke motioned Humble to an armchair.

"Do you mind if I use your phone first, Morton? Couldn't get a signal out there."

"Yes, help yourself. I'll make some coffee."

Humble succeeded in contacting Louisa. He knew there was no point in keeping anything from her but he didn't want her to be distracted from her studies. He told her about the tailgating driver, the damage to his car and the graffiti on his shop window.

"Probably best for you not to drive into Candy right now," he said. "I'd be worried about you but I've got things in hand. My friends are helping. I'll be in touch as soon as I can but just stay put for the moment would you, please?"

"I'd like to help."

"We'll meet up again soon. In the meantime we're going ahead and alerting the authorities so hopefully the thing will be sorted out."

"I feel so helpless. Be careful and stay in touch."

"Of course. Speak to you later. Got to go. This is Morton's phone. Bye for now. Don't worry."

Next he contacted the friend with the garage, Max ('Tiptoe') McGlimpy. Humble had known him for years. Tiptoe had served in the Army and was so-called because of a reputation gained for his alleged undercover activities. Local folklore had it that he had been in the S.A.S. but he was close-mouthed about his former exploits. He had been decorated for bravery under fire.

McGlimpy was large-boned, dark-haired and had a face turned mahogany through weather. The fingers of his hands were like frankfurters. When they gripped anyone else's they were steel yet he was putty in the hands of his petite, sweet-natured wife, Susan.

He owned a hill-farm south-west of Candywood and was as rugged as the hills themselves. He was more than glad to give Humble some help,

"Tell you what I can do. I could bring some of the boys along and keep an eye on that shop of yours if you like. If those bastards try any of that stuff again we'll break their fuckin' faces. Just say the word, Jim."

"Thanks, Tiptoe. I just want somewhere to leave the car until it's fixed. I wondered if I could use that old garage if you still have it."

"No probs."

"Great, thanks."

"Don't let the buggers get you down, eh?"

Parke had quietly left Humble to his calls then poured the coffee,

"You've got some pretty good friends. Want to tell me what else has been goin' on?"

"Morton, this morning's work has not been the only event. Someone tried to kill me last night."

The clergyman's face was a mask, "Go on."

Humble told him about the attempt to force him off the road. Parke was shocked,

"I knew this was really serious and it seems I was right. We need to step up our efforts to get the authorities on our side. By the way there's a senior police officer

218

arrivin' this afternoon from town, about one o'clock. If you can be here that would be helpful. We've also alerted the M.S.P and the Council but not much joy there yet."

"Now it strikes me we're at war. We need to let Kirk know as soon as possible then see who else we can bring on board. Meanwhile we can talk to the media…"

"Not *the Gazettte*," Humble interrupted. "It's possible they're in Falcon's pocket. They're always printing gushingly favourable articles about the place."

"You could be right. That goes for a lot of other local organisations too. We have to go national."

"Remember, Louisa, Kirk and I have photos we can use as evidence."

"Oh yes, of course."

There was a knock at the door. Parke squinted out of the blinds before he opened it and let the two people waiting on the doorstep come in. It was Kirk Andrews and Geordie Hagg.

"Met Geordie in the street, said Andrews. "He's having a rare visit to Candy. He wants to help. I've got some time before I have to get back to work – supposed to be on a home visit. Thought I'd find you here, Jim. Is Louisa okay?"

"Yes, thank God. Do you know what happened?"

"News travels faster than light around here. Einstein should have visited Candy before he perfected his theory of relativity. But I don't know the details. Tell me."

Humble updated him, then said,

"I've noticed people are blanking me, giving me funny looks in the street. Have you had that, Morton?"

"No. They wouldn't dare. They know I have someone more powerful on my side."

He chuckled, offering more food to Geordie who accepted with alacrity.

"Okay, boys," said Parke finally. "Let's review our forces."

"Well, there's us three, Louisa, Geordie, Tiptoe and his boys, Stella, Margaret, Susan and a whole lot of other folk if we thought about it," Andrews said.

"Agreed," Parke said. "Let's start phonin' again."

*

Lady Highwater's contacts replied to her calls or left messages when they were unable to. Her concerns about Falcon were noted and promises were made to investigate. When she had completed her calls she knew she was committed to seeing the thing through, whatever happened. The moral values had won over the commercial. There was nothing more to do but get on with her work and wait.

The hospital in Cruiksdale decided to detain Bromirski. Her shoulder was badly damaged but not broken. She was unable to locate her phone, which in any case would be out-of-bounds in the hospital. It seemed to have disappeared whilst she was being admitted and prepared for treatment. She felt frustrated and helpless. Her friends and fellow activists were unaware of her situation.

She had no idea what their next move would be but she knew they were an uneasy alliance of conflicting views. With the prize in their grasp, the alliance could become unglued.

*

The Falcon scientists listened to another message from Dallas relayed over the inter-departmental communications system,

"Attention, all research staff. This is an important announcement. All work is to be temporarily suspended due to the recent security emergency. Please report to your Departmental Head who will explain the situation more fully. Please continue with routine work if appropriate or take an extended break until further instructions. Security personnel will visit all departments and laboratories to ensure this request is being complied with. Thank you."

The message was repeated several times during the course of the morning, for emphasis. Bowman managed to speak to Prahalad somewhere in the laboratory complex,

"What do you think this means?"

"They may have acquired more information about the break-out and are making sure nothing else goes wrong. While we're alone I want to ask your opinion of Eva Capilus and her friend. I feel a little uneasy about Dos Santos."

"Me too but I can't quite put my finger on it. Funny we should both feel the same. We'll have to keep our eyes and ears open."

His friend nodded,

"I've been reading up on computer-hacking – just a hunch. It's not my field but we all have to have I.T. skills to do our work. It occurred to me that the problems with the created life-forms and the bio-forms might be due to outside interference."

"What do you mean? A computer virus?

"Exactly that. Listen, suppose a software worm - a *vulnerability*, was being used by hackers? It could be a complex rogue code being used as a cyber weapon. I know such *malware* exists. It could have been introduced in a U.S.B drive to target the system via programmable logic controllers - P.L.Cs. It would have to be very powerful with over one hundred lines of codes but if it took the form of a worm-type virus, it just might be able to infect the whole system and cause damage."

"Is it possible that outside hackers could do that?"

"I think so. Remember, Eva is an I.T expert– one of the best in her field. She could have been assisting with the introduction of the virus. If a company, say a rival to Falcon, was involved it would have the means and the financial resources to do this. Even more likely, if another government was behind it. Do you see what I mean?"

"Oh yes. If Eva is involved with this why didn't she tell us?"

"A good question. Why indeed?"

Bowman was silent for a moment,

"Aashish, we haven't been off-site for weeks now. If most work is suspended why don't we go out for a while? Maybe to Carlisle – a change of surroundings? I'm getting cabin fever. We need to think this thing through in a calmer environment."

"Good idea. I'll get my jacket. No time like the present."

He arranged to meet Bowman in five minutes at the nearest exit point and grabbed his jacket, pass, I.D and some spending money. Moving towards the exit, they became aware of the increased activity all around them as they walked through the corridors. Security guards strode purposefully in twos and officials hurried past them carrying clipboards. Reaching the exit, they were stopped by two sentries,

"Sorry, gentlemen. The facility is shut down for the moment. No one is allowed in or out. Orders of the Management."

"But we're only going out for a bit of fresh air and a change of scene. Work is suspended right now. We thought we'd have a break," said Prahalad.

"Not possible, Sir. We have our instructions. Keep listening to the announcements and you'll know when the emergency is lifted. Thank you, Sir."
The guard turned away and resumed his impassive stance. The two scientists looked at each other.

Humble and his friends began their new round of calls whilst Andrews returned to his office, hurrying as quickly as he could in order to avoid hostile looks and curious stares. In his managerial role he was efficient and professional but was aware that gossip was being furiously exchanged when he was out of earshot.

Heading to a smaller office to speak to one of the clerical staff, he paused at the door to listen to voices drifting from inside…

"There were some weird beasts at the farm yesterday you know, Moira – looked like crosses between foxes and dogs. Bloody scary they were. Took all of Dennis' hens and killed a sheep - ate almost all of it."

"Yuk. I heard a giant rat attacked Mrs. Lucken at The Nook when she went out to check the ponies. There were others there too. She said they had teeth like razors. It ate into one of the pony's legs so badly it had to be shot."

Andrews entered the office. The two women inside looked furtive but said nothing. After his brief discussion with them, Andrews left but waited by the closed door. The women were wise to this however and continued their conversation in such low voices he could barely make them out. He decided to try elsewhere.

An increasing tide of gossip rolled through Candywood that morning. As well as speculation about Humble and his friends, there was much talk about encounters with strange animals in the fields and woods.

Reports came in about domestic pets and working animals being killed or maimed by super-sized beasts and freakish entities. People were swapping stories about wandering foreigners raiding vegetable gardens and fields or taking domestic fowl and sheep for food. There were a few reported sightings of weird, expressionless people moving about. Sheep and cattle were found dead, eaten out from the inside, just shells remaining. The atmosphere became tense. A group set off for the police station. Wednesday was a day when it was manned.

Marcus Burn felt besieged and out of his depth. The small station had not been built to hold so many people and he had no full-time assistant to take notes. Under instructions to defend Falcon from undue interference, he could only try to placate the increasingly frantic men and women who filled his reception area. People were drawing their own conclusions about the facility. He telephoned H.Q for advice.

Andrews phoned, informing them of the commotion at the station house. He and Humble were busy with calls whilst Geordie kept an eye on the street outside. He reported it seemed strangely deserted.

"Now we know why," said Parke. "Things are comin' out of the woodwork. I wonder if anyone's seen any escaped prisoners or anything else unusual."

"Yes I've heard some bits about strange creatures attacking pets and stock as well as weird people. I'm listening out for more news."

"Good lad. Stay in touch." He ended the call.

"That's a couple of nationals, the Council and the Scottish Government contacted, Jim. The police will be here in an hour and a half. What now?"

"Is that the time already?" said Humble. "I'd better go and check on the shop. Not fair to leave the ladies on their own like that."

"They'll be fine. They're good girls."

"I know but all the same it's my responsibility."
He made for the door. Parke cautioned him. "Be careful. Remember to come back when the police arrive. Others may turn up too if we're lucky. Take care."

"See you later. I have to see how the car and the shop are doing after the damage anyway."

Humble made his way across the street and down to his place-of-business. To get there he had to pass the entrance of a narrow lane – one vehicle wide, adjacent to the shop. His mind on all the events of the morning, he failed to see the men standing well back in the alleyway. As he drew opposite the entrance, hands grabbed him and covered his mouth. He was dragged into the lane and thrown to the ground, landing painfully on one shoulder. Then the blows began.

225

Instinctively he protected his head, tried to wriggle out of the way. Kicks and punches rained down but he had the presence of mind to grab a leg and push back. Someone fell with a curse. He rolled and made an attempt to stand up. A hard push knocked him over again to bounce off the wall of the alley and there were more kicks to body and face. One landed in his ribs and he rolled again, winded and convulsed with pain.

Attempting to make out the identities of his attackers was difficult but their voices were all local by their accents.

"Try to take away our work would ye? – interferin' bastard. This should get the message through if nothin' else does."

"Aye, fuckin' shopkeeper. Try holding down a real job."

"See how yer Italian tart likes this new face, Humble. She'll soon lose interest when she sees what we've done to it."

More blows then suddenly some new voices – louder and stronger. The beating inexplicably stopped and he tried to clear the blood from his face and check his mouth for broken teeth.

His legs almost collapsed on him as he tried to stand up, using the wall for support. He slid down again, his back to the stonework.

"Steady, Jim. Take it easy now. Just sit for a while. We'll sort this scum out."

Through the haze of pain he could hear the sounds of his assailants being beaten in their turn. They screamed as boots and fists crashed into their faces, groins and ribs. His rescuers were McGlimpy and his men. He could not recognise his attackers at first but then eventually

226

identified Swatte, Coates and some others he had seen around. They all had connections with Falcon.

A few final kicks and severe verbal warnings from McGlimpy then the gang limped away, chastened if not terrified. Their injuries would be clear to see for some time to come but few questions would be asked.

McGlimpy helped Humble gently to his feet assisted by another man. They turned when they heard a strong, female voice from the street end of the alleyway,

"My God, what have they done to you now, Jim?" It was Samantha Leoch and she looked outraged. She surveyed the damaged shop-owner then with a nod to McGlimpy and the others strode off purposefully. Humble's friends helped him out of the alleyway.

"Thanks, Tiptoe."

"Told you we'd keep an eye on the shop for a while. Had a feelin' something would happen."

"Don't think they'll try that again in a hurry. Now let's get you to a doctor."

"No time - too much to see to here."

Humble hauled his body up. Every part of him seemed to hurt. Blood was still running down his face.

"Get in the fuckin' car," said his friend firmly, "You're going to the Health Centre."

"Then it'll be all over Candy. I don't want to give them that satisfaction."

"I can't help that. You need medical attention. Doctor Keene is discreet. We'll just say you were fending off an attempt by a few out-of-town guys to steal from the shop. Come on."

With great reluctance Humble allowed himself to be taken to the Health Centre. A close-mouthed Doctor Keene only asked enough questions to establish the origin

227

of the injuries. It was all over by twelve-fifteen and he was on his way back to the shop to be met by three shocked ladies.

McGlimpy and his men headed off and Humble was fussed over by the women. He made his way back to Parke's house in time for the police visit, released on a promise he would try to sleep it off as soon as he could.

Trade at the shop had been so thin during the morning that he decided to declare an unofficial half-day and thanked the three women profusely before sending them home. He remembered to whisper to Stella that she would receive a full day's pay, as would Susan. He waved away their protests with a weak hand gesture,

"No argument. 'Preciate what you did. Too knackered to talk now. Just let me do this, okay?"

"Okay, thank you."

Andrews was unable to leave his office and was in any case attempting to use his fine honed antennae to listen in on conversations about events in and around the township. An unmarked car drew up outside the Church House and two plain-clothes officers emerged.

The arrivals were a tall, grey–haired imposing officer in his fifties and an equally tall younger man with short, dark brown hair. Both of them homed in on Humble's injuries,

"Detective Inspector Kepple and this is Detective Sergeant Ayle," said the older man. "I see your friend here has met with a bit of trouble."

"He has, Inspector. That's part of what we have to tell you," Parke said. "There are reasons why we did not wish to involve certain local police, as we will explain. Please sit down and I'll organise some tea and coffee."

"Thank you, Reverend. It would be appreciated. We understand that the information you have is serious. The station is currently a little overwhelmed, as we have just found. We called in there before we came to your house. We have contacted H.Q for reinforcements. They're on their way. Our enquiry is technically separate at the moment."

Humble began his narrative and Parke joined them. The officers listened without interruption as the two friends explained the events of the last few days.

*

Samantha Leoch marched along the street to the Lingdale Arms at a brisk clip. Lunches were being served and Craggs was supervising. Leoch arrived by the main door and indicated the back office with her head. Craggs got the message and met her in there, closing the door behind him,

"What's wrong, Sam? You look upset."

"I'm more than upset. I'm bloody livid. Was it your idea to set those goons on Humble?"

"What goons?"

"Don't pretend you don't know. If there's one thing I hate, it's being lied to."

"People are angry," said Craggs by way of defence. "You know how it is in Candy. They do things their own way here. Can I help it if a few locals decided to teach our nosy shopkeeper a lesson?"

"That's crap. I know about the graffiti and the damage to his car too. I thought we were just going to spread a few rumours and let the gossip do the rest?

Violence and humiliation was not part of the deal. It was bad enough when you paid that Guffock tart to whore for you although I believe he didn't bite. Good for him. I'm beginning to think I've made a big mistake here."

"Oh…what do you mean?"

"Rocky, I need to know where I stand. Do you care about me or not?

"Of course I do. You know that."
There was a sickly smile on Craggs' face.

"So do you want to make it permanent – be partners and a have future together? Do you? You've never given me any real idea of your intentions – just hints. I need to know now."

"Well it's not quite as easy as that. You see…"

"I get it. I'm just a convenient bit of totty in the sticks. Is there another woman?"

"Sam…I…"

"I thought as much. So the rumour's true. You've been seeing someone in Gillerston. Don't try to deny it – I can see it in your face. Does she know about me?"

"Not as such. She knows about Shannon though - she doesn't mind that…it's in the past…"

He stopped talking, realising he had just walked into a trap. She continued, quietly seething,

"I was right. There is someone else. What's she like? Some impressionable, young thing or a divorcee hungry for a bit of rough?"

"It sucks, Rock. I've had enough of being your woman of convenience. I want out. Unless you're prepared to give up your screwing around I'm going to the police with all that I know and to hell with it. If I mean anything at all to you, you'll give up all this shit. Otherwise you'll have to take the consequences. Now I'm going to work out my anger with a long horse-ride then I'll wait for your answer. You have until five when I close the school. You know how to reach me."

She turned on her heel and walked out. Craggs sat down on the nearest chair, shock on his face. For a few moments he continued sitting, staring into space, thinking. One of the bar-staff put her head around the door,

"Are you okay, Boss?"

"Aye, fine," he lied. "Just comin'."

He knew he would have to get back to work but this new problem was bugging him.

He surveyed the customers, noticing some of the Guffock family taking advantage of the unspoken agreement that they would always receive whatever they wanted at the Lingdale, without charge. Shannon and other family members occupied two tables. A thought growing in his mind, he walked across to them.

*

In a peripheral area of the forest near the Marchland Stone, members of *An Bile Buada* were preparing for an evening meeting at which they would celebrate the sacred power of the trees. During the early evening they would invoke *Medb* – 'She who intoxicates.' The weather was favourable if a little cool. They possessed a shelter deep in the woods but the night promised to stay dry.

The cult of esoteric mystics would meet at the end of the working day. Drawn from all over the region, they met at intervals to perform the sacred rituals.

The Highwater Estate was aware of the activities of the eccentric outfit and had given them permission to use certain parts of the forest, provided they cleared up afterwards, refrained from using fire and did no damage. Clearings and open glades served as outdoor worship-sites. Four group members quietly made the preparations for the evening. The trees were hung with garlands and areas were marked out for particular ceremonies. Statuettes of the deity were arranged around the site, trestle-tables set up.

As they worked, some of them became aware they were being watched. Thinking it might be deerstalkers from the estate or curious ramblers, they looked up from their work. It was nothing they had previously encountered. They halted their activities and moved apprehensively together.

When the bio-forms entered the clearing, the group attempted to move away but it was no use.
The entities held them in strong grips and, choosing one person, began to obey the promptings of their metabolisms. Whilst the other members looked on in shocked paralysis, iron hands clamped over their mouths, the bioengineered creatures despatched their prey and began to feed, each in their turn.

*

The two police officers seemed to take what Parke and Humble had to say seriously. They had little choice given Humble's injuries, the damage to his car, the graffiti and the commotion at the police station. He told them about the attempt to force him off the road as he returned from Gillerston, explaining that he and his friends had photographic evidence of their encounters.

By this time other officers had arrived to relieve the pressure at the station and statements were taken. The complainants left with promises that their concerns would be investigated.

"Do you have any idea who your attackers were, Mr. Humble?" asked D.I Kepple.

"One was Tommy Coates and another was Charlie Swatte. There were others there I'd seen around but I can't remember their names. They were all Falcon workers I'd say."

"Would you be able to identify any of them?"

"Oh yes, I think so. I saw a few faces before I went down."

"What about the damage to your shop and car?" asked D.S Ayle.

"I can't be sure who did that but I'm guessing it's the same guys. You can still make out traces of the damage and the car's being repaired at the moment. The garage owner will back up my story. My assistant also knows about it."

"You seem to be wary of Sergeant Dalveen and P.C Burn," said Kepple.

"Yes, Inspector," said Humble, his voice hampered by the pain in his jaw. His head hurt as if a large weight was balancing on it and his whole body throbbed with pain. Clearly the medication was wearing off.

"It's a surprising view," continued Kepple, "What's your basis for thinking they're not impartial as far as Falcon is concerned?"

"Just the way they were deflecting me from exploring the forest round about the place. At first Marcus was fairly low-key in his approach. Then when Sergeant Dalveen visited, I realised I was being seriously warned off. Why were they so adamant about keeping me away?"

The telephone rang. Parke took the call. "Yes. Three o'clock you say? Fine. The house is the big one just next to the church. No there's only one. Okay. See you then."

He replaced the handset on its base,

"It's the Press," he said. "They're sending a reporter and a photographer at three. It's *The National Messenger*. There's also an official from the Council due and I'm expecting to hear from our M.S.P."

"Right," said Kepple decisively. "Time to get to work. If you and your friends are correct, Mr. Humble then someone has a lot of questions to answer."

"We've also been contacted by the local council and a different newspaper. "They're looking for a story." He stood up.

At the police station they found a weary officer trying to collate the paperwork mountain he had to deal with. There was no sign of Burn. The officer's manner became respectful when the two senior men entered. They asked all present to move into a back room where there were chairs and a bench. Parke gave the shop-owner some assistance and he sat down slowly.

"Could I have a glass of water please?" Humble asked. "I've got a couple of pills to take."

The police constable disappeared into the small kitchen and returned with a glass. Humble took the painkillers, leaning his chair against a wall and closing his eyes. The telephone rang. The officer took the call,

"Candywood police station, can I help you?"

All except Humble noticed the change in the officer's face. He spoke briefly to the caller. "Yes, yes. Where did this happen? Yes, we'll send an ambulance and a police Land-Rover. One person attacked? Are the others okay? Just shocked. Right. One of you will have to guide the vehicles as near as possible to where it happened. Can you do that? Good. See you in a few minutes."

The constable's face was sombre when he ended the call. He turned to the others, addressing the senior officer,

"Sir, a local nature–worshipping group have been attacked in the woods…by entities they found difficult to describe – like people but not. One has been killed. They said he had been eaten, hollowed out from the inside."

Humble opened his eyes,

"Those half-human things we told you about. Thought they'd do something eventually."

He coughed and slumped forward. Parke grabbed him and easing him back, offered more water. Humble's phone sounded. It was a text from Louisa. The police station was a rare place where the technology worked.

R. U. O.K? Get in touch. L.

He began texting a reply then looked around,

"Do you mind? My girl-friend's worried about me. I won't be long."

Kepple nodded. Humble sent a text back...

O.K. Talk later. J.

"Finished, Mr. Humble?" Kepple asked a little tetchily.

"Er, yes."

Kepple continued,

235

"Sergeant Ayle is going to accompany the police Land-Rover as far as he can. I'll stay here to deal with the press and any other visitors. P.C Collier will meet the surviving nature-worshippers and take statements."

"I will organise a greater police presence and any other support required including armed officers. I suggest you rest up for the time being. We may have to speak to you again later…and yourself, Reverend. Please stay in the locality."

"Yes, Inspector," said Parke. "I'll help in any way I can. Our friend, Kirk Andrews should be available when he's finished work."

"Good. Mr. Humble – a word if you please. Could we step outside for a moment?"

Kepple ushered Humble out of the police station. Ayle followed. When they were well clear Kepple turned to the shop-owner,

"It transpires that P.C Burn has a relative working at the Falcon Centre – a cousin. That in itself is not particularly suspicious but might indicate a bias on his part and account for his apparent ambivalence over the facility. He has been temporarily suspended from duties and has returned to H.Q in one of our patrol cars accompanied by two officers. P.C Collier has taken his place."

"What about Dalveen and the W.P.C who warned me off visiting the forest?"

"The Sergeant is not currently under suspicion and I must caution you against making unproven accusations, substantiated or not. W.P.C March may have merely obeyed orders from a superior officer. If there is a problem we will discover its nature in due course but I wanted to share that thought with you at least. You and your friends have been in the vanguard in investigating Falcon and you in particular have suffered for it. You must let the professionals do the work from now on."

He turned to re-enter the police station. Before he could reach the door however, a panting Sergeant Ayle ran out,

"Sir, P.C Collier has just taken a call from a man setting up to fish in the Candy River. He found the body of a woman by the river path. A horse was wandering loose nearby. Looks like a riding accident."

Humble stepped forward,

"What did she look like?"

The sergeant glanced at Kepple who indicated he could answer Humble.

"Tall for a woman…well made, with long, auburn hair."

The D.I looked at Humble,

"Do you have an idea who it might be?"

"Samantha Leoch – it has to be her."

Fifteen

Knots of disgruntled people still remained in Lingdale Street, the Square and the Heart's Content. The township was beginning to divide into pro and anti- Falcon factions. Those who supported the facility were currently in the majority. Workers did not want to risk their jobs and generous salaries.

The anti group were alarmed about the strange animals, the escaped prisoners, the bio-forms and the secrecy at the core of Falcon. Lines were beginning to be drawn. People gathered in groups and heated exchanges took place. Incidents were talked over endlessly. The township was restless, uncertain, seething with gossip and rumour.

Kepple, Ayle and Collier began their investigations, assisted by reinforcements from Rivers. The members of *An Bile Buada* arrived, still in shock. Their descriptions of the gruesome incident in the woods were graphic. One member returned with the police to identify the site.

Humble's shop remained closed and he continued to shelter with Morton Parke. They were expecting the Press and other visitors. Humble felt unable to eat much but Margaret pressed a little food and endless cups of tea upon him.

Geordie's attempts to return to his woodland cottage were resisted by Parke,

"Wait a little longer, Geordie. Those things are still wanderin' about the forest. Will your animals be okay?"

"Not for long unless I can get back to them. I'll have to go soon because they need attendin' to. I'll take my chances. I've lived out there long enough. I'll be okay. There's not much feedin' on me anyway."

He grinned, showing an interesting array of teeth and gums. It was like looking into an old graveyard.

Kirk Andrews called from the Council office,

"Any news? I hear Jim's been beaten up and his shop and car vandalised. How is he?"

"Not a pretty sight but he's in good spirits. A whole lot of other things have happened as well. I'll tell you about them when I see you next."

"I can come down as soon as possible after work. I've heard some rumours already. It sounds as though it's suddenly gaining speed."

"That's one way of describin' it."

"Is it true about Sam Leoch?"

'Fraid so. There's no doubt it's her. Neck broken as a result of the fall. Nasty business. The police will want to talk to you about the last few days."

"I expected that. You wouldn't think these people would be so stupid as to arrange a fatal accident at this stage would you?"

"It could conceivably have been genuine. She was, apparently, very agitated when she came upon Jim just after he was beaten up. She was seen in an angry state, striding into the Lingdale. If it was a contrived incident, it means they're gettin' desperate. It may also mean she was involved in the conspiracy to cover up activities at Falcon. It makes you wonder who else was. Well, I'll see you later."

"About six, okay?"

"Okay, boy."

239

Geordie slipped out, worried about his animals. The Minister and his wife knew better than to try and stop him. So far the bio-forms had left them alone but Geordie suspected it would be only a matter of time before his cottage was discovered. His slow-paced figure made its way through the groups standing about on the pavements. It was almost a carnival atmosphere.

Anything out-of-the-ordinary was exciting and for many there was an added frisson of danger, even the feeling of being in a movie. There were those who insisted it was exactly that. Geordie resisted all attempts to draw him into conversation. The Old Man of the Woods knew when to keep his mouth shut.

*

Helen Highwater was receiving answers to her calls and emails. Contacts in the Scottish and U.K Governments, business and the legal profession, assured her they would investigate her concerns. In due course, she was able to speak to George Tinto in Edinburgh.

"Thank you for your call, Lady Highwater. I'm shocked that these things are happening on Scottish soil. We were sure the Falcon facility was above board. I would like to bring a small team down from Edinburgh, including myself. We can meet with any representatives from London or from the company. Perhaps a local Press conference may be appropriate. Have you notified anyone else?"

"Yes, Mr. Tinto. I believe the police are now involved and there have been new incidents in the woods as my staff have informed me. I do have concerns about the local economy should Falcon be discredited.Unemployment here would shoot up if the facility closed. People would not thank us for that."

And you would lose a great deal of money, thought Tinto unkindly.

"If the problems are the result of mismanagement or something similar, I'm sure we can remedy that and try to see to it that Falcon continues under a more transparent basis. We have the same concerns about safeguarding jobs," he said.

"The Press may already be alerted or they soon will be. I recently sheltered an injured activist who was involved in the breakout at the facility. She assured me that she and her fellow saboteurs were going to the newspapers about this."

"Then we are into damage limitation. The priorities as I see it are to ensure safety, deal with malpractice or criminal activities and try to preserve the facility as an ongoing source of employment."

"My thoughts exactly, Mr. Tinto."

Ruth Bromirski was released from hospital on Wednesday afternoon, her shoulder still in a support sling. Her phone had been restored to her and she had enough money to top up. Immediately she found a suitable quiet spot in a café and began calling. She had to find out what the other activists were doing.

In due course she established there were four groups of escapees, all in safe houses scattered around the town. This had been prepared before the breakout day.

241

She walked to the main one, located just two streets behind the High Street. It was a second-floor flat accessible by a stairway. There was a tiny, glassed over circular hole in the door. She knocked.

"Who is it?"

An eye scrutinised her through the peep-hole.

"It's Ruth Bromirski."

The door opened...

"Hi, Ruth. I'm Eilidh MacMorran. We've spoken on the phone. Come in"

MacMorran was a twenty-something girl, a little fey, with an angular but pleasant face, intensely blue eyes and long, straight black hair like a crow's wing. She was tall and wore jeans and a sweatshirt bearing the slogan, *Cool Bikers,* and a print of a two people astride a powerful motorbike.

Bromirski entered. The rooms were basically furnished and a T.V rumbled in one corner. The occupants were relaxing or watching T.V. They were a mixed group, including escapees and with activists. There was an air of lethargy about the place.

Accepting a coffee, she began talking and listening. She established that MacMorran and a young man, Darren Newsham, were amongst the original former Falcon employees, dismissed for questioning the ethics of the facility. They had teamed up with political and green activists and others, to form the coalition operating within and outside the Falcon complex. To her surprise they had not yet contacted the media.

"We were waiting until we heard from you," explained MacMorran. "We needed to make sure we had located all those released during the breakout. We knew from our sources in Falcon, that you had escaped and

242

wanted to find out if you had gained any further knowledge. The inside sources cautioned against acting too quickly. We knew you had been in hospital."

"Your information is very accurate," said Bromirski. "I know of course who the inside sources are but I didn't know you were still in touch with them. I imagine Falcon is clamping down hard now and looking for the enemy within. Colin was caught as you know, and will probably have revealed much of his knowledge already as will others who were captured."

"We're aware that things are kicking off down there," said McMorran. "We're guessing the locals who have been investigating the place have contacted the police. Tell us what happened after you escaped."

She told her story, filling in any details MacMorran did not already know. She explained about the Highwater connection and what she knew about the local attitudes to Falcon. MacMorran, now joined by others, revealed that disagreement amongst the coalition partners had prevented swift action to alert the media as originally planned.

"Some of the escaped slaves refused to let us help them and ran away, to the south. They'll try to disappear into the cities. We were also unable to bring in those weird android things. They're still wandering about in there like the other Falcon creations," said Bromirski.

"It's only guesswork when they'll emerge from the forest and move into villages. But they will. The runaway slaves are more of a problem."

"They obviously don't want to be found and now they're at large. We've opened a Pandora's Box. Now we have to deal with the consequences."

MacMorran's pale face grew concerned,

"Just before you arrived we heard that all roads in and out of Candywood have been closed with police roadblocks. Only authorised traffic is allowed through."

"Then we can't waste any more time."

*

Prahalad and Bowman were confining their activities to reading and studying data. No research was permitted as yet. Meeting in Bowman's quarters, they discussed recent events.

"I've heard that some of those bio-forms have escaped," said Bowman, handing Prahalad a cup of tea.

"I heard that too. It's a worrying development."

"How so? They can't last long out there. All they've ever known is a lab in Falcon."

"But they were nowhere near complete specimens. How those saboteurs got them out I don't know but they lack speech, efficient hearing and verbal reasoning skills. Above all they lack empathy. We are not at the stage where a viable machine-supported human has been perfected. It's impossible to know what they might do, but they will try to survive. That much is certain."

"How?"

"They ingest nutrients in semi-liquid form rather than solid foods. I am not directly involved with the work but some of my colleagues have been diverted away from their usual projects to work on this for the military arm."

"Falcon is pursuing the concept of battlefield weapons in the form of bio-entities, which acquire nutrition by using any protein food source they find – dead or living. A machine or robot would run on electricity or another conventional power source but that is inefficient in a military theatre, hence the human-like element. We are a long way from achieving the reality but the concept has been accepted. It would save troop casualties, a sensitive issue in an age of mass communication, but deliver victory on the battlefield. Whatever limitations the current batch have, they are programmed to survive and they will, in any way they can."

"My God, what have we done?"

"Not us…the people who set those monstrosities free. Do you remember the release of mink from fur-farms by animal rights activists back in the eighties?"

"Vaguely, why do you ask?"

"It's the same principle. You release living organisms into the wild for whatever reason but they are out of their normal environment. They cause havoc by having no natural predators and eating whatever they can in large quantities. There is nothing to stop them unless they are removed by human action. In other words they have to be hunted down. Now where's the compassion there?"

"I see what you mean – a false sense of animal welfare - could only happen in this country."

"Maybe. Do you think Management is aware of all this?"

"Of course, hence the way they've been acting lately."

"What can we do?"

"Not much at the moment. We're banned from using the equipment for anything other than study and interest. I've actually done some research and I know this isn't the only country attempting it. The one which develops the technology first will have the edge."

"To the victor the spoils?"

"Precisely."

*

Humble returned to his flat at five p.m as the street outside began to empty of people. Reassured by the police presence and the growing army of officials arriving in Candywood, citizens remembered they had homes to go to, work to do and families to care for. They drifted away.

He had promised to attend the Press conference arranged for the following day and be interviewed by the police or journalists but he also needed to take further rest. With a cup of coffee he settled down, glad of the chance of some privacy. He *Face-timed* Louisa with difficulty. His hands were painfully swollen and his ribs hurt.

"Hi, I've been worried. What else has been going on?"

"You wouldn't believe it. Are you okay?"

"Yes but what happened to your face?"

She sounded alarmed. He told her.

"That's terrible. I knew there was something wrong. How do you feel now?"

"Like a herd of elephants have run over me. I ache all over but nothing was actually broken. Tiptoe sorted them out and the police are here."

"It's out in the public domain. The media are descending on us. Falcon will have some explaining to do at last."

"The roads have been closed. I can't get in."

"At least you're safe. This is a good way to talk at the moment."

"I'll get through somehow. I know the back roads."

"Too risky, besides I'm betting the police will call on you to ask you questions. If they bring you into Candy I'll see you then, possibly tomorrow."

"I wish I could do something to help. I feel so frustrated out here."

"You could put stuff out on social networking sites so the world knows what's happening."

"Yes of course – as soon as."

"Be careful. Use another name. Do you have your photos?"

"Yes. I've kept them so they'll provide proof along with yours and Kirk's."

"Good."

"Okay, better sign out now and let you get on."

He was halfway through a meal when the telephone rang. The calm voice of Kirk Andrews came on the line,

"Can you come over to the Church House as soon as possible, Jim? A few of us are here and we need to talk."

"Five minutes, okay?"

"See you later."

Wincing with pain, Humble made his way slowly to the Church House. It was a cool, clear night. Only a few people were about but he noticed several police vehicles as well as some cars he guessed, must belong to people from the media.

Parke met him at the door and helped him inside. Andrews whistled when he saw Humble,

"My God, is that what they did to you?"

"Didn't imagine it. Bloody hurt at the time but I got some hits in before George and his guys intervened."

"Good job we did, son. You'd have been in a fuckin' wheelchair otherwise. Oh, sorry, Rev."

It was the booming voice of McGlimpy. Three of his friends were with him. Parke ignored the swearing,

"We're holdin' a council of war so to speak. Things are hottin' up but Falcon's far from bein' overturned yet. We're goin' to compare notes and see what conclusions we come to. Sit down and rest yourself. You still look a little uncomfortable to me."

"You're not wrong there."

Humble eased himself into a chair and sighed with relief. Margaret entered with tea and coffee. They talked about recent events and discussed possibilities.

"A lot has happened in a short time," said Parke. "What about this business with Samantha Leoch?"

"She had a thing going with Rocky, we know that," said Humble.

"He's rumoured to have another lover in Gillerston. Maybe Sam found out about her."

"Always got about a bit did Rocky. No wonder Kendra left him," Andrews said.

"But who would want to murder Sam?" asked Humble. "And why?"

"She hinted about us going into the forest didn't she?" said Andrews.

"Yes. She did the same when she was in my shop," Humble said, "Warned me about going there with Louisa. We thought she was just being bitchy."

"Do you remember the night Sticky tried to take the piss out of Bain?" put in McGlimpy, "I was in the pub that night and I remember it very clearly. Sticky said Bain knew a lot about Falcon and that he did too. He implied he was being paid to keep his mouth shut. The funny thing was he said that Craggs also knew things about Falcon. I remember Rocky's face at the time. He looked as if Sticky had walked over his grave."

"Instead Sticky went to his," mused Andrews.

"So did Bain," added Parke. "Now we have Sam Leoch."

"Three deaths all connected in some way with Craggs," Humble said, "And with Falcon."

"Don't forget someone tried to kill you," said Andrews, "On your way back from Gillerston."

"Gillerston," Humble said loudly then winced at the pain in his jaw. "That's the link. If Craggs had a woman in Gillerston and Sam found out, he'd be worried."

"Worried she'd dump him?"

"No," Humble persisted. "That wouldn't bother him much. There's a Falcon connection I'm sure. If Craggs and Sam were in with Falcon and she found out he was cheating on her, she might have threatened to tell all and pull out of her stake in the place."

"Stake?" Parke echoed.

"She'd had a lot of new ponies at her school and new staff," said Humble.

249

"It's also been beautifully refurbished and she had a new 4x4. That didn't happen overnight. Falcon must have paid for that."

"And Craggs has had his pub spruced up with a dining extension added and new waitresses employed," Andrews said. "It's possible they were both being paid a retainer."

"That's it," said Humble. "Maybe Craggs arranged Sam's death and the same with Sticky and Bain. I think he also tried to run me off the road between here and Gillerston. If he'd been visiting his lover he could have been behind me on the way back."

"There's not much doubt that Bain was tryin' somethin' wi' young Tina," said McGlimpy. "That might have been reason enough for Swatte and Coates to knock him off. Bain was out of control and they were gettin' younger. Prison was waitin' round the corner."

"No," said Humble. "It wasn't just that. They beat him pretty badly for the reason you said but my guess is others grabbed him later and placed him in the noose, making it look like suicide. They might have slapped him about a bit to make sure he wouldn't resist."

"I still don't understand what Falcon would get out of it," the farmer said.

"Sam and Craggs could have been recruited as the front line for Falcon in Candywood. As well as supporting the place, they could keep their ears and eyes out for any interference from the outside world – deflect attention away from Falcon, watch out for intruders, breaches of security and so on."

"Like curious shop-owners eh? McGlimpy said.
Humble smiled then touched his jaw tenderly.

There was a knock at the door. Margaret answered it and returned accompanied by Kepple and Ayle. The D.I spoke to the assembled group,

"Evening, folks. We've been to the place in the woods where the nature-worshippers were attacked. It's not a pleasant sight. Some officers are visiting the Falcon Centre this evening and the management team there will be asked for their views."

"We need to interview all of you along at the station. Tomorrow we are bringing Miss Moscadini in from Gillerston."

"A Press conference is arranged for eleven a.m in the morning. Further interviews will take place as required. Any photographic evidence you have can be collected tomorrow. Please have it ready. If you need to contact your families to tell them where you are, do that at the station. If you would come with us please."

The small Candywood police outpost had been turned into a major incident centre with a temporary building tacked onto it. Some police C.I.D officers were lodging at The Three Valleys Hotel and more police vehicles had arrived. The media pack had also increased in number. Locals gathered again now that evening meals were over.

At the station, Collier was hovering around uneasily, trying to keep busy. He was unsure about this sudden posting to the outer limits, as he saw it. Before the first interview Kepple spoke to Humble and his friends,

"Armed officers are now stationed at the entrances and on the peripheral boundaries of the forest. Some are also entering the woods. They will disable or destroy anything considered a danger to the public."

"We are also taking steps to track down the high-risk prisoners who have escaped from the area. All U.K police and security forces have been alerted. I'm telling you this because you have encountered some of the phenomena originating in the Falcon Centre and you have been on the front line as it were. Now please tell us all you have experienced in connection with recent incidents. We'll take you first, Mr. Humble, in view of your injuries."

*

Dallas, Savage and Hardisty were arranging to present the acceptable face of Falcon when the police officers arrived. Their plan was to keep them talking for as long as possible whilst Savage's personnel cleared the way for an examination of the complex. Already the prisoner blocks were being emptied and their inhabitants removed to a pre-prepared, remote, woodland camp, deep within the vast forest. The next stage would be the removal of experimentation and organ-harvesting evidence.

The measures were desperate ones. It was a gamble that the remoteness of the location would be sufficient to hide the camp. When all this had been done, Dallas and Hardisty would take the officers on a carefully arranged inspection of the main site. Savage would remain in the background to deal with any problems. Dallas, McQuade and Hardisty would do the work that evening during the expected police visit. That was the plan - *if* they could make it happen.

252

"That dickhead, Craggs has gone too far," said Dallas. "It could mess everything up big time."

"I know, Sir," Savage said. "Getting rid of Leoch in that way was sheer clumsiness. We could have arranged it better had we known."

"Perhaps he panicked," suggested Hardisty. "Amateurs often do. We cannot be sure it was Craggs himself. . It could have been someone acting for him or someone acting independently."

"Beating up Humble was stupid too," said Savage.

"I don't know where that idea came from but it was stupid as you say," Hardisty agreed, "As was the attempt to cause Humble to have a fatal car accident."

"Have the police fingered Craggs for any of this yet?" asked Dallas.

"Not as far as I know, Sir," said Savage.

"It may only be a matter of time however," said Hardisty. "They'll interview Humble and the others and may conclude that Rocky is their man."

"Under those circumstances, Craggs or any of his brutish sidekicks could talk, especially if the police use divide-and-rule tactics or offer the chance to co-operate."

"What do we do in the worst case scenario?" asked Dallas.

The P.R man stared at the ceiling for a moment. There was a palpable silence.

"Three options, Sir," he finally said.

"Which are?"

"Option 1 – pretend innocence and play the concerned scientists boldly putting the nation's interests first by using cutting edge research and methods to advance the country's competitiveness."

"Option 2 – deny everything and rely on our friends in Government for backing."

He paused.

"And Option 3?" asked Dallas.

Hardisty's face was grim…

"Cut and run."

*

The police came for Craggs at seven-thirty. The pub was busy for a Wednesday but there was a lot of news to exchange. He and his staff were hard at work when the main door opened, filling with uniformed and plainclothes officers. Rocky guessed what was about to happen and ducking out from behind the bar, made for the passageway leading to the rear door.

Of course there was no escape. He was simply not thinking properly. His only thought was to try to flee. It was the fight or flight instinct asserting itself and flight won. Adrenaline was pumping through him. Officers had been despatched to cover the rear exit but McGlimpy and his friends got there first. Craggs began to hurry along the darkened alley, looking over his shoulder as he ran. With shock he found himself cannoning into the wall of men.

"Hello, Rocky," said McGlimpy with quiet menace, "Going somewhere?"

*

Humble found the interview exhausting but he insisted on staying on so he could talk to the others before heading for home.

McGlimpy's interview had been short, which gave him time to unofficially assist in the apprehending of Craggs. The three principal interviewees had turned over their photographic evidence to the police. There was not much more to do until the press conference the next day.

"You look a tired, Jim," said Parke.

"Aches and pains giving me some trouble. Could do with an early night."
He turned to the others,

"However this business pans out I want you both to know I'm grateful for all you've done. It was my bone-headed stubbornness that got us onto this but you've gone along with it no matter what. A man couldn't have better friends."
He looked away.

"You're all wound up," Parke said gently.

"Yet it's been kind of fun," Andrews said. "And it's not over by any means. Adventures like this don't happen often in Candy and I have a feeling there's more to come. Your persistence has exposed some out-of-order practices at Falcon so that's not a bad thing."

"Go home," said Parke. "Talk to Louisa and get some sleep."

"Good night. See you tomorrow," said Andrews.

"Good night, guys."

In the flat he made a mug of tea, took his painkillers and called Louisa. She responded with evident anxiety,

"I'm coming into Candy tomorrow with the police. They want to talk to me and there's going to be a Press Conference. They've asked me to bring my pictures."

"I know. They told me. We all had our interviews today. Rocky has been arrested. He was the one who tried to force me off the road then sent his heavies to do me over. Looks like he also killed Sticky and he may have arranged Samantha's death. However annoying she was, she didn't deserve that."

"Bain was probably strung up by someone else after his beating but Rocky knew about it, possibly arranged it. He's is in so deep now no lifebelt can save him. His sidekicks are being pulled in too. All this justifies what we did. I remember you said you can't keep a Moscadini down but the same applies to a Humble. We're fighters not quitters. How are you by the way? Not too bored I hope."

"Fine. I'm with Jane. I stayed here after I got back from Uni. I have some studies but it's hard to concentrate. Uni are okay about me not going in tomorrow. Are your injuries healing?"

"Getting there but they're going to take a while."

"Better get to your bed."

Before sleep took him, he looked out from his upstairs window at a clear sky. A rose-red sunset had ended and that could mean drier weather tomorrow. Traces of the sun were colouring the horizon above the dark hills etched in silhouette…

Red sky at night is shepherd's delight.

The future was full of promise. He couldn't wait.

Sixteen

The activists in Cruiksdale began their media campaign. Geoff Mulligan turned up at the flat where Bromirski was staying. He had originally been recruited to infiltrate Falcon and release small numbers of prisoners when possible, acting with others on the inside. I.B.A.C was partly funding the sabotage operations. He acted as the link between the company and the activist alliance.

Bromirski talked with MacMorran. She explained that Newsham still harboured a grudge against Falcon. His dismissal had been for his reluctance to participate in controversial technology and the use of captive labour. The other dismissed worker had moved on. Newsham's actions were partly driven by revenge.

The decision was taken to assist the former prisoners to find accommodation, apply for benefits or find work. As many were illegally resident in the U.K, this was the greater challenge. Language was another. Some would have to move to cities where they would merge into the black economy. I.B.A.C would not risk losing credibility by taking on illegal workers.

She was soon able to see at first hand the tension between I.B.A.C people, such as herself and Colin Evan, and the various activists who felt they had purer motives. One supported the other but it was an uneasy relationship. The result was often poor decision-making.

On Thursday morning they began to contact the media in the form of newspapers, T.V stations and social networking sites.

She guessed this would attract the attention of the police so she discreetly spoke to MacMorran, to whom she had taken a liking. She felt the tall girl was a dreamer and perhaps a little vulnerable,

"Eilidh, we're going to get arrested once this is all out there, "she said. "Is that what you want?"

"No, not really but we all knew that would be a risk when we started. I suppose we thought it might not happen. We hoped the public would support us and we could escape prosecution."

"Bollocks. Some of you are not living in the real world. They'll run us into jail before our feet can touch the bloody ground. At least I'll have the backing of I.B.A.C if it comes to hiring a hotshot lawyer. Handled correctly, the company hopes to come out of this smelling of roses then move in on Falcon's territory. That was the original deal but I don't see it happening that way now that the extent of Falcon's operations is becoming known."

"What are you saying?"

"You are being used by I.B.A.C as a means to discredit Falcon. Wake up, Eilidh. Unless your ideals are burnished in pure gold and you're willing to be a martyr for them you need to save your skin. If you stay here with this bunch of no-hopers you'll be in such deep shit you'll never see the surface again."

MacMorran was quiet for a moment, twisting her long black locks around the fingers of one hand,

"What do you suggest?"

"Get the hell out of here and head for Candywood. If we join in the general public outrage against Falcon that's bound to erupt once they're exposed, we can position ourselves as being on the side of the good guys."

"It won't compromise your ideals and it will count in your favour. It's better than just running away because then we'll always be looking over our shoulders. Given today's methods of detection, we would be caught for sure one day and I do not intend to spend my days as a guest of Her Majesty."

"The roads are blocked."

"We can take the van you lot have parked round the back and go in by unclassified roads. There is a way. Once we're near the place we just leave the van and walk through the woods. It's do-able but we have to move fast."

"What about Darren?"

"What about him?"

"He and I are…um…" She looked at the floor.

"Oh I get it. You're in a relationship with him."

"Well there's not much space in here and…"

"You don't have to justify it to me. By all means bring him along but no one else. Let's do it, okay?"

"Okay."

The three slipped away when they judged the moment to be appropriate. The old van was parked in the back street. After a few coughs the engine started and they were off. Newsham drove, Bromirski sat beside him as navigator and MacMorran occupied a pile of cushions in the back. They escaped just in time before the police arrived. She knew the area and quickly guided him up into the hills using a minor road roughly paralleling the main route to Candywood.

*

The Press conference got under way at eleven as scheduled. The population was still divided but the excitement at being in the public eye was thrilling for many. Arrests of Rocky Craggs' paid helpers had been made.

Vincent Craggs was charged with the murder of Sticky Hagg and the attempted murder of Humble by trying to drive him off the road. Coates and Swatte admitted to assaulting Bain and Humble but not to his murder or that of Leoch. They insisted that two bottom-feeders known to Craggs, had lifted the badly beaten and semi-conscious forestry manager into the noose from a flat bed trailer open at the back, and left him to hang.

Information from Coates and Swatte led to the two men being quickly located and arrested. They turned out to be hired criminals from Carlisle, with long records. They admitted their part in the death of Bain but like Craggs, denied any involvement in Samantha Leoch's fatal accident.

This information in a reduced form was given to the general public and the media now assembling in the township. Cameras were deployed and reporters took notes. Inspector Kepple answered questions in a professional way, saying little about Falcon itself,

"Police marksmen are now dealing with any dangerous animals and other elements within and near to Caithland Forest. Former inmates of the facility are being tracked down and all U.K police forces have been alerted."

"Are you confident you have the manpower to accomplish this, Inspector?" asked a reporter.

"I am, but if we have to ask the military for support, we will do so. The situation will be monitored on an hour-by-hour basis."

"Can you comment on reports that strange creatures which feed off living things, even humans, have escaped from the Falcon complex?"

"As far as we are aware, all entities of that nature are being captured or destroyed."

A truculent voice called out from the assembled audience,

"Not before they ate some of my best bloody sheep."

"They were indeed caught when feeding on a sheep," said Kepple. "We know their numbers are few and are confident we have the situation in hand."

Another reporter asked, "Is it true they are androids, robots or half-humans?"

"Their exact nature is yet to be determined and this is something we are discussing with Falcon management," said the D.I smoothly. "In the meantime, speculation does not serve any useful purpose. Everything will be explained as soon as our investigations are complete."

"What about compensation for the animals eaten and the stuff pinched from farms and gardens?" a different voice called.

"All that will be dealt with in due course. I would ask everyone who has lost livestock, pets or produce, to make lists of the items and we will organise claims for compensation," Kepple answered.

"Worse than that damned foot-and-mouth," added another voice. "At least you knew what you were dealing with then."

Humble and his friends attended the meeting but made no comment, as advised. There was a good deal of staring at his injuries. The issues of captive labour, experiments and organ-harvesting all surfaced, resulting in a myriad of questions and an emotionally charged discussion. The police dealt with this calmly, urging people not to speculate, despite the increasingly hyper-elevated media output.

Louisa arrived at eleven-thirty accompanied by a female police officer and her parents. Humble met them for the first time. They were a good - natured British / Italian couple. He felt it was better to remain discreet at this point.

*

The van toiled up steep, hill-roads and around tight bends. The interior was dirty and smelled of oil and damp. Rust stained the inside walls. It was not the most comfortable ride and MacMorran was obliged to stretch out in the rear by holding on to a metal projection.

"Are you okay back there?" Newsham asked, concerned, as they hit another rise in the road and the vehicle bounced.

"F-f-f-fine," MacMorran lied, feeling sick. Her normally pale face was even paler, causing her bright blue eyes to stand out. Red spots showed on each cheek.

"Almost there," said Bromirski. "Stop at the next forestry road end and drive up a bit. You can park the van in a picnic area I know. We'll walk in from that point."

Newsham stopped the van at the suggested place and they clambered out. MacMorran immediately ran into the forest to throw up.

"Travel sickness?" asked Bromirski.

"Must be," he said.

"When she feels better, we'd better take a walk in the woods. You'll have to look after her on the way."

"I know." He took Eilidh's hand as she emerged from the forest. She leaned against him as they walked.

The track held to the high ground above Candywood at first, eventually bringing them down to a farm, after which, they tramped along a muddy path into the built-up area. There were few people around and they realised why when they emerged into the main street. Most people seemed to have congregated around the community hall, talking in groups. There wasn't enough space inside to accommodate everyone.

"Right," she said as they merged into the crowds of people. "Keep calm and wait to see what transpires. Are you okay now, Eilidh?"

MacMorran nodded. Some of the locals gave them curious glances in the way of country folk but concluded they were out-of-towners there to see the fun. Bromirski and the others gradually worked their way around the crowd. Louisa was allowed to sit with the group on the stage. Parke and Andrews shifted their chairs to let her to move next to Humble. Still in a slight daze after recent events, he was unaware of this until he felt a cool hand squeezing his. His face lit up when he saw her.

"Hello," she whispered. "Been wrestling bears I see."

"You could say that," Humble replied.

The conference was drawing to a close and people were drifting away. The media and other visitors were providing extra income for Candywood but the Lingdale Arms was closed. Bromirski and the others decided to find somewhere to have lunch whilst the police gathered Humble and his friends together.

*

Tinto arrived at the manor house accompanied by two officials from Edinburgh. Refreshments were organised and they settled in one of the ground floor rooms to talk. A secretary took notes. Lady Highwater exhibited her usual self-possessed poise but Tinto seemed on edge, concerned for the image of the Scottish Government as the extraordinary developments at Falcon emerged.

"This is beyond a simple repair task, Lady Highwater. If everything I've heard has indeed occurred we are looking at something quite momentous. We have apparently been kept in the dark by clever manoeuvring on the part of a few rogue politicians and unscrupulous management at the Falcon Centre."

He sipped his tea, reaching for a piece of cake,

"In some ways I have been taken in too," said Helen Highwater. "My position vis-à-vis the local community is precarious. The border is very porous in these parts and most people here regard themselves as Borderers or "Candys." Local identity is very strong."

"I know. Most of my colleagues in the Central Belt have never heard of the place. That's why it was chosen both by Edinburgh and London."

"Your generous granting of a lease meant the facility could be located in a remote area and provide jobs. We thought we had secured a long-term future for the region as well as technological innovation, which would propel our country into a leading position in Europe."

And get you more votes, she thought but carefully said,

"I think if we keep our heads we could yet emerge from this with some credibility. Most people realise Falcon has gone way beyond its original remit although there is a vociferous group supporting it at all costs."

"Yes I agree," said Tinto. "Of course there are two governments involved as I have pointed out. When Falcon was first established there was no Scottish Government as such - now there is. If the facility survives, any benefits, which accrue must be shared proportionately."

"I will leave that for the future. The main thing is to ensure its continuation but in a different form and under new management," said Helen Highwater.

"Any criminal activity must result in prosecution as well," said Tinto. "However high up it goes."

"Quite, but we must try not to throw the baby out with the bathwater."

The doorbell rang. Belinda Anfield answered it and was admitted to the room,

"The visitors have arrived."

"Thank you, Belinda. Would you show them in please?"

"Visitors?" asked Tinto.

"Why, yes. In order to reach an amicable agreement we must have U.K government representatives here too. I have invited the appropriate people as well as officials from the local Council. I have already received a visit from members of the police today and have told them what I know. There is in fact a Press conference in Candywood today but I felt our meeting had the greater urgency. A member of my staff is there however, and will report back."

Tinto frowned,

"Hopefully we can unmask the faction behind all this and bring them to justice."

Helen Highwater said nothing.

*

In the Falcon complex the security and management teams were as satisfied as they could be that the police and other visitors would not see anything incriminating. They were gambling that a more thorough search would not be undertaken. It was a high-risk strategy. An internal media conference had been arranged and the appropriate feed-line to the press and television had been decided. Dallas, Savage and Hardisty were on alert, together with Senior Administrator, Lucinda McQuade.

"Have all the ordinary workers been sent home?" asked Dallas when they had time to talk.

"Yes, Sir. Those who carry out day-to-day tasks have been sent home on full pay."

266

"It was explained that due to an unexpected security situation and technical problems, the facility will continue on a maintenance basis until further notice. They have now returned to Candywood and the district round about."

"Good. Do we have enough people to carry on?"

"Apart from research and experimental work, yes. Some of my staff can help if required as well as some of the scientific and engineering people. The hydroponic farm complex and other regular activities will continue to run."

"We have only shut down the more controversial work and moved anything or anyone we do not wish the police to see, out into the forest. The location is just over the border and should be remote enough to be hidden until this has all passed."

"Excellent. What about the research scientists, especially those from abroad?"

"They are under discreet surveillance and are being encouraged to carry out routine work or take time out altogether. The facility is sealed."

"Right. Well, the police should be here any moment. Let's hope we can pull this off."

They looked at him and murmured the expected responses. Lucinda McQade felt as if she was on the deck of *The Titanic*. She glanced at Hardisty and sensed he felt the same.

The scientists arranged to meet in one of the recreation areas. Most of the research staff at Falcon had changed from lab-coats to ordinary clothes. There was little work for them to do at present. Bowman and Prahalad both felt it was important to keep in touch with the others, as their uneasiness had not abated, especially with regard to Dos Santos.

They were uncertain of his motives and the Lithuanian was also something of an enigma. All were a little on edge but Capilus and Dos Santos seemed more so. Bowman decided to probe a little,

"So, Antonio, what do you think of the recent developments?"

Glancing briefly at Capilus, Dos Santos replied,

"Not good. It is frustrating being confined like this. After the breakout and what followed, it feels more like being under siege than ever. When will we get a chance to tell the outside world about Falcon?"

"Who knows? What would you tell it if you had the chance?"

"That capitalist greed has resulted in a place where normal rules and moral values no longer apply. Falcon is a company motivated by profit even though it is supposed to have Government support. Ultimately both politicians and corporate business leaders will share in the success of the venture and fatten themselves on it."

Now we're getting real, thought Bowman. *He's one of those anarchist types – a pain in the arse.*

"Do you think our research should be shared for the benefit of everyone?" he said.

"Of course. There are some aspects of life which do not fit into the business model."

"What do you think, Eva?"

"I agree with Antonio," said Capilus. "In Lithuania we had a communist regime imposed by the

268

Soviets but now that we are free it does not mean we should go wholesale the other way and do anything to make money. There is a balance to be struck."

"What about the experimental technologies and the organ-harvesting?" asked Prahalad.

"Immoral," Capilus said, with a voice rising in anger. "Disgusting!" Several other people in the recreation area looked around. She continued in a quieter tone,

"Those filthy creatures, those *mistakes* – they are unnatural, against the Law of God. If we had not met up and agreed to try to avoid using those obscene methods, I would have got away from here and told the world what was going on long ago."

"I didn't know you felt so strongly," Bowman said.

"Yes and I am not alone. Some of those who helped to engineer the escapes and were caught, have disappeared. They are being held somewhere, probably being tortured. They felt as strongly as I do. I talked to them before their capture."

"The humanoid machines, whatever they are, reflect the ethos of Falcon – they feed like vampires, they suck blood, they are like the money-obsessed system they came from," said Dos Santos with venom, "Feeding off the weak."

His dark face was even darker with anger.

"Yes I've heard about that," said Prahalad. "Rather unpleasant aspect of their physiology."

"Where do you two stand on all of this?" Capilus asked, "Do you agree with us?"

"Of course," Bowman lied, "I've not thought much about the political angle but now that I know more

269

about the questionable methods and the even more questionable technology I oppose the whole ethos of the place."

Have to pretend to share their views, he thought. *I'm not keen on some of the stuff in here but I'm a realist.*

Prahalad added his voice,

"And it is run like some oppressive dictatorship."

"My intention is to destroy the stem-cell research equipment and the other ungodly machinery of death," declared Capilus, "And tell the world what has happened here."

"It should all be cleansed," said Dos Santos as if on cue…"Purified and made harmless. Morality must be restored and the vampire profiteers defeated. When the chance comes I will help to destroy it along with those devil creatures."

Right on son, Bowman thought, wearily.

*

The police visit to Falcon took place as scheduled at two p.m. Dallas and his team answered questions in turn, as carefully and politely as possible. With their media-savvy skills, they attempted to convey an atmosphere of normality in a hard-working, purposeful environment. The visitors were given a carefully organised tour of the facility. Kepple explained that police marksmen were trawling the forest looking for dangerous animals and other entities. He was particularly insistent on discussing alleged escaped prisoners.

"It is true we do have a resident labour force here, Inspector but they are migrants from the E.U and the

Commonwealth for the most part. They are looked after and paid appropriately," said Dallas.

"Our information gives a different impression, Mr. Dallas, "said Kepple. "For example there have been allegations of prisoners being used for experimentation and organ harvesting. Some of the workers here appear to be from non-E.U or non-Commonwealth countries. The massive security you deploy smacks of a forced labour camp rather than a research centre."

Hardisty cut in - "If I may, Director?"
Dallas nodded. Hardisty turned to Kepple,

"Volunteers have often been used to test new technology Inspector, especially in medical research. The Common Cold Centre is a case in point – very respectable and well established. In keeping with other research stations, we of course, have to use animals and you know how vociferous some animal rights activists can be. We have to have strict security in place in order to avoid incidents or sabotage, even attacks on our staff. The location of Falcon was chosen for that purpose."

"Yes, but we understand this has gone far beyond the use of animals. There are too many sightings as well as photographs and verbal accounts to write the thing off as simply the work of a few idealists. Information is being posted on social networking sites. The media are here. There are credible witnesses as well as so-called 'activists'. It will justify a deeper investigation of the premises, which we will begin as soon as possible."

"Meanwhile what can you tell us about the escapees, currently being rounded up by my officers?"

"It appears that activists infiltrated Falcon and

engineered escapes," said Dallas. "They must have been well organised to get past our security-checks and be employed here. This was proven when outsiders obviously in league with them, broke down part of our security barrier and released some of our, ah…bio-experiments."

"You see, Inspector, we are involved in vitally important work but problems can occur even in the most controlled conditions. Internal and external sabotage holds up our work and prevents the successful breakthroughs we hope to achieve. The economic future of the country is at stake if I may put it that way."

"You mentioned medical research but I understand Falcon's brief was originally for agricultural research only," said Kepple.

"Things change and one technology informs another, "Hardisty replied smoothly. "When our work began to show promise, it also pointed in other directions, which have direct human benefit. It is rather like space-exploration technology, which also has spin-offs, useful to humanity. This is how leaps forward occur – often in unexpected ways. We felt we were in a very good position, given our location and security-level, to pursue exciting new research in all fields."

"I think you need to know that we have made a number of arrests in and around the Candywood area," Kepple said, unimpressed, "For example, a Mr. Craggs and his associates. They are giving us some quite disturbing information about developments in connection with this facility. The recent Press conference and interviews of witnesses have opened up the investigation further."

"This is now an official police enquiry and I must ask you to remain here and co-operate fully with my staff. Police officers, some armed, will remain here whilst we carry out an extensive search and interview staff as necessary. All weapons carried by your security personnel must be handed in as soon as possible. Please issue the appropriate instructions, Mr. Dallas."

He waited. Dallas looked at Savage and Hardisty who shrugged their shoulders. He moved to the communications microphone.

"May I ask on what charges Mr. Craggs was arrested, Inspector?" said Lucinda McQuade suddenly. Savage turned to her in surprise, his suspicious mind detecting a connection. The D.I hesitated for a moment,

"It will be in the public domain by now so I can tell you. The charges are the murder of Mr. Peter Hagg, the attempted murder of Mr. James Humble and conspiracy to murder Mr. Adam Bain."

"Two men, acting on behalf of Craggs, have been charged with Bain's actual murder. They have supplied us with information about these deaths. Another death has recently occurred – that of Ms. Samantha Leoch of Brookbank Riding School. She seems to have suffered a fatal fall from a horse. We think she had a relationship with Mr. Craggs but he denies any involvement with her death. Do you have a particular interest in this man?"

"Er, no…" McQuade said. "I just happen to know him slightly. We have a mutual acquaintance in Gillerston."

Kepple looked at her steadily for a few moments. She became increasingly tense under his gaze but outwardly cool.

"Is that the only connection you have with him?" he asked finally. "Any information you may be able to supply would be welcome."

"The name is just familiar to me."

He wondered if she was lying. McQuade met his eyes calmly but it was an effort. Dallas and Hardisty tried to control their expressions but the Director's face showed the pressure he felt,

"Are we under arrest, Inspector?"

"Not as such but that situation could change should you or your staff, decline to give us your full and complete co-operation. Remember I have asked you all to stay on the premises. I will begin the search as soon as possible. Please issue your instructions when you are ready."

He left, accompanied by some of his officers, to begin the search.

Savage turned to McQuade,

"Lucinda, we knew Craggs and Leoch were lovers. We saw that as a convenient link with Candywood. He and Samantha thought they knew everything about Falcon but they didn't know it all. If I've read the situation correctly, you were in a relationship with him too, as the gossip implies. Am I right?"

"With respect, Kenneth, my private life is not your business and I have already explained my tenuous connection with Vincent Craggs to the Inspector."

"You live in Gillerston," persisted Savage, changing tack. "Do you ride by any chance?"

"Yes, for your information I do. I learned as a child. I'm not originally from Gillerston of course."

274

"I'm from Glasgow as you know but there are riding schools in the countryside there. I haven't ridden much since I came here. How is this relevant, exactly?"

"What are you getting at, Kenneth?" asked Dallas.

"I am trying to establish if Lucinda has compromised our security through a personal relationship with Craggs."

He turned to McQuade again, his cynical mind looking for any sign of a double cross,

"Lucinda, you're one of the few people here who can come and go as you please. You knew Craggs and Leoch were an item. You also know about horses. Did you cause the accident, which killed her?"

She stood up, cold anger showing in her normally controlled features,

"How could you accuse me of such a thing? Most people know Rocky is weak when it comes to women. My guess is he kept seeing Sam Leoch to stop her from grassing on him. Maybe he did have another woman – it wouldn't surprise me, given his track record."

"Yet he continued to see her," said Savage, "That must have been galling for whoever it was. Were you the other woman? Is that what this is about?"

She controlled her anger with difficulty,

"So what if he was having a relationship with that stuck-up cow? My work here has been exemplary, as my appraisals show. I resent your inference, actually. What sort of a woman do you think I am?"

"Maybe Rocky got into a panic and either did the deed himself or got someone else to do it for him. Either way, I didn't spook that fucking horse. I've been here for the last three days, as you well know. How could I have engineered an accident?"

275

Savage sat back, astonished at her outburst. He decided not to push it further, despite his suspicions that McQuade may not be entirely loyal. She was normally very polite and professional. He had never heard her swear before.

"Sit down, Lucinda," said Dallas, equally surprised. "This adds something to the mix. It means that you may come under suspicion even though you're innocent. That inspector may suspect you of complicity in the death."

She said nothing.

Dallas turned to Hardisty,

"Which option have we reached do you think, Nathan?"

The P.R man did not smile…

"Straight to Option 2."

McQuade excused herself and hurried out. The others looked at each other. Savage asked if he could leave to check on the situation on the site and Dallas agreed. He moved to a telephone and began calling. Hardisty activated his own phone.

Seventeen

Bromirski and the others had little money but they managed to scrape together enough to buy food at the Heart's Content. The café was packed, some people still reluctant to go home. Little groups gathered to talk about the events, which had suddenly overtaken the remote community. The activists were unsure of their next move but knew they would have to find somewhere to spend the night or move on.

After further talks with the police, Humble and his friends were allowed to leave. Andrews and Parke, arranged to contact the shop-owner at a later time. Humble invited Louisa'a parents for tea, feeling it was the polite thing to do. He made them comfortable in his flat and busied himself organising refreshments. She offered to help. They whispered together at the far end of the kitchen.

"We'd better tell them everything I suppose. They must wonder why I look like a war casualty."

They told Louisa's parents about their attempts to investigate Falcon and why Humble had been attacked. Guiseppe and Rosa Moscadini knew their daughter could be a little headstrong. They were happy she had survived the dangerous encounters and were impressed with Humble's good manners. The atmosphere grew calmer.

*

At Falcon, Capilus and Dos Santos began their sabotage efforts by heading towards the secure

277

laboratories where they hoped to disable the machines and equipment, destroy the bizarre animals and if possible, the bio-forms. Bowman and Prahalad went with them, ostensibly as allies but in reality to see what they intended to do.

Other sympathisers were gathered en route. At first they succeeded in bluffing their way past the security guards but this became increasingly more difficult as they approached the sensitive areas. Suddenly a flurry of activity was apparent. Squads of security personnel began moving along corridors. The internal communications system crackled into life,

"Attention, all security staff, attention all security staff – we have an instruction from the police. Please hand in all your weapons to Mr. Savage in the main hall then return to your workstations and await further instructions. Attention all security staff…"

"Looks as if you might get your chance sooner than you thought, Antonio, "said Bowman.

The police officers left in Falcon oversaw the handing in of weapons. Bowman and the others, seeing an opportunity, moved towards the secure laboratories. On arrival at the first lab, they were disappointed to find all the controversial equipment and experimental creations missing.

Angry, the internal activists went from lab to lab and discovered the same.

"Where is it all?" shouted an enraged Dos Santos.

"They've stripped it out and hidden it," someone else answered. "But where?"

"All the freaky things have gone," said someone else.

278

"They must have moved them off-site," said Capilus.

"And the prisoners?" asked Bowman.

"Those too. The police will check the living areas eventually."

"Then they'll realise their purpose," said Prahalad, "Those units can't be there for anything else."

"We need to find someone who knows where everything is hidden, "said Dos Santos. "All the evidence of this dirty work."

"Can I be of assistance?" a voice asked. They turned. It was Lucinda McQuade. In her right hand she was holding a weapon pointing upwards.

*

In Candywood most of the people still remaining after the press conference began to move out and head for the Research Station. It seemed to be an accepted decision suddenly arrived at – the collective crowd mind. They picked up supporters en route. People joined them from the houses and cottages as word spread that a delegation was on its way. They streamed out in various forms of transport or on foot, making for the minor road into the forest.

Humble travelled with Andrews, Louisa, Parke and Louisa's parents, using Parke and Andrews' cars. Humble was still too injured to drive comfortably. Bromirski and her fellow-activists retrieved their van from the forest track and followed as quickly as possible.

Delayed, they found themselves trapped between the main crowd and a group of Falcon supporters moving west. Despite being in a minority, the pro-Falcon group were clearly angry and anxious. They felt their jobs and futures were at risk. No one recognised the group of activists.

McGlimpy and his helpers joined the main group. They were in two Land-Rovers. Other vehicles joined the procession as the crowd passed farms en route. Scuffles began to break out between the pro and anti-Falcon groups. Police moved in to keep the two factions apart. Other police were arriving from Divisional H.Q in vans with steel mesh across their windscreens. The scene was beginning to look like a civil disturbance.

Some were arming themselves with sticks, garden implements and other improvised weapons. A few of those who lived on farms had shotguns, carefully hidden. The situation was getting ugly. Police officers on the scene contacted Kepple in the Falcon complex and he then asked for 'Special Ops' police to be sent in. There was an atmosphere of heightened tension.

*

"Senior Administrator," said Bowman. "What do you want?"
The others stopped searching and joined him, staring at the Falcon officer.
"To help," she said in a reasonable voice. "I know where everything is – the equipment and other things you're looking for."
She had changed out of her dark blue business suit and wore a sweater, jeans and a flak jacket. Her usually

flowing hair was tied up behind her head. She wore a baseball cap.

"Why should we believe you?" asked Prahalad.

"Falcon is finished in its present form," said McQuade. "I'm jumping ship."

"You'd turn against Dallas and the others?" Bowman said. "Why?"

"I don't have a future with them actually," McQuade said, "In fact I've never been one of them. I'm a deep cover operative working for I.B.A.C. I was infiltrated in here soon after the place opened. I keep in touch with outside activists by email and phone, when I can get a signal. Even the inside activists were unaware of me – an extra security precaution – apart from two. Isn't that right, Eva?"

Capilus nodded silently.

McQuade continued,

"I personally ensured that activists and potential saboteurs got through the security screening. I fixed the records and the databases so that could happen. If you don't believe me that's fine, but can you afford to ignore what I'm saying? I have information, which will interest the police and the media as well as I.B.A.C. This place has been more than a little sloppy in its security vetting."

"As soon as we could, Eva and I assisted outside computer-hackers allied with the activists, to introduce a software worm, which infected the computer-systems. This is what caused the anomalies with the bioengineered life forms."

"I knew it!" shouted Prahalad. Bowman had rarely seen him so animated…

"What did I tell you? *Malware* targeting the systems. Just as I suspected. At least I know it wasn't my mistake."

"Absolutely, Doctor Prahalad," said McQuade. "Well, folks?"

"What have we got to lose?" said Dos Santos. "Lead on."

"How many of you can use guns?" asked McQuade.

Capilus and Dos Santos held up a hand each.

Why aren't I surprised? Bowman thought.

"Right, you can come with me," she said. "The rest stay here. It could be dangerous."

"Sod it," said Bowman. "Aashish and I want to come. We're part of this too."

Prahalad looked startled but nodded.

"Okay," McQuade said, seeing their determination. "Just be careful."

Bowman said nothing. He thought,

This is a totally different woman...All the time I've worked here and I never realised.

"First I have to make a couple of calls," she said. "Some of you can retrieve the files and databases. I'll show you where they are. Then the others can move out into the forest with me. We'll need transport. Hold on."

She called a number and listened. Bromirski answered. Fortunately she was in an area where a signal could be received, still amongst the mob moving on Falcon. It helped to ensure her words were not overheard. McQuade's next call was to on-side staff from the security cohort whom she knew could be trusted.

282

In the forest, armed police were closing in on the station, mopping up the bioengineering products as they went. Not all could be located, however. The thick undergrowth covered a wide area. Officers were in communication with Kepple and the other police approaching the centre and those inside it. The operation was almost military in character.

Internal disorder was breaking out in Falcon as people began to choose sides. Some stayed loyal to Dallas whilst others chose to move towards the activists, greater in number than Bowman and Prahalad realised. Others were undecided. Kepple, still on the site, was co-ordinating efforts to take control of the facility.

Some security staff made the decision to try and grab back their confiscated weapons. As a faction in the military had an interest in Falcon, there were some handpicked army personnel, whose weapons had been carefully concealed. There was an assumption they would be on-side, whichever emerged as the victorious one. Developments at Falcon were beginning to mirror the external ones.

*

"I suggest one group stay to go through the files and databases," McQuade said, "I could take four to six people with me to the location. There will be three pick-ups carrying security personnel who have also jumped ship. I've just called them. They've retrieved their weapons. They will provide protection."

"There are 4x4s outside. I'll be lead driver. Sort out amongst yourselves who is doing what but we'll have to hurry."

She checked her gun – a Falcon-issued Uzi.

Bowman, Capilus and Dos Santos opted to travel in McQuade's vehicle, Prahalad in the second with two other activists. Another would drive.

"The lifts are at the end of the next corridor," said McQuade. "Follow me quickly."

She jogged off to the left, carrying her weapon. They were on the ground floor. A basement floor was reachable by stairs or elevator. They could hear the growing chaos in other parts of the facility. Feet pounded along corridors and voices were raised.

They crowded into the two lifts. Those who would ride in the second vehicle went first. McQuade stood guard outside the lift-shafts. This was not the smoothly efficient administrator the Falcon staff saw every day but a tough operative. Her face was set under the baseball cap and her eyes looked all around. She was clearly well-trained and experienced.

*

Dallas made contact with Galliard over a secure line,

"It's all unravelling here, Roland," he explained to the senior civil servant. "What do I do?"

"Just keep steady, Campbell," was the reply. "Give me the details."

The politician listened carefully whilst Dallas explained all which had transpired. There was a short silence. Dallas became apprehensive,

"Hello, can you still hear me?"

"Yes I can. Actually I already have a fair idea of how things are going out there. Social media sites and the Westminster rumour mill are carrying all sorts of information or misinformation. I'm glad to have your input however."

"What do you suggest?" asked Dallas, trembling a little.

The patrician voice returned,

"In terms of the politics of this I will deny everything. My colleagues will do the same – I mean those who were instrumental in setting Falcon up. If the worst comes to the worst I have a little bolthole prepared. As far as we down here are concerned, Falcon is a legitimate facility using conventional methods. We will not admit to knowing about anything illegal. Some of us may fall but others won't. I intend to be one of those who don't."

"My advice is to get out of there if you can. Save yourself. You may be able to brazen it out but then again you may not. I'll leave you to be the judge of that. Goodbye and good luck, Campbell."

The call ended. Dallas controlled his temper with difficulty,

"Bastard! Fucking upper class bastard!"

Hardisty entered the room. He at once noticed Dallas' agitation,

"Any news, Sir?"

"I've just been on the phone to Galliard. That posh piece of shit has abandoned us."

"He's in complete denial of everything and is moving to put distance between himself and Falcon."

"In that case, Sir, I suggest we're at Option 3."

*

The lifts stopped at the basement level and they stepped out into a spartan area of concrete walls and floor. The main feature was an underground car park. A fleet of the dark green Toyota Hi-Lux pick-ups was lined against one wall. The other vehicles were vans and two chunky 4x4s bearing the Falcon logo. McQuade walked to a wall-mounted key-box and took out two sets of keys.

She threw one to the driver of the second vehicle and took one herself, whilst activating the remote locking system. There was a second remote device in her hand,

"I'll open the doors ahead with this other remote. They'll close behind us after we leave. A censor picks up the number plates of vehicles leaving then allows twenty seconds time before automatically sealing the doors. Everyone take flak jackets from the wall hooks and fasten them as we go. Let's move."

They were met by three 4x4s filled with security personnel of both genders. They appeared to have mustered at the rear of the building from another direction. The vehicles had high metal arches over the rear sections so the occupants could steady themselves.

Once into the forest, the vehicles swayed and slewed along the muddy, pot-holed track, throwing their occupants from one side to the other. Only McQuade and Dos Santos had experienced off-road driving. Bowman swore when his head hit the interior roof.

Capilus was grimly silent. He wondered what she was thinking. McQuade drove fast but with surprising skill. Bowman realised he had seriously underestimated her and wandered idly who she really was. In her normal role she had seemed like the *Ice Queen*. Today she was all action, her movements fluid and efficient.

He had stopped speculating about Capilus – too noble. She was probably involved with Dos Santos anyway. They would imagine they were going to change the world together. He looked back. So far there had been no sign of pursuit. The track twisted ahead through the thick forest.

Savage and Hardisty had decided to take the same route out of Falcon, using the underground exit. The security chief urged Dallas to do the same,

"It's all over, Sir. We need to get away. If we're quick we can make it out of here and start again somewhere - live to fight another day - take our knowledge to another country maybe. We can take as much cash and whatever we can use. What do you say?"

"No, I'll stick it out. Falcon is my baby and I'll go down with it if I have to. I appreciate your loyalty over the time you've been here – you too, Nathan but I can't ask you to stay. Just take off as soon as you can and good luck."

"Good luck to you too, Sir. Are you sure you won't…?"

"My mind is set. You'd both better go before it's too late. I've no idea where Lucinda is but if I see her I'll advise her to do the same."

With final waves, Savage and Hardisty headed for the lifts. Dallas opened the door of his office and listened to the chaos outside,

Damn them all to Hell, he thought.

Eighteen

Before the narrow entrance to Falcon's access driveway, a large cleared space existed in the forest. A memorial stood at its centre. It was a sandstone obelisk dating from the nineteenth century, commemorating a popular Highwater who had developed the estate successfully and considerably improved the conditions for the workers. The opposing groups met at that place.

Vehicles stopped as police vans and some military vehicles blocked the way. There was a general melee then everything came to a halt – impasse. Armed police closed in, drawing a tight ring around the facility. The two sides faced off. The military contingent had gone over to the police, obeying the instructions of their commander who knew the power balance had changed.

The renegade group within the Defence Ministry had been unmasked. It was unclear how their identities had been established but fault lines were opening up within Government. Someone was giving information freely, possibly through an immunity deal.

The fugitives descended to the basement area and looked for transport. They had briefcases containing documents, memory sticks and cash.

They chose a Toyota Hi-Lux as being suitable for forest tracks and operated the automatic doors of the parking area. Their plan was to head north and east, hoping to reach Edinburgh Airport.

From there they would try to obtain a flight to London. After that their plans were unclear. It was possible they would then go to ground or approach a rival company in order to sell their secrets.

The heavy vehicle roared out of the underground space and turned onto the forest track. They made good time, negotiating the muddy, undulating way easily, Savage driving. Pheasants and rabbits in their path were crushed inexorably but Savage was more careful when larger animals were encountered. They splashed through puddles and powered on.

Mud was their undoing in the end. A huge mass of it was at the side of the track when they had to swerve to the left after a near miss with a deer. The wheels sank into the glutinous black mess and the vehicle stopped.

"Engage the differential," said Hardisty, looking back for signs of pursuit.

"I'm trying," Savage replied. "I know what to do but it's not making any difference. This fucking mud is too thick. That last wet spell must have made it worse." The wheels continued to spin.

"You'll burn out the starting motor," shouted his companion.

"Shit!" said Savage. "Find branches and put them under the wheels."

They jumped down from the vehicle and began rooting amongst the conifers for fallen branches. There were tools in the Hi-Lux and they found saws and axes. Frantically they set about making a supportive bed for the wheels. Aware of possible pursuit, they worked with intense concentration and so they failed to notice the group of bio-forms emerging from the forest, until it was too late…

290

*

Frequent clashes were taking place between pro and anti Falcon supporters in the cleared space around the monument. Police tried to restore order. There was confusion and congestion as more vehicles and people arrived and ranged around the area. Eventually a kind of settling occurred. Police units continued their tightening grip on the Falcon buildings, assisted by military personnel.

The tension was palpable. With difficulty, Humble, Andrews and Parke pushed their way as near to the edge of the crowd as possible to face the Falcon supporters and guards. McGlimpy and his men came up behind. The tall farmer stood next to Humble,

"Any sign of the top Falcon staff, Jim?"

"Just the security guys and a few loyalists. Most of the staff have either melted away or joined our side as far as I can see but these people are blocking any clear view of the main building."

Kepple was making an announcement through a megaphone,

"Please put down your weapons and step back. Allow us to approach the building. There are civilians here. My officers have surrounded you. There is nowhere to go. Give up. Your situation is hopeless."

There was a stirring within the pro-Falcon faction. Humble asked if he could borrow the megaphone. Kepple agreed, sensing that this could be a way of avoiding casualties. Humble spoke through the instrument,

"Falcon workers – please listen. It's no good trying to protect those armed guys behind you. If it comes to a fight they'll allow you to take the flack. You'll be a human shield. Move away and we'll see what the hard men are made of. This isn't doing you any good. If the place is smashed up there'll be nothing. Remember most of you have families. If you let the police take care of this, it will sort itself out and you'll be able to continue working here. Think about it."

Humble glanced around. He had asked Louisa to stay further back for safety reasons. The presence of her parents had tempered her habitually headstrong tendencies. He noticed she was still where he had asked her to be. He faced forward again, relieved.

"Look, something's happening" Andrews said, pointing.

Gradually pro-Falcon supporters were moving away to left or right. Those with weapons were placing them on the ground, now beaten into a flattened mud expanse from the many feet. A way was opening up to the main Falcon building.

The ring of loyal security personnel remained intact. All had retrieved their arms. There was no sign of Dallas. Inside the Falcon complex. Police were imposing order, corralling the loyal Falcon scientists in the main hall under guard. Any security personnel in the buildings were either surrendering or putting up a fight. The few who resisted were dealt with. Occasional shots were heard.

The D.I spoke again,

"You can hear what's going on inside. You can't escape. Put down your weapons, I repeat, put down your weapons."

Humble sensed a presence at his left elbow. He turned. It was Geordie Hagg,

"Still buggerin' about are they?"

Humble grinned then felt the pain in his jaw,

"It's being sorted. We should be able to go in soon I think."

"Where's the bastard who pushed Pete into the river?"

"It was Craggs, remember? He's been arrested."

"Did someone tell him to do it?"

"We don't think so but he worked for Falcon and probably thought poor Pete had to be shut up in case he gave away any secrets when he'd had a drink. Rocky wouldn't want anyone to know he was in with the top people at Falcon and he'd be scared Pete might blow his cover."

"Aye, Pete knew a lot about this place – too much for his own good."

"I know. But we're turning the tables on Falcon now. It'll be over soon."

Geordie Hagg was wearing a substantial jacket more suitable for wet weather. It was dry and mild on that evening. As they watched the frozen tableau ahead he spoke again in his smoky, growling voice,

"So it's down to the boss of this place that Pete suffered the way he did?"

"In a way, though there's no evidence Craggs acted under direct orders. What are you getting at?"

"The buck stops with the boss doesn't it?"

"I suppose so, but look, something's happening."

The Falcon security guards were giving up. Police moved forward to arrest them and take their weapons.

Two tried to break away and run into the woods but were brought down with some crisp shots to the legs. A figure was suddenly seen at a first floor window.

"It's Dallas!" someone shouted. The figure disappeared.

"That the boss?" asked Geordie.

"Not for much longer," said McGlimpy moving forward. Humble and his friends moved with him. It was time to enter the building.

*

Falcon's secure holding facility was built around a venerable, stone cottage called South Mossbank. Its counterpart, North Mossbank stood on the opposite side of a small stream marking the Scotland/England border. The one on the Scottish side was used for storage and was also owned by Falcon. A small, timber footbridge lay between them.

There was a cabin on the southern side, which served as an administrative centre. This was the remote place where McQuade was leading the scientists and on-side security personnel.

McQuade signalled to the following vehicles to stop. A wider space on either side of the track came into view. She jumped from her vehicle as the others parked. With her Uzi in one hand she beckoned to the leader of the security force. He came forward and she began issuing instructions again,

"If we keep quiet we can approach without them seeing us. Then we'll take them and get into the place."

"I don't know how many there are but I'm guessing not many. Most would be needed back at the main building."

She turned to Bowman and Prahalad,

"You two will have to stay back. You can go in when it's all over. Guns please."

The security men gave spare pistols to Dos Santos and Capilus. They themselves were armed. The combined group began moving carefully towards the cluster of buildings ahead. There were lights in most of the buildings including the administration cabin. McQuade and the security force leader directed the armed group to break into two...one to surround the small structure, the other to fan out amongst the buildings. They closed in. Bowman and Prahalad followed, ignoring her instructions. Surprising the guards in the cabin, she kicked the door open and aimed her gun,

"Stay quiet, gentlemen. I'll use this if I have to."

Once more, Bowman felt he was in an action movie with some kind of tough, female lead. She ordered two of the security men to disarm the guards and tie them to chairs. As the group moved further within the site they encountered resistance.

One of the troopers shot a guard running out from behind a building, his gun firing. The man dropped, wounded. There were more shots as the group advanced. At one stage Bowman and Prahalad saw Capilus snap off a shot and a man fell with a shoulder wound. Eventually the remaining guard contingent surrendered, overwhelmed by the surprise attack. McQuade led the way into the nearest housing unit.

The place was filled with cells ranged along a central corridor.

The accommodation was basic but clean and the majority of the inmates were either lounging on bunk beds or reading. They began to approach the bars as their liberators entered. Most were Middle Eastern, Asian or African in appearance. They regarded the newcomers hopefully.

McQuade's gun spat at a guard who had burst out of a small office at the rear of the building. He collapsed, his legs shot from under him. As the pain kicked in he began to scream. She turned, sweeping her gun in an arc and another guard fell, wounded in the arm. Calmly she walked along the corridor scrutinising the prisoners,

"We'll release the safe ones," she said. "We can take them back with us but only if they co-operate. We'll get one of the captured guards to tell us who is safe and who isn't. If in doubt we keep them in. We don't want any crazies running around the place. See if you can find someone with medical training to see to these guys."

This was directed towards one of the on-side security men who duly ran off to do as she had instructed. When all the guards had been located, McQuade left some of the group to stay with them, especially the wounded, and walked away from the prison units to search the remainder of the site. The rest went with her.

What they found was astounding. Beyond the prisoner blocks were caged areas where various mixed-species creatures were kept in a series of enclosures. Most were blends of familiar animals but others were simply super-sized versions of their original types. They appeared to be well cared for.

In a building standing slightly apart from the others, they found more bio-forms, carefully guarded by two Falcon personnel who swiftly surrendered.

The building was secure and quite substantial. The beings had space to move around but could not leave. What sickened the arrivals however, were the animal corpses, clearly food supplies. The Brazilian was incensed,

"Devil creatures! Satanic horrors! I will destroy them all now!"

He lifted his pistol.

"No!" shouted McQuade.

"What?" he asked. "You want to keep them?"

"I work for I.B.A.C. The company will be interested in these things if only to study them. So will other organisations, including the Government. Back off."

"Screw you, McQuade!" he shouted and prepared to fire.

"No thanks," she said calmly. With neat accuracy she shot the weapon away, shattering his hand in the process. "You don't have the *cojones*."

Capilus raised her own gun. McQuade turned and aimed her Uzi at her…

"Drop the gun, Eva. I'll do the same to you if I have to."

Bowman put his hand on Capilus' shoulder,

"Do as she says. She means it."

Capilus dropped her gun. McQuade kicked it away,

"Now we'd better get some help for him."

She indicated Dos Santos who was in intense agony on the floor, his hand a mess of blood, bone and ragged flesh. "Hurry up, woman… move!"

Capilus moved. Prahalad went with her to find help. McQuade retrieved Capilus' gun, continued to search the building and entered an office at the rear. It was empty. She had been ready to shoot anyone she found there. Bowman followed her, fascinated.

She leaned against the wall and closed her eyes, lips parted. The air was filled with smells of cordite, sweat and blood.

They made the guards, who were now prisoners themselves, fully secure. Checking the records and using the knowledge of the guards, they released only the harmless captives who milled around looking disorientated. One of the Falcon staff was a paramedic and was able to give emergency help to the wounded. One guard was dead. It was not clear who had shot him.

Eva Capilus was drained, burnt out. She slumped on a chair staring at Dos Santos who lay on a mattress nursing his wound. McQuade on the other hand seemed invigorated. She spoke again to Bromirski on the landline from the administration cabin,

"Ruth?"

"Yes?"

"We're finished here but there are casualties. Ask whoever's in charge at Falcon to get medics out as soon as possible. We don't want to move the injured. We'll need transport for the released prisoners."

"The police inspector, I believe his name is Kepple, is in charge," Bromirski said. "We don't know where Dallas is but he's still inside. Savage and Hardisty have vanished."

"Right. We're coming back once the injured are taken care of. Oh and there's a body too. We'll need a body-bag. Please tell the Inspector all of that."

"A body? Oh, God, what's been happening?"

"Only one. Could have been worse. Don't know yet who shot him. Don't lose your bottle. See you later."

*

At the main Falcon building things were moving along. The light was fading and dusk was giving way to darkness. Some of the local people had brought torches. Others began to organise a fire. The forces ranged against Dallas moved forward to enter the complex.

There was little resistance. Some loyalists still remained holed up inside but the formerly pro-Falcon supporters outside had been neutralised. McGlimpy spoke quietly to Humble,

"Me and the boys will go in after the police and finish the bastards off."

"I don't think you should. You've done enough already. I'm going in myself though. I can't wait to see what's inside."

"Jim, you've been hurt. It's not a good idea. We'll learn soon enough what Falcon is all about."

"If you're going I'm going."

"And me," said Andrews.

"They might need spiritual comfort," said Parke.

"I doubt it, Reverend. Well if that's the way you want it, okay. I can't keep out of the action myself either. I'm all fired up and so are the boys but we should be careful. Let the professionals do the hard work."

They followed the armed squads into the building. As in the secure woodland location, the few loyal guards and staff who resisted were arrested if they were unarmed and challenged if they were not. No one was killed. Dallas was nowhere to be found. The cells housing the imprisoned activists, including Colin Evan, were discovered.

Some of the prisoners showed signs of torture. Many were listless and hardly knew they had been freed.

The squads proceeded through the labyrinthine corridors and laboratories. Humble, McGlimpy and a few others, followed in their wake. In the growing dark they succeeded in slipping past Kepple's men. Once inside, they were able to take advantage of the general confusion. At one point, as they moved carefully along yet another corridor Humble realised Geordie Hagg had sneaked up behind him.

"Geordie," he whispered. "What are you doing here?"

"Helpin'," said Hagg. "And seeing what all the fuckin' fuss is about. I've wanted to see inside here since it was built. It's been the death of me brother after all."

"Okay, I can see that," said Humble. "We're keeping well back though. There's no telling what's in here."

They reached the hydroponic farm complex. Huge ponds of liquid nutrients slopped gently under plants deeply rooted in the mixture. The surfaces looked as if they had been lacquered. There were pathways between the waterbeds. The plants were healthy - future food for a hungry world. There was no one tending them. They were normally cared for by basic robotic feeding devices roaming on tracks, administering top-up nourishment. Human workers oversaw the process.

Armed officers walked slowly around the vast area, searching for Dallas and any remaining loyalists. The place was eerily still. Their footsteps echoed despite their attempts to walk quietly. Humble and the others followed at a distance.

Passing the door to an adjacent laboratory, Humble lingered and opened the door carefully, curious to see what was inside. The others had all drawn ahead. Without warning, a strong hand emerged from behind the door and pulled him in. Something hard pressed against his spine,

"Come inside, Mr. Shopkeeper. There's a gun in your back."

The hand pulled him further inside. It was Dallas. The Falcon Director's face was wildly manic, his eyes staring. The others had not seen what had transpired, except for one person who turned and waited by the door, listening.

"You're going to be my ticket out of here, Humble, you prick," said Dallas, "We're leaving by a back stair, which leads to the helicopter pad on the flat roof. A helicopter is standing by. The pilot has remained loyal to me."

"It's not going to work. They'll scramble jets and shoot you down if necessary."

"Not if you're aboard they won't...as my guest. This country does not appreciate my talents so I'm going where they'll be rewarded."

He indicated a backpack he had on a table,

"U.S.B drives, laptop, paperwork – all I need to start again. I also have cash, D.N.A and other useful things salvaged from Falcon. You could call it a starter pack."

He grinned. It made his face look ghastly – *The Phantom of the Opera.*

"What makes you think they'll not shoot you down just because I'm on board?"

"Come on, shopkeeper. This country has scruples and a free press. It's not some fucking shit-hole like Uzbekistan or Zimbabwe. The media will be all over the place by now. We'll give them my ultimatum then fly out of here. Once we've cleared British airspace I'll pitch you overboard."

"How do you propose to force my compliance during all of that?"

"Like this." His hand shot out and Humble felt a stinging pain in his left thigh. A syringe had penetrated through his trousers and into his flesh. Dallas moved him forward and sat him on a chair,

"You'll pass out in a moment. Then my friend and I will take you up into the helicopter and you'll awake trussed so tightly you'll hardly be able to move. It will be easy to drop you overboard after that. Like they say in Sicily – you'll sleep with the fishes."

He laughed manically.

Humble's head began to swim. He was losing his focus. Dallas was busy getting organised and did not notice the door easing open until it was too late.

A hand holding a shotgun appeared in the now open doorway. The gun fired. A dark hole appeared in Dallas' head. He looked surprised for a few seconds then pitched forward to the floor. Blood pooled under his cranium. Before he fell into unconsciousness, Humble looked around to see who had fired. It was Geordie Hagg,

"That's for Pete, y' bastard," he said.

Nineteen

Officials arrived in 4x4 vehicles, apart from those who were particularly important, who came by helicopter. Armed police raced up the stairs from the room where Hagg had fired his fatal shot. They ordered Dallas' pilot out of his machine. The man knew there was no escape. A circle of guns trained directly on him, concentrated his mind.

The crowds dispersed for the most part when it was clear the crisis was over. Some stayed on to make a night of it by the substantial fire. Food, beer and whisky were miraculously produced, like the feeding of the five thousand. Louisa was anxious when Humble emerged unconscious, on a stretcher from the Falcon building.

"What's happened to him, Kirk?"

"It's okay. He's not hurt. Dallas jagged him with a syringe full of something to knock him out but he'll be okay. We'll get him to hospital and you'll see him soon."

"Are you sure?"

"Don't worry, lass," said Parke. "Jim's tough. He'll be fine in a day or two. A sleep will help him rest after his injuries and all that's happened. The main thing is this seems to be finally comin' to an end."

"Aye, it's been a long day," McGlimpy said. One of his men walked up to him and spoke in a low voice.

"Back in a little while folks. Got a small job to do," said the farmer. He moved away with his men. The others tried to see what was happening in the dark. They heard muffled cries and thumping sounds. Several people yelled out.

Then there was a movement away from the scene as a group drove off in the direction of Candywood. The farmer returned,

"Just a bit of tidyin' up," he explained cheerfully.

"What?" Andrews said.

"Well, there's still a few turnip-heads who blame Jim for all of this even after tonight. They were mutterin' about doin' over his shop again and so on. The boys and I just thought we'd give them a wee reminder."

He glanced around with satisfaction then went off to find food and drink, followed by his cronies. Andrews and Parke shook their heads and looked at each other.

"Candy justice," said Andrews. They stood waiting as Kepple walked over to them.

"I want as many people as possible to return to their homes," he said. "I would like you to help with this. Miss Moscadini and her parents need to be safely away from here as well as the others who came with the crowds from Candywood. The area is now controlled by the police and military and will be out of bounds. I'm going to announce all this in a moment. There will be another Press conference as soon as we can convene one. Thank you everybody."

He looked utterly exhausted – a small town police officer in his twilight years pitched into dealing with a major incident. It would be to his credit in the end, however. Not every policeman got the chance to deal with something like this.

*

During the mopping up operation the bio-forms still at large were rounded up. A group of officers also found the remains of Savage and Hardisty. It was not a pleasant sight. The Press retuned to Candywood after a briefing. The politicians and officials were accommodated in the Three Valleys or at Highwater House. The Falcon Centre was placed under twenty-four hour guard and sealed off. Louisa and her parents returned home. All roadblocks were lifted.

McGlimpy found Geordie Hagg near the fire where the food and drink were located,

"Thought I'd find you here," he said. "Listen, it might be a bit hot for you for a while after you took out that Dallas guy in there."

"Twat deserved it," said Hagg.

"I know that and your friends do too. I dare say most of Candy will feel the same. That's not the point. The police and the P.F may want to pin it on someone and you're the main man."

"They can stick it up their arses."

"I know, Geordie, "McGlimpy said soothingly, "I'm on your side but you know how it is don't you? What do you say to hiding out at my place for a while? There's a vacant cottage on the land and we can bring your animals in and take care of them. A couple of my boys will kook after your place for you and see it's okay. You can stay as long as you like. Think about it – Susan's cookin', a chance to keep your head down and you'll be amongst friends…How about it?"

Hagg stared into the distance for a few minutes then came to a decision,

"It's a good offer and I'll take it. You'll definitely keep an eye on my place will you?"

"Oh aye, and you can come and go whenever you please. If the Law comes nosin' around you just disappear, and I play the daft laddie until they've gone - I know nothin', okay?"

"Okay, Tiptoe."

"Good lad. Now let's get out of here. This place gives me the creeps."

*

McQuade was enjoying the leadership role she had assumed. When the vehicles arrived she directed the transfer of the still captive prisoners and the moving of the released slave-labourers to safety. Those who needed medical help would be taken on by ambulance to hospital in Gillerston. A token presence was left at the secret facility until something could be done about the entities there.

A subdued Capilus was ushered on to one of the 4x4 s. They moved in convoy back to Falcon's main building. The fire had been extinguished and only the 24-hour guard, Kepple and a sergeant remained on the scene.

Bromirski and the others were suddenly aimless, unsure of their next move. After establishing their identities, the D.I ignored them. He was too busy examining the interior of Falcon and making some interesting discoveries. They sat around with coffee and sandwiches left over from the feast. Kepple also had to organise the removal of the formerly imprisoned activists to hospital.

McQuade obtained permission to enter the Falcon Centre and organise sufficient funds from the budget to pay for accommodation for Prahalad, Capilus and Bromirski's group. As Senior Administrator she knew what to do. She left the arrangements open-ended. It was not clear how long the authorities would require them to stay in the area.

"Can you take some in your van, Ruth?" she asked. Bromirski nodded,

"Two or three."

"Right. Can you take a vehicle into Candywood, Doctor Prahalad? You'll be covered by Falcon insurance."

The scientist was still a little dazed but rallied,

"Er...oh yes, I can do that."

"Good. Then we'd better get out of here." She moved away to her vehicle after informing the police officers they were leaving.

Prahalad looked at Bowman,

"What about you, Lance?"

Bowman turned his head in the direction of McQuade. On cue, she looked back at him and gestured to her vehicle.

"Oh, you're fixed up. Well...er...see you then."

"Goodnight , Ashish. Get some sleep."

He gripped the other scientist's shoulder briefly. His friend nodded and smiled, returning the gesture.

Twenty

Galliard had hoped to put some distance between himself and the events at Falcon. It was a vain hope. The 21st century media could not be denied for long. He was arrested at Heathrow trying to board a flight for the Republic of Honduras. There followed a clear-out of Government departments and a rolling of heads. The Government tottered badly, almost succumbed then rallied.

The second Press conference was scheduled for five p.m on Friday. The Lingdale did not open but Humble's shop did, manned by Stella Gill and Susan McGlimpy.

A mini-conference got under way at Highwater House as a working breakfast, beginning at eight-thirty a.m. There were a number of officials from both governments around the table, including Tinto and representatives from various U.K departments. Inspector Kepple attended. Over coffee, the estate-owner opened the proceedings.

"This has been an extraordinary week, ladies and gentlemen. I am still attempting to come to terms with what has happened. My concern at this moment is to preserve the facility as a working research-centre and retain as many jobs as possible. I hope that that can be achieved, despite its current lurid reputation."

One of the U.K junior ministers had just travelled from London and answered the question. She was serving until a new minister was appointed,

"We hope so. When all this is over our intention is to preserve the facility as you described, removing the controversial technologies and methods, ensuring it is open to scrutiny and to the public – truly open that is."

She was referring to the stage-managed tours formerly practised at Falcon. Not entirely au fait with events, she was winging it a little. Tinto asked to speak,

"Whatever becomes of Falcon it must be a shared facility – for the use of both nations."

"Of course," the junior minister added hastily, on a steep learning curve. She had only recently read her brief...

"Any benefits will accrue to both on an equal basis."

"The Falcon management and those behind them, essentially conned us on this," said Tinto.

"Agreed," said Lady Highwater. "But that is behind us now. I intend to campaign to keep the facility open but under new operating conditions and with a different remit. Jobs are needed in this area."

"We will have to rename it," said a senior official. "But when enough time has passed the public will forget. It's been done before."

"The knowledge should not be lost, however," said Tinto, "In spite of the way in which it was obtained."

"Is it possible to say what will happen to the captive workers?" asked Helen Highwater.

An official from Immigration spoke,

"Genuine asylum seekers or migrant workers will go through the normal process and allowed to settle if their cases are proven. The rest will be deported to their countries-of-origin. Those who stay will be offered assistance with housing, medical needs and to find work."

The Justice Ministry Representative, said,

"Actual criminals will have to be brought to trial unless they are already serving sentences. In that case they will be returned to prison. Our counterparts in England and Wales are currently looking for those who escaped to the south. We hope that all of them will be detected but it is possible a few will melt into the black economy."

"Will there be other prosecutions?"

"Yes, those who took part in the deception carried out unlawful actions and used violence against inmates, including medically inflicted violence; will be brought to justice. Expect a few weeks of media attention around all that."

"There's a bit of mystery surrounding the undercover agents working in Falcon," said Tinto. "Do we know where they are or anything about them?"

Kepple answered Tinto's question,

"It seems there were both insiders and outsiders actively working against Falcon. We have not yet identified all of the outsiders but there are safe houses in Cruiksdale and we have raided those. It will be up to the Procurator Fiscal's office to decide whether criminal proceedings are appropriate."

"As for the insiders, they were a mixture – some motivated by ideals, others by loyalty to another company. They have all been identified and are staying in Candywood. One was wounded in the fighting around the secret Falcon annexe at South Mossbank. He remains in hospital. There was also a death there…a security guard. We are not sure who fired the fatal shot as more than one person was armed during that skirmish."

"What about the scientists and other staff who from Falcon's point-of-view were renegades – Ruth Bromirski and her friends?" she asked.

"One of them, Dos Santos, was wounded and is receiving treatment. It appears he was shot by Lucinda McQuade, formerly the Falcon Senior Administrator but actually working for I.B.A.C. as Bromirski was. The shooting took place during the raid on the secret location. Others had their own agendas, such as animal rights, anti-capitalism, religious beliefs, etc."

"Two of the scientists, Doctors Bowman and Prahalad, became concerned about the breaches of ethics and the use of captive labour as well as the more bizarre experimentation. They took a moral stand. Lucinda McQuade is another issue altogether."

"Oh?"

"Yes. A highly intelligent and capable woman, she was also a deep-cover operative for I.B.A.C. While serving as Senior Administrator for Falcon, she was aware of everything and chose not to reveal this to the outside world until the crisis occurred. She was operating in at least three roles, two of them, covert. Bromirski, Capilus and Dos Santos were the only ones aware of her real motives."

"It seems she knew how to use a range of weapons and displayed professional toughness during the conflict at Mossbank. We do not think she fired the shot which killed the security guard but one of her squad may have done so."

"A bit of an enigma?"

"It appears so. She was trained by Falcon as an officer in the Security Echelon but secretly manipulated the system of vetting, allowing activists to obtain jobs

311

inside. She and Capilus also helped to introduce the *malware*, used as a cyber weapon to sabotage the bioengineering processes. The consequences were not what they had imagined, however."

"I have also heard she was seeing Vincent Craggs, now under arrest."

"Some people had heard that rumour and it appears to be true, however she had ended their association before all this occurred. Craggs had a much deeper relationship with Samantha Leoch."

"One of Falcon's eyes and ears in Candywood," said Tinto.

"Who met with a riding accident," added Lady Highwater. "Has anyone shed any light on that yet?"

"No, said Kepple. "My officers are convinced it was not an accident but there is no proof at the moment."

"Who could have staged an accident, if that is what happened?"

"At first the main suspect was McQuade but she had not left the research station when it happened. She does not seem to be the type who would give way to emotional over-reaction, despite Craggs cheating on her. The enquiry goes on."

*

Humble woke in the hospital ward at nine a.m with a crushing headache. In addition, his injuries from the beating were giving him discomfort. A nurse arranged for food and fruit juice,

"Lucky you're here, Mr. Humble. We can now properly attend to your hurts. All that carry on down in Candy won't have helped them."

"How do you know about that?"

"It's in all the news media. The whole area's talking about it. Now let's get you better before you have to face the world again."

The first contact was Louisa. She called the hospital at nine a.m and he was allowed to speak to her. She was all concern

"You've done it again. When are you going to be out of the wars?"

"Hello, Louisa. Are you okay?"

"Yes. I heard what happened to you. How you managed to get into Falcon with the police there, I'll never know."

"It was all very confusing. It was easy to slip in. I couldn't wait to see inside the place."

"Well you'll be able to do that eventually but not yet. It's under guard. When are they letting you out?"

"This afternoon, about three. Somebody will have to collect me as I'm not supposed to drive for a while and I wouldn't be entitled to an ambulance."

"I'll do it. Should I bring Kirk and Morton?"

"I'll see them when I get back. I need you to myself for a while, on the return journey. You can tell me all that I've missed since I passed out. How are your parents by the way?"

"Puzzled but relieved, as well as concerned about the things you get up to."

"I'll try to settle down when life returns to normal."

313

"That may not be for some time. See you at three."

*

In McQuade's home in Gillerston, she and Bowman watched the 24-hour news channels and learned that the police wished to talk to her about the skirmish at Mossbank. The question of who had fired the shot, which killed the guard, was settled when a squad member admitted to it. Her position at Falcon and her links to I.B.A.C were also being debated. Bowman was mentioned as a Falcon agronomist, last seen at the facility at the close of Thursday.

"It's scary how fast news travels these days," said Bowman. "The events only just took place."

"That's how it is in today's world. I've got some thinking to do."

"Make it fast," he said, "We'll have a police visit unless we call in soon. Best to get it over with."

*

Louisa drove to collect Humble after the conference ended. He had recovered from his involuntary removal from the world and they had plenty to say to each other as she drove home along the narrow country road.

"My head's mince at the moment. I can hardly believe only a week has passed since this whole thing began," he said.

"I know. It's changed our lives hasn't it?"

"It's affected the whole district. The pace of events has been staggering. I'm hoping it'll be for the best."

"It will. I've heard they're going to try to keep the place going and it might even expand. That's all down to you," she said.

"Down to my stubborn nature and intense curiosity but if it hadn't been for Falcon's activities, I might never have got up the courage to ask you out."

She smiled.

The road passed over steep gradients and round tight bends. There was very little traffic apart from the ubiquitous white van. Dense clumps of mixed woodland came into view on their left. A lay-by had been provided. A pathway led from it into the woods.

"Pull in here," he said. "I need to walk for a while."

They walked together along the track. Beech trees interspersed with rowans arched overhead forming a natural tunnel. Pheasants raced in panic across their path. A sparrow-hawk rose from a fence post on their right. From the trees came the clacking of crows and the chattering of small forest birds. It was cool but dry.

The path rose slightly then they came to an open space fringed with gorse and bracken. Humble began to relax.

"What are you plans for tonight?" he asked.

"After the Press conference and all that, I'll drop in to see Mum and Dad and the girls in Gillerston. Then if you like I can come over and make you a special Italian dinner."

"Sounds good to me."

"Tonight I'll start work on your Italian by naming the ingredients when I cook."

"I'll look forward to that"

*

Bowman and McQuade arrived in Candywood at two p.m and were interviewed by the police. She had already emailed I.B.A.C and secured their backing for her former position as their agent. Their line was that they had placed her in Falcon because of their concern about dubious methods and unfair competition. The notion of industrial espionage was quietly parked. It was accepted she had been legitimately trained and authorised to use weapons.

The casualties resulting from the incident at Mossbank were viewed as regrettable. It was noted that McQuade had been actively working against Falcon at the time. The incident was treated as a conflict situation. Bowman had worked with Falcon's unethical methodology but so had others. A general amnesty was tacitly accepted.

Those at the top had been held to account or had perished, literally and politically. There had been suicides and resignations of some senior politicians.

The second Press conference got under way at five p.m. in the community hall. Cameras were present and the group of senior officials, top police officers and politicians arrived from the manor house together with Lady Highwater and Sir Alexander. As before the hall was crowded and a throng gathered outside.

The atmosphere was more subdued this time. Kepple was there. A considerable number of questions were asked that day and decisions made. Tempers flared as people relieved the tension bottled up during Thursday when the Falcon crisis emerged and grew legs. The media scrutiny was intense.

The community and the district round about experienced something of a boom. Guesthouses and campsites were inundated with visitors and the shops enhanced their profits. This included Humble's business manned by the redoubtable Ethel Moans and Susan McGlimpy. Many citizens rented out their properties at inflated prices and moved in with friends or relations in the area. Farmhouses suddenly sprouted B&B signs.

There was now a post-event vacuum in Candywood as if the community had gone through a disaster. It allowed for a collective emotional release. The small township enjoyed a mixture of international fame and notoriety. The Press conference was more like a 'Truth and Reconciliation Commission.' Most people simply wanted a new beginning.

Tinto chaired the meeting and made some announcements,

"The bio-forms, ladies and gentlemen, have already been shipped to a location further south and will be studied in a secure setting. Colin Evan and the other captured activists are being treated in hospital until they are well enough to provide information. Some have clearly suffered torture."

There were gasps around the hall. Tinto cleared his throat and held up a hand for silence,

"The most dangerous of the bizarre animals have been destroyed and the remainder sent for study in the

317

same location as the bio-forms. Antonio Dos Santos will be deported to Brazil when his injury has healed. His work and immigration papers were forgeries. We now know that Capilus and Dos Santos had been the co-ordinators of the sabotage efforts inside Falcon, with McQuade secretly assisting them."

"This included the introduction of the software worm, which I.T experts are already working to disable. No progress had been made in solving the case of the death of Campbell Dallas at the hands of person or persons unknown."

"The weapon was missing but the wound has been identified as caused by a shotgun, confirmed by ballistics experts. The Procurator-Fiscal has ordered an autopsy."

McGlimpy kept his head down.

Tinto explained further,

"Prisoners will be returned to serve out their original sentences. Former slave-workers are receiving assistance and medical treatment. Burn, Dalveen and other officers have been charged with corruption. The conspiracy to hide Falcon's activities was deeper than we guessed."

"The Centre will be examined and cleansed before being reopened. Lady Highwater and others have successfully argued for its retention under new management and with a remit to pursue non-controversial research."

He ended his explanation and sat back. Other officials as well as Kepple added further information, answering questions from the floor. The conference closed after exhaustive discussion. People made their way home, glad tomorrow was Saturday. Capilus and the activists were still being accommodated locally, paid for by Falcon. Bowman and McQuade were released from the police station at eight p.m.

*

As promised, Louisa arrived at Humble's home for dinner. She carried a large carrier-bag and an overnight case.

"I've brought the food. Do you have any wine? Red would be preferable."

"No problem."

She hurried to the kitchen to prepare the meal. He watched her as she moved around, singing softly to herself. She sensed him looking and smiled,

"You could get everything else ready – the wine, the cutlery and all that. It will save time. Then I'll tell you the Italian names for the parts of the meal."

"Of course. I was just dreaming a little."

"How are the injuries now?"

"Getting better. They won't hold me back."

"Good. We'll eat in twenty minutes. How about some music whilst we're having the Italian lesson?"

It was after ten when they pushed back their chairs and moved to the sofa with coffee. They sat together closely and she leaned her head against his shoulder,

"It's a relief to have it all over."

He suddenly had a thought, expressing it impetuously,

"I looked up some Italian phrases on the Internet, Louisa - to impress you. For example, *sei bella* - you are beautiful."

"I know what it means," she said, laughing.

"You promised to tell me the meaning of those words you used during our night out." he said. Her gazelle eyes focussed on him,

"Oh yes. Let's see. There was, *Mi rendi felice* – you make me happy."

"Do I?"

"Yes you do, actually.

Then there was, *Ti pense sempre* – I always think about you."

"And do you?" he asked.

"Pretty much."

"It's the same with me where you're concerned," he said.

"Then we'll have to do something about it. What do you say - should we begin?"

"Directly."

Epilogue

October – Five weeks later.

Saturday - eleven a.m.

There was a slight autumn chill in the air. A pale sky held piles of cloud but the sun was bright, close to the horizon, moving to its winter position. Humble, Parke, Andrews and Louisa stood outside the former Falcon Centre. The place had changed considerably. The high security barrier was gone, replaced with a simple perimeter fence. The gates had only two guards. They checked I.D. but were unarmed. The new name showed a commitment to move on from the recent past.

They had travelled in Andrews' car after meeting in Candywood. The community was beginning to return to normality. Kepple had kept in touch and the enquiry remained ongoing. Decisions were still awaited from the Procurator-Fiscal's office.

"What do you think of the new name, Jim?" asked Andrews, looking at the collection of buildings, "*The Caithland Centre?*"

"A good choice I'd say. Now run as a not-for-profit charity under an elected Management Board. Better that way."

"As long as people don't think it's for educational behavioural support or young offenders," said Parke.

"Or alternative therapy," Andrews laughed.

"The prisoner blocks are closed now," Humble said,

"Although I believe they may be adapted as accommodation for resident staff or visitors. They're working on a make-over at the moment."

"What a difference a week makes," the Ulsterman said.

"Yes, time seemed to speed up in a strange way and everything changed here."

"Have all the jobs been kept?" Louisa asked. "Mostly, and I hear they're taking on more workers," Andrews said.

"Shows how wrong people were about losing the Cash Cow," said Humble.

A neatly dressed figure with a white lab coat over a jacket and tie was approaching them from the main building. At the same time they became aware of a car moving up the drive. As Doctor Prahalad walked through the gates the car drew to a halt. Inspector Kepple stepped out followed by Ayle. The groups met and mingled.

"Congratulations on your appointment, Doctor Prahalad," said the D.I, looking a little weary. The effect of that momentous week in Candywood had not quite worn off.

"Thank you, Inspector," the scientist acknowledged. "An unexpected development," he added in his polished English.

"But quite appropriate," said Humble - "Director of the Caithland Centre no less. What about the other scientists? Have they returned to work now?"

"Yes, the Board has re-appointed them all apart from those who were too obstructive to work here again. That included Eva Capilus and Antonio Dos Santos. She has returned to Lithuania."

"He was deported to Brazil. I doubt we will ever see them again. Doctor Lance Bowman is now my Assistant Director. Sadly, it means we're both too occupied in management matters to personally carry out as much research as we used to but we have found an efficient Centre Administrator in the person of Dawn Barclay."

"I also understand congratulations are in order for Miss Moscadini and yourself, Mr. Humble?" he said, "Your joint business enterprises seem set to have a bright future."

"Call me, Jim, please," Humble said, "And thank you."

"You look after him now, young lady," said Parke, pretending to be serious. "He's such a delicate flower."

Andrews snorted.

"So what research are you actually doing here now?" asked Humble.

"Most of what we did before but no cloning, organ-harvesting or other illegal stuff. Naturally we only use legitimate workers paid at a good rate and we are always open to inspection. I invited you here partly to offer you a full tour of the site – and you gentlemen too of course," he added to the police officers.

"Thank you," Humble said. "I've been inside once before but under different circumstances. I only saw a small part of it and I was otherwise occupied at the time."

"You'll notice some changes. By the way the Board has decided that Mossbank will be completely demolished once the investigations are finally over and the Procurator-Fiscal's office has made its decisions with regard to what happened there. There is full co-operation from the C.P.S in Cumbria."

When the tour ended they sat in the comfortable private lounge for the use of senior staff. Kepple shared some information with them – tying up loose ends as it were,

"The activists working against Falcon have gone their separate ways although some have slipped the net and may still be in the area," he said, "They were never a cohesive bunch and have splintered into various groups according to their particular ideals. Some have gone to London I believe or other cities. You could say they've achieved their ends."

"The technology which produced the bio-forms cannot be ignored can it? Humble asked. "Isn't the genie out of the bottle now?"

"You're right," agreed Prahalad. "In future humanity is going to change whether we like it or not. As you said it cannot be held back. That goes for the other breakthroughs too. We can only hope it can be successfully managed and used for the public good."

"But there are no guarantees are there?" said Andrews.

"Indeed not. We face some turbulent times ahead. The life-extension research is serious and will have worldwide repercussions if it succeeds. The question of who will be first to benefit from the process will arise…will it be the wealthy and the influential or will it be shared amongst the bulk of the population? Other nations will want a piece and there will be military and commercial pressures to deal with."

"We have to accept that a new era has begun. In the future we may see a new species emerging – the bioengineered, regenerative human."

"The impact has yet to be determined but they're very significant developments, like robotics and the Internet. We don't know where they will go."

"Given human nature it will be messy, driven by money, greed and characterised by double-dealing and conflict," said Kepple, cynically, "I guess only the rich and powerful will have access to the technology in the first instance. The rest of us will get a few crumbs if we're lucky."

"The bioengineered entities could become human look-alikes," said Humble.

"Dear God, I hope it doesn't come to that," said Kepple.

"But there is a credibility gap," said Prahalad, "Sometimes referred to as, *The Uncanny Valley.* It's when androids, bio-forms or robots don't look human enough and people get worried. Conversely, when they *do* look human, people are scared if they show machine-like characteristics. It would be a hard sell."

"There are a lot of unknowns with this development," continued the scientist. "We must be careful not to let it get out of hand."

"It already has," Humble reminded him. "In a way. We just knocked it on the head in time before it went out of control."

Parke had a sudden thought,

"Inspector, did you ever find out who frightened Samantha Leoch's horse and caused the accident, which killed her? Some people thought it was Lucinda McQuade but it turns out not to have been the case."

"That's one of the things I came to tell you about. Witness evidence places McQuade inside Falcon when it happened so she was ruled out. We were baffled for a while until we extracted a full confession from Vincent Craggs. He was hoping it would help his own situation if he came clean with us. We've now begun making arrests. According to Craggs the perpetrators were the Guffocks - some of the men to be precise."

"Well I'll be damned," said Andrews.

"Karma," Humble said.

Prahalad nodded.

"Candywood was really on the map for a while wasn't it?" Andrews volunteered after a short silence.

"And you folk are local heroes," added Ayle, "Celebrities - the ones who saved the place and boosted its economic strength."

"It needs to be left alone now," suggested Parke.

"To hopefully revert to its former peaceful self now the dust has settled," Kepple said.

"I wouldn't bet on it," said Humble. "In truth it's never really been peaceful. That's just an illusion. I have a feeling there's another issue or two waiting to surface."

He thought of the community he had grown up in, with its undercurrents, invisible to the casual observer. Somehow he knew the extraordinary events they had experienced, would not be the end of the story.

326